Journeys Through Faladon

THE TITAN DIVIDE

From The Ruinsong Order

2020

Journeys Through Faladon: The Titan Divide
Copyright © 2020 by ForgeFiction, Inc. All Rights Reserved.

All rights reserved. No part of this book may be reproduced in any form or by any electronic or mechanical means including information storage and retrieval systems, without permission in writing from the author. The only exception is by a reviewer, who may quote short excerpts in a review.

This book is a work of fiction. Names, characters, places, and incidents either are products of the author's imagination or are used fictitiously. Any resemblance to actual persons, living or dead, events, or locales is entirely coincidental.

From the Ruinsong Order
Journeys Through Faladon: The Titan Divide

It has been centuries since the Mountain Birth, a magical calamity that turned the Jödmun from men into... something else.
Part curse, part blessing, the Jödmun need neither food nor shelter, living as veritable stone men. One among them, Ürbon the Wanderer, will emerge from his people's centuries-long isolation.

A chance encounter with an unusually violent elvish people leaves Ürbon without a ship, without his men, and without direction, changing the course of his life forever. In a journey across the vast world of Faladon; from the sandy Savarrah desert to the lush Forgotten Isles, the Human Kingdom of Ravenburg to the bustling port-city of Venova, Ürbon will gather to him unlikely friends and dangerous enemies, each seeking a weakness in his stony flesh. This is his tale.

First Printing: Jul 2020
ISBN: 9798669898632

Written by

Majorkill
Eugenio Comelli
Connor Leo Pfeifer
B. W. Quacke
Mace Steven Garza Velarde
Chad Corbett
John Doe
Allan Sawyer

Powered by:

ForgeFiction.com
A Platform for Community-Driven Story Writing

2 0 2 0

Acknowledgements

Worldbuilding:

Troy Smith
Şerbănoiu Eduard
Carolina
Thiele
Terra
Mason Hooper
Machiche
Januk Bolek
Volkovh
Joshua Barry
Jānis Starks
Nathan Sanctis
Hanael Merali
Tyler Williams
Henry Mccoull
Tiziano Donatello Pizzuti

Harry James
Steelwind
Thomas Menzies
Miatrox
Edward Smith
John
Sander Jensen
Adam
Patrick Roberts
Clarke
Reece Brown
Pairtree44
Nobr4in3r
Alys Empress of the Silk
Silverthorne

Cover design: Anush Abyan
Editing: Firstediting.com, Judi Soderberg
Map illustration: Alessia Sagnotti
ForgeFiction.com

Chapter 1:
Into The Deep

"Damn that rotten toothed bastard!" Ürbon cried out into the still sea air. "Two weeks we've been sailing, with no sight of land or ship!"

"That's what happens when you trust an urchin; you never know what you'll be getting," answered one of Ürbon's lieutenants. The veteran sailor was close enough to speak freely in his captain's presence but far enough to not fear his rage.

"I know what he'll be getting from me if I ever see him again," Ürbon retorted. He desperately wanted to punch something but knew that giving in to that urge would be unwise. Very little could withstand a hit from the tall and fearsome Jödmun. They were a people with flesh quite literally made of stone, a condition arising from a calamity known as the Mountain Birth. But that was a long time ago.

The Mountain Birth changed not only the skin of the Jödmun but freed them from the basic survival requirements of mortals. Not only were they able to forgo food and sleep, but they were endowed with superior power and strength. At first, they thought this a blessing, but before long, they came to see it as a curse.

One aspect of this curse was their inability to produce children. And although they lived an unnaturally long life, each death became that much more significant. Nevertheless, the Jödmun lived on, using their strength and endurance to build mighty ships able to bear the weight of the world, if necessary. Ürbon's own craft, *The North Wind*, was no exception.

The North Wind had taken him and his crew on countless voyages as they sought out legendary treasures. It was sailing them now to a prize greater than all others. According to a lone urchin, who gave Ürbon and his crew coordinates to an archipelago, it was there they would find what they seek.

That is, if the wind would just pick up, thought Ürbon.

"Ship sighted! Starboard bow!" came a call from further down the ship.

Ürbon grabbed his spyglass and ran to the prow of the ship, the crewmen on the deck following him; they had not seen anything but open water for days.

Looking through his spyglass, Ürbon saw a beautiful ship cutting through the waves like a knife. Its white wood and elegant design could only mean one thing, as no other race crafted with such grace and beauty.

"Elves!" Ürbon shouted. "Double the oars, follow them!" The crew spurred into action, the boat gaining momentum. As if the wind itself heard Ürbon's command, the sails filled and surged them forward through the water. Though the urchin's information was not very detailed, he had mentioned elves to be the inhabitants of the island that they sought.

The Jödmun did not tire, and with this fortunate sighting, their morale picked up and spurred them to narrow the gap between the two ships. Ürbon closed his spyglass; he would no longer need it to keep an eye on their quarry.

The elven ship was nowhere near as fast as Ürbon initially thought. By now, the elves were visible on the deck, huffing and puffing in their frantic attempt to outsail *The North Wind.*

An arrow whizzed through the air and thudded into the prow of the Jödmun vessel. Ürbon clenched his fists as the elves scrambled to grab their elegant weapons. It was not his intention to fight but to follow them and gain some much-needed information. But it seemed as if these elves had no desire to be followed, so he'd resort to violence if he had to.

Ürbon had to react quickly as more arrows hit the ship's wooden frame. While he may not have wanted any bloodshed, he couldn't risk losing the elves, either. So, fighting it was.

"To arms! Ram them!" Ürbon cried out as the gap between the two ships shortened. The crew grabbed their weapons, ready to board the elven ship.

With an ear-splitting crack, *The North Wind* crashed into the smaller vessel, dragging the boat sideways and ripping off a large chunk of the elven wood. The impact threw many elves into the water, and the fortunate ones who stayed aboard grabbed hold of whatever they could.

The Jödmun grimly jumped onto the remains of the elven ship. There was no joy in taking on this weaker opponent, but they had their reasons. The elves tried to defend themselves with their slender blades, which screeched and cracked against the stone flesh of the Jödmun.

Their efforts were useless, as Ürbon's crew picked up the squirming elves with ease and threw them down onto *The North Wind's* deck. The fight was over almost as soon as it began. The elven vessel was pulverized to nothing but white splinters floating in the seafoam.

Though one step closer to their much-needed information, the Jödmun met with yet another obstacle. The elves — defeated, quiet, and tied to the mast, refused to answer Ürbon's questions.

"Where were you headed?" he asked yet again, only to be met with more silence.

Many members of the crew had enough of this dead end and were suggesting torture or execution. Ürbon knew that if none of them would speak, it would have to come to that. Afterall, there was no food onboard the ship and the elven ship was sunk.

"Yes, execute us and rid us of the painful sight of you, foul creatures!" one of the elves retorted.

"I thought elves liked rocks, moss, and other such things," Ürbon said, turning to the elf.

"There is nothing natural about you. You're a monster, twisted and warped by magic," said the prisoner in response, and spat on the deck.

"Watch it, elf!" Ürbon snarled. "I'm the only one keeping you from brutal torture." He was almost ready to let his crew do things their way. After hearing the elves and their insults, many of them had already decided on the best ways to get them to talk. They even brought up rope and hooks from the lower decks.

But that would have to wait, since for the second time that day, one of the crewmen yelled.

"Land Ho!"

Ürbon looked straight ahead through his spyglass, and there it was, between the hazy mist and sea spray — hints of an island. As the mist parted and *The North Wind* drew closer, the first thing Ürbon noticed was the enormity of the land. Along the shoreline, he could see a cluster of jetties where various ships were docked. This seemed to be a harbor of quite a large settlement. He could see elven structures stretching far inland. Lush jungles with flowing rivers surrounded the village, but what really caught Ürbon's attention was a volcano, billowing smoke up to the sky.

Ürbon commanded his crew to prepare to land as they steered *The North Wind* alongside a port jetty.

So far, there was nobody to be seen, though one could tell this was no deserted city. Fish, spices, and other trading goods could be seen lining the stalls, but as Ürbon and his crew stepped down from the boat, they saw no people behind the stocked counters or walking in the streets.

"This doesn't seem right," said one of the crewmen.

"Where are all the people?" asked another as they reached the end of one street and found themselves at a five-pointed plaza. It looked as if amidst the activity of a busy afternoon, all the residents had vanished into thin air, leaving their day half-finished. Amidst the silence, even the weakest winds could be heard, gently pushing empty wicker baskets across the narrow streets.

The silence gave way to the noise of marching feet as all the streets were suddenly blocked by groups of elves. Seeing they were surrounded, Ürbon and his crew turned to go back to the harbor, only to find another group of elves marching forward. They were trapped.

Ürbon looked around at the elves; they were well prepared to ambush him and his crew. Behind every group were mages, each holding staves glowing from magical runes carved into the wood. *Not good*, he thought, *not good at all*. The Jödmun had become magical creatures from the Mountain Birth and in turn had become especially vulnerable to all forms of magic.

But this was not all that crushed his hopes, since amongst the last group of elven warriors, four of his guards flowed forth enveloped by a blue, glowing haze.

"I'm sorry, Captain, they appeared out of nowhere, surrounded us," one of them croaked. Ürbon had left some of his crewmen to take care of the ship and prisoners, though now he saw that the elves had also captured their only means of escape.

"Be gone from our island, savages!" an elf shouted, approaching Ürbon and his crew. He was taller than the rest of the elves and seemed to hold an air of authority as they parted respectfully to give way.

In a sense, Ürbon was relieved; at least he and his men wouldn't be killed without a moment to explain themselves.

"We did not intend to capture one of your vessels, O noble one. Your elven compatriots were the first to raise their sword and then, by chance, we happened upon this island. We do not wish you any harm!"

"Do not wish us harm?" the elf scoffed, pointing to a group of cut and bruised elves, the prisoners from *The North Wind*. "You claim to not wish us harm, yet just now you destroyed one of our boats and took our people prisoner?"

Ürbon could not find any words to reply. Clearly, the elves would never believe that their people were the first to take up weapons, that destroying the ship was an act of self-defense, not an unprovoked attack.

The elf saw the doubt and hesitation in Ürbon's eyes and after a moment shouted, "Mages! Take them to the dungeons!"

With swift movements, the blue glow of the staves shot out and engulfed each one of the Jödmun, lifting them up into the air. With a contingent of guards to protect them, the mages led their prisoners along the path to the volcano.

Ürbon watched the city slowly come back to life as the procession made its way out of the city. Elves looked out of their windows in fear; others walked out of their doorways, whispering to each other with nervous glances. It seemed they rarely saw members of other races, let alone a race from so far away, and some, overwhelmed by curiosity, even followed the marching soldiers.

Eventually, the procession reached the end of the city, where the path leading up to the volcano was blocked by an iron gate. Upon reaching this point, those who had followed from their homes retreated back to the town, as if frightened of whatever lay beyond.

The bold elf leader from the plaza now seemed frightened himself, as he conversed in hush tones with something beyond. Ürbon craned his neck to see, but all he could make out was the elf talking to the gate. Abruptly, the gates swung open, and the procession moved on. After a while they entered into some sort of structure and they were led down many hallways, continuously turning left and right. The blue glow covered his vision, and he couldn't make sense of his surroundings. Without a warning, he was tumbling to the damp stony ground, and an iron door was slammed shut behind him.

The blue glow ebbed away, and he could move freely once more. He looked around and saw that he was left within a circular pit, surrounded by slick and smooth walls he could not climb. Ürbon desperately tried to think of a means to escape. He had been put in a chamber separate from the group, and for all he knew, they wouldn't have any idea where to find him if they were to make an attempt to escape.

The realization of failure made his blood boil. For weeks, they had sailed with no hint of land. After meeting nothing but dead-ends for months, they finally seemed able to move forward with their plans, only to be met by what appeared to be a conclusive impasse. He paced and stomped around the walls of the chamber, trying to get a grip on his anger, but instead his rage came to a head. He saw only red and a wall in front of him. With a roar that shook the chamber itself, he let his anger loose, hitting the stone with awesome fury. His fists felt no pain as his hand broke through; he ripped his hand out and hit the wall even harder, breaking it to pieces revealing a tunnel of black, glasslike stone.

He punched again only to find air as the wall had crumbled under his blows. He took a step back as his rage subsided. He felt an uneasy stroke of good luck; it seemed as if he would be able to escape, if only this tunnel led to somewhere useful. But what of his crew? It would be impossible to rescue them on his own, what chance would he have against elven magic? His only option would be to make his way back home and muster an army to rescue them.

Having no other option he took a deep breath and leapt into the tunnel. Where he thought to find ground, he found only empty air.

This was not a tunnel but an entrance into a chamber, a chamber inside a volcano, illuminated red. And where he expected to find ground, he instead found a pool of lava...

The further submerged in lava he became, the more his head pounded. Groaning, he tried to climb higher. The last time his head felt like this was after drinking a cask of firemead. It had seemed like a good idea at the time, until he woke up in the morning.

Slowly wading out of the hot lava he hauled himself onto a platform of solid granite. Looking around, he saw that the chamber consisted only of a pool of lava, with slabs of granite above the surface. Ürbon looked up to see shards of stalactites on the high ceiling. There was a small hole right above him that showed the tunnel from which he fell. Climbing up there would be impossible; besides, he'd just find himself trapped yet again.

Ürbon looked across the magma; he could see a small tunnel on the other side of the chamber. He stepped down from the granite once again and waded across to the tunnel. Though he could still feel the heat of the magma, after a while it felt more like a hot bath than anything else. Once he made his way across, he stepped into the tunnel and walked along its winding path. He could tell from the rising heat that he was walking towards the volcano's heart, but to turn back would be pointless. So he continued along the path, across smaller caverns dotted with little lava puddles.

Eventually, he found himself in a truly enormous cavern, illuminated by an icy blue glow that filled the vast space. The source of this light came from an object in the center, and there was some unknown pull that called Ürbon towards it.

Curious about the glowing light, Ürbon made his way through the cavern, moving through the shallow puddles of magma dotting the surface. The eerie darkness of the cavern was nothing compared to the wonder of the blue glow radiating from its center.

As he reached the middle, he found the mysterious object to be a block of ice. How did a block of ice come to be in the heart of a volcano? And how did it not simply melt on the spot? Ürbon could not know. He gazed in wonder at the mysterious thing, marveling at how it kept its form despite the heat. What also gained his attention was a handle sticking out of the block. Upon further inspection, he noticed the transparency of the ice and a curious shape within. He thought he could see a large horned head and rows of teeth bared at him. The edges and hairline cracks of the icy container amplified a certain power within.

Ürbon did not know why he grasped the protruding hilt. It could easily have been either an act of fate or simply the enactment of childish fantasy; the hilt being the arm of a blade of yore, and he, Ürbon, the legendary hero to lay claim to the fable.

But no amount of fable or legend could have prepared him for this.

As his hands gripped the leather, a white flash engulfed his vision. He tightened his grip to keep himself steady. An ear-splitting crack rang through his ears, the white flash growing stronger. He closed his eyes to escape the blinding light, but it was no use. He felt himself engulfed by it, lost in its freezing glare. He shuddered from the icy light, and, for the first time, Ürbon felt fear, gut-wrenching, heart-stopping fear.

The flash dissipated as suddenly as it began, and Ürbon opened his eyes, still dazed from the blinding light, to find himself in darkness once more. The icy blue glow was also gone, and where once was a block of ice now was an empty space. Yet he still held the hilt in his hand, free of its icy lock.

What was now in his hands was an axe of ice and steel, the haft wrapped in soft leather. He recognized the steel of the axe's pole. It was a metal used by Jödmun craftsmen, a formula of steel and a rock substrate, creating a virtually indestructible material. What was more impressive, however, was the ice sculpted atop the pole, a visage of a wyrm, whereas the wyrm's fiery breath was of steel, forming the blade.

Ürbon knew this axe but could not believe it to be in his hands. There was only one such weapon in existence. Bjarl, the rune axe of legend, crafted by the greatest blacksmith of the Jödmun, Volstagg the Mad Smith himself.

He looked at the axe in awe. He could not avert his gaze, its wonder and beauty captivating him. This was a true legend within his grasp. How it ever came to be here, so far from home, he could not fathom.

His eyes barely tore away from the legendary weapon as a scorching fire erupted in the darkness. Ürbon saw red and orange flames, coiling and twirling around a great horned head. It rose amidst a rumble of rocks. Two blazing eyes glared at him as its mouth opened in a snarl, the flames burning ever stronger. Sharp black scales peeked out from behind tendrils of flame which flowed out from a large jaw lined with pearlescent teeth.

As if one legend within this cavern was not enough, Ürbon held back a gasp as yet another rose from the darkness. Any Jödmun would know well what creature this was, for only one could breathe flame, and they were revered as the most terrifying yet majestic of all. It's cold-blue eyes stared as Ürbon stood his ground, holding

Bjarl firmly in his grip. Fear would only inflame a full-grown dragon.

"You do not cower in my presence, thief?" The dragon's voice seemed to resonate from the cavern itself. A jet of fire shot from its mouth and streamed past Ürbon, lighting a brazier at the other end of the cavern. Now Ürbon could see the true magnificence of the creature. Covered in scales like shards of obsidian, its wingspan could reach from one end of the cavern to the other.

"I am no thief; I merely seek that which belongs to my people!" Ürbon replied, standing his ground as the dragon stepped closer, peering at him and Bjarl with a keen and intelligent eye.

Bjarl crackled with lighting in his hands, giving Ürbon confidence. "I will go through whatever trial necessary to restore this axe, even if that means to go against you, dragon!"

At this, the chamber erupted. Rocks fell from the ceiling as a growling cackle echoed off the stone walls. The dragon seemed to convulse as fire rhythmically erupted, unchecked with each breath.

"Your naivety amuses me. You cannot know how long it has been since a soul has entered my home, especially one with an ounce of courage. Or perhaps it is simply lunacy that gives you such confidence. Those elves were right; you are odd folk, odd folk indeed!" The cavern shook as the dragon took a step closer to Ürbon. "That axe does not simply belong to the Jödmun, Wanderer. It was forged by the great smith Volstagg and only his descendants may wield it!"

The dragon's attention shifted from Ürbon to Bjarl. He stared at it as if in contemplation, a gust of smoke drifting from his nose. "I suppose there is only one way to know whether you are worthy to carry such a gift."

With a deep breath, he exhaled a stream of fire, giving Ürbon barely a second to react. He ducked his head under his elbow, ready for the fire to kill him, for dragon fire was one of the few things that could. Yet he didn't feel the burning touch of fire, and after a moment, he raised his head to see a barrier surrounding him. An icy blue shield stemmed from between Bjarl's two pointed horns. The dragon, seeing his fire was obstructed, closed his jaws, extinguishing the flames.

"I suppose you do have a right to the axe after all, Jödmun," The dragon snorted, once again looking at Ürbon with an amused glint in his eyes. "Go, take the axe. I have no right to keep it from Volstagg's kin."

With a single glance, the brazier burned out, leaving Ürbon once more in darkness.

Not knowing whether to trust that the dragon would truly let him go, Ürbon stood there with no light to guide him except for Bjarl's icy glow. For only a moment, the dragon's massive head was visible once more, as a great fireball shot out towards the wall, revealing a new pathway.

"Will this suffice for you to leave, now? Or would you like me to carry you out?" the dragon roared.

Without wanting to anger the dragon further, Ürbon walked towards the opened path. But his curiosity took hold of him, and he could not help but ask.

"Why are you letting me leave with such a valuable piece of your hoard? Or is this some kind of a trick?" Ürbon asked into the darkness.

"Perhaps there is a bit of foolishness to you after all. How quick you are to assume I have a need for tricks. You mortal races are all the same; elves, dwarves, humans...Jödmun," the dragon spat with contempt. "You all think yourselves so powerful, when you have no knowledge of the true sources of power in this world. You're all little more than ants crawling on a round table, oblivious to those sitting around it. If I let you leave with this *valuable piece of my hoard* it is simply because I choose to...Now leave!" The dragon's grumble reverberated through the dark cavern.

For some time Ürbon trudged through the mountain path, pondering the dragon's last words. Then his thoughts turned to his captured crew again. Bjarl, still firmly in his grip, was a formidable weapon, but, even with it, he himself didn't stand a chance against the elven mages.

Eventually he made his way out of the volcano and found himself in a dense forest. It was only just sundown, and the sky illuminated his surroundings in a deep blue glow. He walked through the undergrowth, the moonlight barely lighting his way. Still engulfed with thinking up a rescue plan, he knew he couldn't risk getting trapped again, for then they would all be lost forever. He would have to make his way off the island, find some way he could get back home and recruit an army powerful enough to withstand the elven magic. Engrossed in thought, he didn't notice when the path gave way to loose rocks. Before Ürbon realized what was happening, he found himself falling.

He tumbled down a steep cliff, crashing into rocks and foliage, desperately trying to grasp whatever he could reach, but nothing would hold. When he finally reached the ground, he was once again dazed. Finding himself in another series of caves, he clenched his fists, growling in frustration. But at least Bjarl was still with him. Looking around the series of caves and tunnels, Ürbon could swear he saw a flash of eyes peering through the darkness. He blinked to make sense of it, but at that same moment it disappeared. He dismissed the thought, assuming the fall had simply dazed him.

Taking a moment to gather himself and clear his head, he looked up the sheer wall to the night sky far above him; there was no hope of climbing back up. The only possible trail was a cavern to the right, though obscured by shadows. With a determined sigh he gripped Bjarl and walked down the path. The axes glow lit the way and he took care not to misstep this time.

As he continued to walk, curious markings began to dot the rock walls. The further he walked the more densely they appeared. Most of them he couldn't understand, but some of them he recognized. On his travels, he had learnt bits and pieces of various tongues, and he knew at least some of these glyphs belonged to the ancient Gataran language. He had stopped to take a closer look at a portion of glyphs when a flash of movement caught his eye, and he heard a scrabble of loose rock. He turned to see the source and had just missed it, save for a white reptilian tail, scurrying around a corner.

Ürbon gave chase to the mysterious creature, following the flash of white and scrabble of claws. Turning left and right, he ran through the caverns when at last he caught up to the creature, barely glimpsing it before it disappeared through a tiny gap in the rock walls. No use even thinking of getting through that tiny gap, so he did all he could do and hit the wall with his axe. Bjarl made quick work of the solid rock. With just a few hits, he had opened a gap in the wall, wide enough for even him to get through, and found that he had created an opening to another cavern.

Ürbon stepped through the entrance and found himself surrounded by carved hieroglyphs, and the reptilian creature cowering in a corner, holding its shaking tail with thin, spindly fingers. Its white scales and ridged spine, along with its thin and wiry features made it look sickly, like its strength had long since seeped away. It did not meet Ürbon's gaze, instead looking at the fragments lying at the Jödmun's feet, hieroglyphs carved into the wall he had just knocked down.

Ürbon looked at the shattered rock shards. He could still make out the images — a black-winged shape much like a dragon surrounded by flowing lava. Another shard was dotted with white and icy blue specks like a blizzard, an axe in its center. Yet another fragment showed a bolt of lightning, or something similar. There appeared to be more to the image, but it was too shattered and broken to decipher.

He turned around only to find himself surrounded by reptilian creatures. They stared at him inquisitively; most of them were smaller than the one he had followed. Three significantly larger figures stepped forward on webbed feet, they towered over their smaller brethren, who bowed and parted respectfully to give them way.

They stood there simply staring at Ürbon as if waiting for something. But the Jödmun's patience had grown thin, and he didn't have time to stand around all day. Judging from the language of the hieroglyphs earlier on, he was sure these creatures would speak some sort of Gataran, and he knew a bit of the language himself.

"What?" Ürbon said to the crowd of curious reptiles, who jumped back in surprise. Only the three larger ones held their gaze, though their eyes seemed to light up in excitement.

"At last, he has come!" one of them answered, raising its spindly arms. Ürbon knelt to be level with the old wrinkled reptile; clearly it was not in its right mind.

"Show me the way out of these caves," he said as gently as he could.

"Long have we waited for the savior from above! Long have we Geck'teks hidden in these dark burrows, waiting for the day he shall break down this wall, its painted image turned into reality! And now he has appeared and shall raise us out to walk free upon the land once more. At last he has come to help us take back our rightful place as rulers of all the Gatarans!" it cried, its arms still raised as more of the Geck'teks joined the crowd.

Ürbon tried to comment that he was definitely not interested in anything but getting out of these caves, but it was of no use; the frail elder kept to its long and drawn out speech.

"The time has come for those inferior Gatarans to regret the day they turned on their masters! They shall pay tenfold for their insolence! Their homes shall burn and they shall all live in chains! For the savior from above has come, and the Geck'teks shall rise up..."

Ürbon was done paying attention. His thoughts wandering back to his purpose, getting out of the cave and off the island.

Finally the elder stopped talking, and beckoned sharply to a distant Geck'tek, who hurriedly scurried over. This one was much larger than the rest, and carried two spears crossed between his shoulders. A vast array of small jars were strapped across his chest, and a tiny dagger of jagged black stone upon his waist. The Geck'tek leaned in to listen as the elder whispered into his ear, but his gaze never left Ürbon, who looked back at the reptilian creature with a cold, implacable stare.

The elder whispered a final word and turned back to Ürbon. "Behold, Tlupic! One of our most prized warriors; he will be your guide! Now go back to the surface and fulfill your destiny!" The elder spoke as the cavern erupted with the noise of scrabbling feet. Small Geck'teks scurried away, disappearing through tiny holes, emptying the cavern. Tlupic gave a final nod to the elders, walked past Ürbon and beckoned him to follow. Ürbon followed the Geck'tek warrior, only wishing to get back to the surface, even if it meant playing into the frail elder's mad fantasies.

After a long walk through the winding caves, they made it to the surface. The sky was brightening as dawn broke; the air was filled with the sounds of the lush and humid forest. It almost felt like they were in a jungle. Ürbon looked at the awe-struck Geck'tek, frantically moving to a fro, observing everything from the trees to the grass. Its stupefied gaze looking up at the sky covered in hues of purple and blue.

Ürbon stomped past the reptile; he didn't have time for this...

***

Tlupic wallowed in his freedom, taking in the fresh air, the sounds of life and the beautiful colors of the world. Leaving the burrows was a punishable offense for the Geck'tek, only allowed when a sacrifice was needed for the gods. And even then, only for a short period of time. But sometimes he would sneak out of the caverns to catch a glimpse of the world's beauty. There was a time when all of the Geck'teks lived out in the open, under the eternal sky. They used to be the elite, ruling over the lesser clans. Everything changed when a sacrifice was made of an important Gataran. Despite being ruled over by the Geck'teks, the lesser clans had leaders of their own. And upon seeing one of their leaders sacrificed the Gatarans and lesser clans rebelled against the Geck'teks, driving them into exile. Now Tlupic and his people lived underground, hunted and killed whenever they ventured out.

He did not know much of the surface and the races who lived there. The elders only spoke of such things when a sacrifice was needed, or when a raid would be organized to strike against wielders of magic. Magic belongs to the gods and any mortal who used magic was a thief. For magic did not belong to them, and only by sacrificing them would that magic be restored to its rightful owners. Tlupic would occasionally be a part of these raids, capturing a user of magic and taking them to the altar. Like a sixth sense, the Geck'teks could feel the presence of magic from miles away, and their basest instinct was to return this gift back to the gods, an instinct devoid of hesitation.

It was this sense that had drawn him to the cavern. Others of his brethren had already made it there and stood staring at the stone monstrosity standing in front of the elders. The strange creature had a truly impressive stature. Taller than any Gataran he had ever seen, it had no scales or tail and was armed with an impressive axe. Resembling a roaring dragon, it seemed to be made entirely out of ice, yet it showed no signs of melting. The elders called the giant *Azmekui*, the "savior from above." A sacred figure, shrouded by myth, but this creature of stone would only be a half of the prophecy, for the *Azmekui* was not a single entity but a pair linked by fate itself.

The elders saw Tlupic approach and beckoned him forward.

"Tlupic, guide him on his journey, for he will need your aid," the elder said in hushed tones.

"But an *Azmekui* is not one, but a pair! What of our own bringer of light from among our people?"

The elder silenced him with a gesture, "You are the second *Azmekui*, young Tlupic, together you will guide our people out of these caves, but for now, your journey begins on the surface."

With no room to argue and a duty to obey his elders, Tlupic walked over to the stone creature. "Fellow *Azmekui*, I am Tlupic the Sky Seeker. I will be your guide and companion."

But it only scoffed and moved quickly, in a hurry to move things along.

***

The unlikely pair made their way through the lush forest, carrying the supplies the elder's provided. At first, Ürbon had been going his own way. Since this was an island, logic dictated that if he kept walking in one direction he would eventually end up at a shore. But he was stopped by Tlupic multiple times. Though he hadn't spent much time on the surface, Tlupic knew the territory better than Ürbon, and steered him onto better trails. Heading east was their wisest option, as to the north and west lay Gataran territory and to the south were the orcs. All that mattered to Ürbon was getting to a shore as quickly as possible, avoiding all confrontation, and though he was initially too stubborn to take the Geck'tek's advice, eventually he gave in.

Ürbon walked through the forest with long strides, eager to get to the shore. Though the Geck'tek had trouble keeping up with the taller and faster Jödmun, Ürbon did not seem to care, unwilling to slow down their progress. Indeed, he barely noticed that Tlupic had fallen behind, or that he was utterly alone when a group of Gatarans surrounded him.

The creatures were taller than the Geck'teks and looked far more vicious, with a long, scaly, crocodilian snout that had long sharp teeth protruding from their jaws. They stood on two legs and brandished various weapons of crude metal, their upper bodies supported by their strong tails.

Ürbon looked around to find Tlupic but the Geck'tek was nowhere to be seen, and so he turned to meet the Gatarans' vicious glare as the circle tightened. The Gatarans were talking to each other in what sounded like snarls and hisses. It was much more guttural than the Geck'teks more refined tongue; Ürbon couldn't understand a word.

He brandished Bjarl and prepared to meet a charging Gataran. The creature moved faster than anticipated, and he barely met the blow of its halberd in time. Occupied with parrying and dodging the attacks, Ürbon hadn't noticed the other Gatarans behind him slowly closing in. Feeling a weight upon his shoulder, he realized his mistake. Moving fast he caught his current opponent off guard and killed it with one mighty blow. He then turned to meet the Gataran who was bearing him down.

When he turned, expecting to find a Gataran on his back, he found one crying out in pain as a spear was dug deep into its chest.

This weight upon his back was no Gataran, but Tlupic, who had killed the Gataran before it could strike at the unsuspecting Ürbon.

It was then that Ürbon realized the value of Tlupic's aid. He watched as the Geck'tek jumped swiftly around with agile movements, ducking and dodging every blow against him. Tlupic dispatched yet another Gataran before jumping back onto Ürbon's shoulder, a spear in each hand.

The two of them continued to fight the Gatarans, Tlupic lunging with his spear and Ürbon's Bjarl, trailing its ethereal glow, wreaking havoc upon their enemies. The crude metal of the Gatarans' weapons often broke during a parry or shattered against Ürbon's stone skin. Gatarans sprawled upon the ground, either dead or heavily wounded. Both allies were consumed by rage as arrows whizzed past, narrowly missing Tlupic and bouncing off Ürbon. With long strides, the Jödmun caught up with the Gataran archers. Tlupic's spear pierced their chests with powerful jabs, knocking them back. Ürbon caught up with two others and with quick blows finished them off.

Seeing Ürbon and Tlupic fight with such ferocity, the remaining Gatarans gave up the fight and disappeared into the woods as quickly as they had appeared. Alive and unscathed, Tlupic and Ürbon continued towards the shore with a newfound sense of camaraderie.

Ürbon no longer let Tlupic fall behind; from now on, the Geck'tek was always welcome on his shoulder. He sprawled there day in and day out, discussing his culture and traditions as the Jödmun repaid in kind by teaching Tlupic the Common Tongue.

It was during one of these conversations that Ürbon asked what Tlupic could sense between Bjarl and himself.

"We are both warped by magic, of course, my people are under the power of a spell, which made my flesh the way it is," Ürbon asked.

"With you, yes, the gods have given your people their gift. You have not stolen their power. The axe, well, the axe is strange, strong magic, much power. Too strong for Tlupic, it gives me a headache. But I can tell that this is not its true power. No, the axe is asleep!" the Geck'tek replied.

"The dragon spoke of the axe as if it was a living thing. Like it chooses where it goes or with whom."

"The dragon speaks true, the axe appears to have chosen you." Tlupic uncurled on Ürbon's shoulder and looked up to the sky where there were large white birds with black-tipped wings flying across. "Once we reach the sea, what's next?" Tlupic realized he hadn't asked before.

"To a port, to catch a ship headed to Maldora, from there we'll sail further north to my home. There, I can get more men to rescue my crew from the elves," he replied.

"Elves!" Tlupic said "Magic wielders! Let's go kill them!"

"Their magic is too strong even for you, Tlupic." Ürbon smirked. Though he was wary of the dangers ahead, the readiness of the Geck'tek amused him. "We cannot do it alone. We will need more men."

Eventually, they reached the shore and luckily had to look no further for a port. They had reached the renowned port city of Servialdes, a major trading center in the area. There were ships harbored on the jetties and many traders stopped to stare at the ten-foot tall Jödmun and the Geck'tek upon his shoulder.

Scraping together whatever gold they could find, Ürbon and Tlupic had just enough to bargain for passage over the sea. Though most of the ships were too small to carry Ürbon or too large to be discreet, one in particular caught the Jödmun's eye. *The Swift Eel* was written on its bow, and a woman called Amuliea was its captain. She was a keen-eyed woman, and clearly a good haggler judging from the large sum she was able to get for giving them room on the ship.

And so the Jödmun and Geck'tek boarded, bade farewell to that fateful island, and sailed off into the horizon.

Chapter 2:
Through Uncertain Waters

Upon the bow of her ship, Captain Amuliea looked out over the seas. She was a sailor, always had been, and was born to the salty breeze of the sea. Her ship, *The Swift Eel*, was currently crashing against the waves of the open ocean. She was on a job, quite an odd one at that. She turned behind her to glance at the two passengers.

She looked at the stone giant named Ürbon, who was reading a comically small leatherbound book he brought aboard with him. Ürbon was one of the Jödmun, a stone-like humanoid race hailing from the north. They were often spoken of in reverence and treated as a myth by humans like her who came from the south, but this one was clearly real. He had a massive axe the likes of which Amuliea had never seen, seemingly sculpted from ice, yet refusing to melt in the heat of the sun. In tales, it was told that the Jödmun were mythical smiths, and this axe was nothing short of a masterwork.

Turning away from the stone giant, her eyes fell onto his companion. A small thing, and seeming to be a lizardman of some sort, it wasn't even tall enough to reach her shoulders. It spoke in a strange language, rasping and dry, and she had caught glimpses of a tongue forked like that of a serpent. It was highly alert at all times, constantly moving around, its eyes, with pupils like that of a jungle cat, constantly exploring its surroundings. The lizard had two spears crossed upon its back, which were designed to perfectly match the reptile's white skin.

Honestly, Amuliea didn't like it, not one bit. But, she would persevere, as the giant promised a hefty sum for this transport. She was ordered to take her ship to the Shattered Isles, saying he was on important business. So she tore her gaze away and continued to stare out onto the open sea. Milton, her second in command, was piloting the ship; he needed the experience. He was practically still a child, and so that left her with some time to contemplate. *The Swift Eel* was not very impressive, with a singular sail as well as a hull tiny in comparison to one of the Maldoran trading vessels, but so far it had always done its job.

Captain Amuliea leaned with her arms across the ship's railing, watching as storm clouds rolled their way in. "Damn," she thought to herself, as she realized they weren't going to be able to steer clear of the storm. The clouds stretched a long, dark line across the horizon. She stoically marched towards her two passengers, it's best they stayed out of her way and under the deck during the storm.

As she approached, the lizard stopped its flurry of twitching movements and tensed, its yellow eyes fixed firmly on Amuliea, as if she was a threat.

Ignoring its wary glare, she directed her attention at Ürbon, who looked up from his book with an indifferent look. "Storm's coming," stated Amuliea. "I suggest heading under the deck and taking shelter before it hits."

The giant looked as if he were about to respond, but seemed to think better of it and simply nodded his head, closed his book, and stood. His reptilian friend protested, but Ürbon ignored him and went below deck, crouching to enter the stairwell at the stern of the ship. The lizard creature hissed, and after glaring at Amuliea, fled down the steps to join his companion. As it ran out of her sight, she let out a sigh of relief. That had been easier than expected.

***

Ürbon calmly walked down the stairwell to the lower deck. He didn't think much of the captain, but she was the only person willing to take a Jödmun overseas.

"Why didn't you do anything? That was humiliating!" Tlupic said in Gataran. Ürbon was in the process of teaching him the Common Tongue, but so far he'd been reluctant to practice. "She demanded far too much of us."

"She is the captain of the vessel, and if we don't treat her with respect, then we will not be able to get to the Shattered Isles," Ürbon replied smoothly, having some difficulty maneuvering around a turn in the stairwell. "We must simply remain calm and collected, so we won't have to triple our price."

"Still, she should know her place! We should be treated with greater respect. Better food and better beds!" The small lizardman was furious, clearly not used to the conditions of travel.

"They act according to their own customs, Tlupic, and we must follow those customs if we are to befriend them." Ürbon said wearily, for what seemed the hundredth time.

"I do not understand why we must be so kind to them, we are the..." the Geck'tek stopped short as he realized they had reached the inner hull, and that the rowers were staring at them. Hurriedly, he shut his mouth and scurried behind the Jödmun.

While Ürbon had learned to be patient with long stretches at sea, the Geck'tek's constant complaints were testing his patience. Setting Bjarl to the side, he once again opened the leather-bound book he had been reading on the deck. However, just as he began to get into the book, one of the rowing men began to wheeze and groan. Attempting to ignore the man and focus on his book, he found the man's labored breathing incredibly annoying. Finally having enough, he set his book down and went up to the man.

The rowers turned their heads as he approached. When the man looked up at Ürbon amidst his coughing fit the Jödmun motioned for him to move aside. The message was received clearly and the man scurried out of the way allowing Ürbon to take his spot.

Rowing wasn't hard work, at least not to him. The curse granted him the luxury of never getting tired, he saw no reason not to ease both his irritation and the rower's labored breathing. So with one hand, he rowed the oar, and with the other, he turned the pages of his book.

***

As *The Swift Eel* fought the murky waters, Amuliea watched the stormy seas. The ship pitched and turned as she fought for control of the vessel. Lightning flashed overhead, illuminating the dark seas in brief flashes as the wind howled like a wounded animal. The ship rolled towards the starboard, and Amuliea grabbed the wheel with all her might, heaving in the opposite direction, barely regaining control of the ship.

The rain was coming down in blinding sheets, and the storm had been going on for at least a few hours, causing her to lose her sense of direction when the clouds blocked the stars. The storm showed no signs of letting up, as the ship once again listed to the side. She could barely see where they were going through the blistering rain, and it took everything she had to keep the ship under control. All she had to do was endure the storm for only a few more hours, but she was almost completely spent. Just as she thought she had no more to give, she heard a set of footsteps approaching. They were so loud she could hear them over the howling wind and constant drone of the rain, and she was greeted with the sight of the Jödmun approaching.

"It's not safe up here!" she shouted, barely able to hear herself over a blast of thunder. "Get back below deck!"

However, the stone giant was undaunted and continued to stand still. After several seconds, he offered a hand, asking to take the wheel from her. "What? No! This is my ship, I will handle it!" Amuliea was outraged by this slight. Her ship was everything to her, the culmination of a life's hard work.

"I am a sailor too," the Jödmun said, "The storm is too strong, it's not safe for you up here. Let me help you."

Amuliea was about to respond in anger, but the giant spoke true. She was almost at her breaking point, and if what she heard about Jödmun was true, they had unlimited energy, without a need for rest or sleep. She could tell that he understood the code of sailors, the unspoken rules of the seafaring, and she knew he meant well. So, she begrudgingly accepted the offer.

When she let go of the wheel, she feared the ship would spiral out of control and sink to the ocean deeps, but her fears went unrealized as massive stone hands grasped the wood and held it steady. The warmth of relief swept through her body, and she knew that she had made the correct decision. As she watched the rain patter off the Jödmun's stone skin, she realized that the feeling of warmth was rapidly replaced with that of horrid cold. With a start, she realized she was shivering. Giving in, she took to the shelter of her quarters and the pull of her bunk.

***

Tlupic writhed in boredom in the inner hull of *The Swift Eel*. He was surrounded by unknown humans, trapped upon the sea, completely at their mercy and that of the nature spirits. When he had set out on his journey with Ürbon, who had fulfilled the centuries-old prophecy of his people, he had hoped to find adventures that were slightly more...invigorating, to put it lightly.

Here he was, forced to stay amongst beings that had no knowledge of him or his customs, and thought him a mere animal. It was degrading, and he had considered total slaughter of everyone aboard the ship several times but had been forced to reconsider, as his rock companion counseled otherwise.

Several minutes after Ürbon had left, the captain herself came down, drenched and shivering. Tlupic watched as she unlocked a door and wondered what could be on the other side. What could possibly be so important to warrant such secrecy? Overcome with curiosity he stealthily slipped into the room before the captain slammed the door and turned the key.

Tlupic silently sprinted to cover behind a bed that was much bigger than any he had slept in and took in the room around him. It was as large as the entire living quarters of the sailors, and better furnished. There were two beds — the one he was hiding behind and a smaller one complete with a pillow. Both were built into the wall to ensure stability, as was every other piece of furniture or seating arrangement. The beds were opposite each other, and in between them was a table.

As his eyes peered out from behind the bed, he watched as the captain ripped the blanket off the large bed he was crouching behind, and wrapped it around herself, before sitting down in a chair next to the table. Upon hearing her enter the room, a shape under the blankets of the smaller bed shifted and rose.

As the figure sat up, the blankets fell away, revealing a boyish face, with blonde hair and sky-blue eyes. He was young, no older than eighteen, and as he rubbed the sleep from his eyes, his eyes settled on the captain, shivering at the table.

"Oh no!' he exclaimed, "Are you alright, Captain?"

"Of course I'm alright, you dolt!" She retorted.

Their conversation was horribly awkward after that, even Tlupic could tell with his limited grasp of the Common Tongue. The boy kept trying to help the captain but was continually getting rebuffed until he finally sat back down on his bed, dejected.

Clearly this was pointless, but it was still more entertaining than sitting on a bench and playing with his tail. Tlupic watched the pair in silence for a few minutes until the captain looked like she was about to make up with the boy. But as luck would have it, it was at that moment that the boy's gaze met with his, and they both froze at the contact.

The captain said something, but Tlupic did not catch her words, instead focused on the boy slowly raising a finger pointed straight at him.

That is not good at all, thought Tlupic, as the captain followed the finger. Upon seeing the Geck'tek, her gaze filled with rage, and she lunged at him, screaming something he couldn't quite understand, but could guess was something along the lines of "get out of my quarters, you bastard!"

Tlupic thought fast and jumped, scrambling over her as her head crashed into the wall. He landed on the table, and the boy's face paled before he collapsed onto his pillow, unconscious. Tlupic watched him fall, stiff, and blinked in wonder at how strange humans were. He was interrupted by another screaming lunge by the captain, which he again dodged. The captain crashed into the table, her face twisting in pain, and as her eyes met with that of the lizardman, rage that increased tenfold burned within her eyes.

***

After hours of fighting the wind and the waves, the storm overhead passed, and calm once more reigned over the sea. Ürbon still stood at the wheel, once again reading through his leather-bound book. Finally at a moment of peace and quiet, he took out an ink pen and began to write down the events of the previous night. Though it used to be his captain's log, and was accordingly enchanted to be water-proof, since losing *The North Wind* it had become his private journal.

As he began to write, however, a very distressed and angry Amuliea came up from below deck, dragging a reluctant Tlupic by his tail. Ürbon glared at Tlupic as he fought uselessly against Amuliea's grip, and his struggles stopped.

Amuliea swung her arm around and threw the lizard at Ürbon's feet with a grunt, where the lizard was fixed with an icy glare by both the captain and the Jödmun.

"Please explain to me how I came to find your friend sneaking around my room?"

The lizard looked up at Ürbon for support, only to meet a gaze as hard as the mountains.

"I expect you to pay *double* when we get there." The captain added.

Ürbon nodded, keeping his face stone cold. As the captain stomped back down below deck, Ürbon focused his gaze upon the lizard beneath him.

"I told you to not upset them," Ürbon's gravelly voice was deep, and upset, and beneath it hid a vast fiery pool of anger at his scaly companion. "Do something like this again and we're done."

***

Several days had now gone by and the crew aboard *The Swift Eel* had realized that the storm had blown them off course. Thus, they would be several days late to the Shattered Isles. But the wind was in their favor, so it wouldn't be much longer.

Ürbon looked out from the bow of the vessel, watching the waves churn and break upon the ship's hull. The boy who was the second in command was currently piloting the ship, as instructed by the captain. He looked at peace behind the wheel, though it was easy to see he wasn't as confident as he should have been for a second in command. Ürbon was about to go down below deck to see if he could soothe Amuliea's temper, and potentially get the price down, but as he turned away, something caught his eye. There was a small speck upon the horizon, then two more appeared next to it, on the port side of *The Swift Eel*, blocking their path to the Shattered Isles.

Ürbon cursed under his breath and ran down to the captain's quarters, having to slow on the staircase. As he reached the captain's door, he gently knocked on the wood. Muffled grunts could be heard from within, and so he knocked again. The door opened, and a very disheveled and annoyed Amuliea greeted him, as it appeared she was sleeping.

"Get back on deck, right now!"

"Last I checked, I'm captain of this ship, and I go where I please, when I please," Amuliea retorted, turning away from Ürbon, "I need my rest."

"There's ships heading straight towards us."

"Merchant ships, that's all."

"You and I both know that merchant ships don't block another's path," the Jödmun replied.

He felt sorry for the captain; with an incompetent crew, and an inexperienced second in command, running a ship would be endless work. She probably barely slept at all since they set sail.

"I'll be up in a moment," she said, walking towards her gear determinedly. Closing the door, Ürbon went back up the stairs to notify the second in command.

When Ürbon came up to the deck, the previous specks had gotten closer. Though they were still too far away to tell if they were friend or foe, it was best not to leave anything to chance. As the minutes passed, Amuliea came back onto the upper deck followed by the six rowers from below deck, each armed with a small arming sword. The wind kept strong, so there was a chance that they could still escape from the ships.

However, such hopes were dashed against the waves as the vessels grew ever larger and looked as if they were coming directly for *The Swift Eel*. Soon they were close enough to distinguish features of each ship. There were three, with two flanking the center vessel. The two flanking ships were similar in structure to *The Swift Eel*, with only one sail and a set of six oars. However, the biggest threat was the central ship. With three massive masts, each boasting two sails, the ship was clearly of Maldoran make. Though one of their smaller versions, it still dwarfed the others.

The size of the vessel was not the main concern. Maldoran ships were known for their deadly weaponry. And despite its name, *The Swift Eel* was not capable of evading such a massive ship, even with such favorable winds.

As the crew waited on deck, Tlupic scampered up the steps of the ship, wondering why no one had chosen to wake him when everyone had left the lower deck. He clambered atop Ürbon's shoulder and asked what was happening, to which Ürbon replied by pointing a stone finger. Tlupic's eyes narrowed at the sight of the incoming vessels and his face grew serious. He then whispered something unsettling in the Jödmun's ear.

"They have magic," was all Tlupic said, and Ürbon knew the Geck'tek spoke the truth. The Jödmun considered warning the others but decided against it. If they knew they were up against such impossible odds, then they might be moved to simply surrender.

The ships drew inevitably closer, until finally one of the smaller ships came to the side of *The Swift Eel*, the other two close behind. After someone shouted orders on the other ship, a plank was put between the two.

Three men climbed aboard *The Swift Eel.* They were wearing clothes befitting people of the Shattered Isles, though they were notably dirty and ragged. Their sunburnt faces, as well as how comfortable they were in crossing the plank, showed that they had been out on the sea for quite a while. The leader of the group stepped forward.

"We wish to see the cap'n, so please be kind enough to bring 'em 'ere!" The man spoke as if drunk with a heavy accent on top of the heavy smell of alcohol.

"You're looking at her," replied Amuliea, calmly. She clearly didn't like the man or his cohorts, and her nose wrinkled at the smell of his breath. "What do you need, and how can we help you?"

"We're just 'ere to collect our tax, ye'see. Sailin' these here waters don't come cheap!" The man smiled, revealing large gaps between yellow and blackened teeth.

With every word, spittle flew in every direction. They were clearly pirates, making a living by attacking and harassing trade routes on the open waters.

Wiping the spittle from her face, Amuliea replied. "I've never heard of this tax you speak of, and I've been sailing this route for over ten years!"

The man's smile faltered, and he scratched the stubble on his chin, looking thoughtfully up at the sky. "Well, it's one o' them new taxes, ye'see. Now, I'll just be telling the cap'n that this 'ere lass ain't no payin' 'er taxes!" The other men laughed at this strange joke, either that or how the man's speech seemed to be getting more broken by the minute.

"Fine!" snapped Amuliea, prompting a nod from Ürbon. At least she had some sense. "How much?"

The man laughed again, before replying, "Well, first we need's to be lookin through this 'ere vessel to make sure nothin' illegal be on it." He stomped on the deck for emphasis on this point. "Then, we decidin' what stuff we's to be takin'."

Amuliea, starting to lose her cool, shouted back, "We don't have anything of value on this ship, bilge rat! We aren't a trading vessel!"

The man's smile grew bigger at this outburst. "Well, that there would mean ye can't pay the tax there, lass. But..." the man's eyes roamed down the captain's frame, hungrily.

His eyes met with the fire in Amuliea's gaze, and swiftly turned away. "I could agree if ye' gave me them two." He lifted his finger to point at Ürbon and Tlupic, his words slurring even worse than before, "and ye could get off fer free. How's that sound?"

Amuliea turned towards them, as if weighing her options. Unafraid of these pathetic creatures, Ürbon opened his mouth, ready to assure her he'd go with the pirates to save her trouble.

But before he could utter a word, another sailor ran across the plank towards the drunken pirate. Whispering something into his ear, the sailor pointed at Amuliea. In an instant, the pirate lunged forward, grabbed hold of her arm and motioned to the rest of his crew. The cutthroats grabbed hold of Amuliea and pulled her off her feet, running back to their ship and kicking the plank into the sea.

Unable to follow, the crew only watched as one of the sailors threw their concussed leader back to their ship and pulled away. As the distance between the boats grew too large to jump, the crew stopped in their chase. They were unable to reach their captain, forced to watch as she was dragged across the other ship.

Ürbon would not be so easily dissuaded, however, and began to back up across the deck.

"What exactly are you *plaaanning!*" screamed the Geck'tek on his shoulder as Ürbon sprinted across the deck.

Without answering, he leapt the distance between both boats and dug Bjarl into the ship's hull to stop himself from falling into the water. The crew of *The Swift Eel* shouted encouragement from the ship, before rushing back to their posts to attempt to follow the ship.

Using his stone hands, the Jödmun tore a path into the inner hull of the ship, terrifying the rowers within the vessel. As one they turned and fled to the upper deck. Pausing to retrieve Bjarl, the Jödmun reached onto his shoulder to grab hold of Tlupic and put him down onto the deck.

Charging up the steps, Ürbon delivered a crushing blow to one of the fleeing pirates. Not bothering to stoop or slow himself, he crashed through whatever wood was in his way like a wrecking ball. Not wanting to miss out on the action, Tlupic drew one of his two spears and threw it at one of the fleeing men, catching him in the ankle, before spinning and delivering a precise blow with the other spear to the man's neck. Stopping to pick up both of his spears, the Geck'tek turned to see nothing but broken wood and blood on the steps.

***

From the window in his cabin, Captain Caultere of the Maldoran ship *The Pinnacle* watched the scene unfold. This was supposed to be a simple raid on a small transport vessel, but it seemed as if nothing had gone to plan. He was the leader of the pirate clan Eschnov, which, although relatively new, had shown promise to become a great power among the underworld of the seas.

They had successfully conducted raids on ships and seized them, all while gathering manpower and prestige. This all culminated in them acquiring the resources to attack and capture the Maldoran ship named *The Pinnacle*, where he earned his reputation as a pirate lord. And now, all this was being threatened by this single defiant ship. He had been searching for it for a while, and now that he'd found it, they were confronted with far more resistance than expected. It seemed when one of his smaller ships had approached the merchant vessel, two members of the merchant crew had gone rogue. Jumping across and wreaking havoc on board.

His thoughts were interrupted by his cabin door opening to his second in command, an elf named Arthurian. Arthurian was an inhabitant of the Shattered Isles and had belonged to a wealthy family. Something must have gone wrong since he chose to turn to a life of crime on the open ocean. Despite being an elf, he was kept aboard for his ability to utilize magic, a useful asset to the Eschnov clan.

"We have captured her, my lord." The elf spoke fluently and gracefully. He held a strange wooden staff that seemed to be covered in seaweed. His robes were purple, and like most elves his face was fair.

"Thank you, Arthurian. Bring her to me and send all available personnel to defend the starboard side. I believe we have visitors."

"It would be a pleasure, my lord." Arthurian was always like that, always willing to be a servant, to obey. Caultere knew the elf was envious of his position. He didn't know why Arthurian even bothered with the pleasantries, for he knew that the elf could easily best him in a direct challenge. However, while these thoughts might plague him, they would have to be dealt with another time. There was a spectacle to watch.

***

Ürbon reached the upper deck of the smaller vessel, with Tlupic close behind him. They were greeted with the sight of a motley group of sailors surrounding the drunken pirate. Some of them were still struggling to restrain Amuliea. She fought wildly in an attempt to escape, but received a hit to the head and fell unconscious. Seeing this, the Jödmun charged.

Closing the gap in a few strides Ürbon swung Bjarl high before bringing it down upon an unlucky sailor. Joining the fray, Tlupic threw a spear across at another man's chest. The lizard then spun through the air using momentum and his other spear to impale the man's head before continuing his spin by ripping out the first spear and throwing it once more. Ürbon cut through guards like they were made of butter while swords shattered on his stone skin. Tlupic nimbly avoided every strike that came his way and continued to fly through the enemies ranks, slicing through them with uncanny accuracy.

Overwhelmed by the sudden attack no one had stayed behind the wheel, preferring instead to scramble for cover. Before anyone could correct its course and save them all from disaster, the directionless ship crashed into the Maldoran vessel with the sound of cracking wood. Seeing that all was lost, the remaining sailors seized their chance and escaped onto the larger ship, taking Amuliea with them. Before Ürbon and Tlupic could do the same, they were stunned by a sound like a roaring wave as a bright purple light flashed before their eyes.

The light was gone as soon as it had appeared, and in its place stood an elf, tall and fair, dressed in purple robes and wielding a staff made of gnarled wood and seaweeds. Tlupic hissed in fanatical anger and threw his spear at the elf with all of his might. However, the elf merely looked at it, and it stopped in mid-air before clattering to the wooden deck. Not even waiting for the spear to hit its mark, Tlupic was already on the move, hurling himself at the mage, attempting to stab him with the other spear. This ploy nearly worked, but the elf blasted the reptile back with a bolt of purple energy shaped in the visage of a tentacle. It struck the Geck'tek in the chest, throwing him backwards, knocking the spear from his hands.

The elf staggered back before seizing Ürbon in a similar grip. "My name is Arthurian." the elf panted, as if the spells he had cast had drained his energy. "And I, shall be your doom." The elf cast another purple bolt at the struggling Ürbon. But before it hit him, Bjarl released a flash of blue light, freeing Ürbon from the magical grip and allowing him to duck for cover, narrowly missing the magic missile.

"What? Impossible!" yelled the elf as Ürbon swiftly recovered and sprinted towards the mage with fury in his eyes.

The mage, in a panic, launched another bolt at him. The bolt was faster this time, and Ürbon was forced to block it instead and raised Bjarl to meet it. The bolt collided with the magic weapon and began pushing Ürbon back, the wooden floor breaking as he braced himself against it.

Ürbon inched backwards, the bolt growing stronger as if drilling into Bjarl. He knew he could not hold much longer. But in a twist of fate, it was the elf who faltered, his concentration broken as he clutched his side. The purple bolt exploded in a burst of energy.

Arthurian screamed in agony, the area around the mage flashed with purple light, and suddenly the mage was gone. Looking around the wrecked ship's deck, Ürbon saw Tlupic where the elf had stood, holding a bloodied spear. Before they had time to rest however, the ship once again began to drift away from the Maldoran vessel, and the two were forced to jump aboard the larger ship before they were left behind.

***

Caultere cursed under his breath as he saw the lizard creeping up behind Arthurian and stabbing him in the side. Hurriedly, he put his spyglass away, and readied himself to dispel the invaders himself. A flash of light inside his cabin alerted him of Arthurian's presence. The elve's face was drawn tight with pain, and he was holding his side to try and staunch the bleeding.

"Welcome back. You're just in time to see one of my ships sink to the abyss."

Arthurian scowled, and turned away. "They were stronger than expected."

The door to his cabin burst open, and three figures came through, carrying someone unconscious between them. The captain's face twisted into a smile as he recognized the woman. Amuliea, the whole reason he had gone through this ordeal.

Returning to consciousness, she began to struggle against her captors. "Release her!" commanded Caultere, and the sailors immediately obliged. Unrestrained, Amuliea immediately spun around and punched a sailor directly in the nose, attempting to push her way past.

"Come now, Amuliea. Let's be civil. Have a seat." Caultere said. His guards made a move to restrain her again, but he waved them off. Hearing her name, Amuliea froze.

"Please, sit down. We have much to talk about."

Amuliea hesitated, and turned towards the door, but then sat down at the captain's desk.

"Glad to see you have come to see reason." Caultere said, leaning forward and grinning from ear to ear. "We have much to discuss, cousin."

***

Ürbon heaved Tlupic up into the hull of The Pinnacle. Water was pouring through the gap left by the smaller vessel. If not fixed soon, it would become a serious threat to the ship. A team of two dozen sailors emerged, each carrying a bailing bucket.

Seeing the pair, the sailors drew arming swords. Those who were not armed, grabbed hold of anything in the vicinity; planks of wood, or even their buckets. Ürbon was frankly tired of fighting, and so instead of hefting Bjarl to charge the enemy, he walked towards the group of pirates, with deliberate steps.

One of them charged at the pair, but didn't make it far. Ürbon caught the man's throat, and lifted him into the air.

"You cannot win here." Ürbon said as his gaze swept across each and every man, most of them trembling from his show of brute force. "Run and live another day. I am tired of pointless bloodshed."

To emphasize his point, he threw the man in his grip to the floor, not hard enough to kill him, but enough to make a point.

The sailors turned back and fled up the stairwell, pushing and shoving their way past each other to escape the Jödmun's fury. While Ürbon patiently waited for them to all flee, he walked over to Tlupic, and placed him gently upon his shoulder. The magical bolt that had struck Geck'tek in the chest had hurt him badly, and the scales around the area were icy cold.

After making sure the Geck'tek was secure on his shoulder, Ürbon set off up the empty stairs, stooping to ensure the safety of his reptilian companion. Reaching the upper deck, he was greeted by dozens of pirates, each one holding a weapon pointed directly at the two.

From among their ranks came the elven mage, his brilliant purple robes stained crimson on his left side, his hand covering the gruesome wound. His eyes narrowed as he saw the duo, particularly the Geck'tek in his weakened state. "Well, well, well, look what we have here!" The mage grimaced in pain, before he smiled, and slowly approached the pair, the pirates parting to let him pass. "I do believe we have unfinished business. Particularly with that lizard on your shoulder."

"That magic does not belong to you, thief. It belongs to the Gods!" Tlupic hissed. But the mage did not understand the Gataran language, and instead laughed at the Geck'tek's anger.

But his laughter was drowned by a sudden ear-splitting shriek. The cry was like the sound of screeching metal, cutting its way through the air like the edge of a sword.

At that same moment a massive writhing tentacle shot out from over the edge of the ship, and it lashed out and grabbed a pirate off his feet. As the shriek faded, everyone turned towards the tentacle as the man screamed, and watched as he was pulled off the ship. Arthurian paused for a second, torn between his enemies and the mysterious tentacle, before rushing to the side of the ship, only to see still water.

***

Cousin? What was the man thinking? She had no connection to this brute, this despicable employer of revolting swine!

Appearing to guess at her feelings, Caultere stood up, despite asking her to sit. "I'm sure you have no idea what I'm talking about, and for good reason." The man had begun to pace as he spoke, the spyglass swaying at his side parallel with the sword on his belt. He stopped for a moment to stare down at her with a smile on his face.

"Your grandfather had only one child..."

"Don't you mention my grandfather, you vile serpent!" Amuliea burst into a rage, jabbing a finger accusingly at the other captain, "You aren't fit to speak his name!"

The man raised his hands in surrender, though he kept his smile. "I know, I know. You'll forgive me eventually." Amuliea glared at the man, who ignored her and continued pacing.

"Now this might be a shock. But your grandfather only *raised* one child," the friendly look on his face faded for a second, replaced with an insane — almost fanatical — look. "I am his bastard child."

Even seeing it coming, he barely dodged the furious punch thrown aimed at his nose. Anger boiled in her eyes as Amuliea launched herself out of her chair, screaming incoherently at the man, throwing blow after blow, before eventually managing to shout out a few coherent sentences.

"How dare you accuse my grandfather of such abuse! You worthless pig farmer! You wretched sack of orc shit! You vile, foul, brain-dead, spineless, whore of a creature!"

After dodging several more punches, the captain clearly had enough and caught her next punch.

Still screaming, Amuliea struggled in his grip, launching another punch at Caultere's head, which was also caught by the pirate captain. Shoving her away, he used the time to reach within his extravagant coat, and pulled out a small portrait of three people.

Amuliea pushed herself back up, and geared up to charge at the pirate captain; then she saw the picture. It showed a man in his early thirties, holding two children; a girl under his arm, and a baby in his other hand. Amuliea recognized two of the people in the portrait, she had known them all of her life. "Is that...my mother and grandfather?" She gently took the picture out of the captain's hands, staring at it in disbelief.

"Indeed it is, a long time ago." Caultere pointed at the baby held in the man's hands. The baby was wrapped in a white cloth and was no more than a few weeks old. "That's me."

Amuliea barely heard him. For most of her life, she had been looking for more information on her late mother, talking to old acquaintances and trying to squeeze details out of her grandfather. Now this apparent stranger, and a thug at that, had a near perfectly preserved picture of her?

"How did you get this?" Amuliea's voice was barely a whisper.

"I've always had it." He put a hand on Amuliea's shoulder, which prompted her to look up at him. "They gave it to me to remember them by before leaving me out on the streets."

"What? My family would never have done that!" Amuliea pulled away from him, Caultere's hand falling back to his side to rest upon the spyglass. "We look after our own!"

"Oh, I wish. But I understand why they did it, and if I were in their place, I'm sure I would have, too." He began to pace again, his hands behind his back, and he continued to let words spill from his lips. "The family was poor, and could barely feed itself as it was. With another child, they would have starved to death." Amuliea's eyes swept from the picture to Caultere, who continued to get more agitated as he ranted.

"But, I survived! I was rescued from my sorry fate by a woman whose own child had died of disease. She took me in, fed, clothed, and raised me. She turned out to be a leader of the Eschnov pirate clan, and I followed in her footsteps when she passed. I have searched for my parents across the seas while amassing fame and fortune for the clan, and here I am." He slammed his hands down on the desk, as if finished with his speech, but almost immediately he began to pace once more.

"I learned about you from an anonymous letter a few years back. One look at the handwriting and I knew in my heart it was from my father, even if it did not mention his name. But what it did mention was a mysterious captain I could call my relative. I have traveled far to reach you, and now that I see you before me, I know it was all worth it. Please, join me! I would have you as my Empress, a woman garbed in red and black, a great and terrible queen who could shake the oceans with her commands! Together we will take over this pitiful pirate underworld and remake it into a maritime empire, our offsprings will rule for an eternity..." The captain was cut brutally short by a kick, aimed directly between his legs.

Before he could recover she smashed her fist directly into his nose knocking him unconscious.

Though far beyond angry, she reigned in her rage and grabbed the captain's elegant sword before storming out of the room. She was making sure the picture was secure in her pocket when a shrill shriek swept through the ship.

***

As Arthurian stared at the surface of the ocean where the sailor had been dragged under, the water started to bubble. Soon, a writhing mass of tentacles appeared out of the waters, and Arthurian recoiled from shock. Out of the writhing mass of limbs emerged a head of flesh and sinew. It was enormous, the length of five men across each way, and was a color somewhere between red and purple. It had several smaller fleshy lumps at four points around the center of its body, which was essentially a very large circle. These smaller extrusions were also circular in shape and were equidistant from one another, and it was from these that the tentacles grew.

As it rose a single, massive yellow eye showed itself. It blinked with a fleshy pink eyelid, the same color as its skin, and it was alight with the gleam of intelligence. Out of sheer horror, Arthurian leveled his staff at the creature and screamed at the top of his lungs, conjuring a huge, purple ball of energy.

The ball of energy surged forward, splitting off into countless tiny magical arrows raining down onto the creature. The purple arrows struck the beast, each one exploding in a cloud of purple mist, and the creature released a low droning cry. As the cry faded, Arthurian slumped forward on his staff, weak and spent from the spell.

However, as the purple mist cleared, the beast reared its ugly head, its mass of tentacles twitching around in pain. With astonishing speed, it lashed a tentacle at the weakened mage, and brought him up to its singular eye, which was full of sorrow and hurt. The mage struggled against the iron grip of the tentacle, as the monster grabbed the side of the vessel and revealed its massive underbelly to the elf.

Its underside was white and smoother than the skin on its head, but what was truly horrifying, was its gaping maw. Located in the center, it was perfectly circular and ringed with needle-like teeth. As its muscles moved, its mouth constantly shifted, and Arthurian cried out in horror as the tentacle shoved him forward towards the gaping maw. Before the creature could complete the horrific death that awaited the sorcerer, however, a bolt of lightning exploded against the soft flesh of the tentacle holding the elf.

The elf fell to the deck, coughing, as the pirates rushed to him, swords and halberds at the ready. The mage cast a glance at the source of the lightning, and to his surprise saw the Jödmun, the dragon's horns upon his axe leveled at the spot the tentacle had been. With a final effort of will, Arthurian cast a final teleportation spell, and disappeared in a flash of purple light.

***

Ürbon saw the mage disappear in the blink of an eye, the men around closing their eyes in pain and stumbling to and from the sudden burst of light. More tentacles reached over the side of the deck and swept the men off their feet before grabbing several of them and pulling them over the ship's edge. Ürbon quickly rushed towards one of the tentacles and severed it before it could pull another sailor off the ship.

The man who had been wrapped inside the tentacle now struggled to free himself from the dead appendage, which was much heavier than it looked. More tentacles lashed out from the water, and another ear-splitting roar screamed across the deck as the creature pulled itself over the side of the ship. It bared its massive mouth as it jumped atop a man who screamed in agony as blood pooled beneath the creature. As the creature fed, it seemed to grow slightly, its body swelling, and several of its tentacles beginning to regrow.

Ürbon began to cut his way towards the abomination, his axe cutting through nearly all the tentacles that shot towards him, severing and mutilating the fleshy limbs that tried to throw him back. Those tentacles which slipped past his guard were driven back by Tlupic, whose agility let him leap to meet each tentacle, darting under Ürbon's swings and past falling severed limbs. Soon a group of men rallied around the two, their halberds and swords drawing attention off Ürbon and Tlupic.

The monster had swollen to twice its previous size as it finished devouring a fifth man. Its eye, bloodshot and full of anger, swept over to the Jödmun and the Geck'tek charging towards it. Shouting another shrill cry, it lunged towards the two and the gathering of men behind them.

It concentrated completely on its full assault, dedicating all of its offensive assets to shatter the ranks of men. Lightning-quick tentacles grabbed men around the waist, slamming them through the wooden hull, crushing them with its immense strength. It even resorted to using multiple tentacles to pull men apart slowly and painfully, and then devouring the pieces to regenerate its wounds.

Beneath the ferocious assault of the sea monster, the pirates' charge faltered, and they fled from its brutal onslaught. Before long, Ürbon and Tlupic were isolated against the full force of the creature, barely able to keep the thrashing tentacles at bay. The leviathan slowly raised itself above the two, and readied itself to smash down to swallow them whole. The duo could not escape this rather gruesome death, as they could not cut their way through fast enough to flee the swirling mass of tentacles. Just before it slammed itself into the pair of champions, Bjarl glowed brightly, and a bolt of lightning flew out of the sky, striking the beast upon its fleshy head.

A shriek louder than any other pierced the air as the monster threw itself off of the ship, back into the water, its head smoking and blackened. Moments after the beast vanished beneath the hull of the ship, several wounded men began to drift back out from their hiding places and pick themselves up off the deck, if they could. Ürbon began to march towards a man buried in wooden planks who was crying out for help, but before he could reach him, the sailor was sucked down through the deck with a horrified scream.

Soon the sound of cracking wood resounded throughout the deck, sending shockwaves of fear rippling through the already terrified sailors. Several sailors tried to get below deck, but as soon as they reached the steps, several tentacles burst out from below and dragged them to their deaths. With a shrill cry from below, the deck of the ship began to shudder and quake, and slowly crack apart.

The shrieks of the sea beast cut through the air as men attempted to flee, but they had nowhere to go. As the deck began breaking apart, from the stern of the ship came a familiar figure, the one that Ürbon and Tlupic had come to rescue. Amuliea waved frantically from the back of the ship before covering her ears as another high-pitched shriek filled the air. Ürbon picked Tlupic up and once more placed him upon his shoulder, then ran towards the captain. But before he could reach her, the deck began to break apart, pieces of the floor falling away into the inner hull.

From these holes, they all witnessed a sight out of nightmares. The inner hull of *The Pinnacle* was covered in fleshy tentacles, each reaching and holding on to the wooden structure. The fleshy body of the leviathan had swollen tremendously and now was easily five times the size it had been before. Its massive eye was completely bloodshot and partially swollen as a result of the lightning bolt. It fixed its hateful glare on the duo, but did not attempt to attack. For the real horror was in the center of the ship.

The massive gaping mouth had grown to insane proportions, and was now steadily moving along the outside of the ship's hull, eating away at the wood. Seawater was rapidly pouring in from the tremendous gashes in the wood that the monster had created. It was devouring the ship straight up the center, causing the deck split in two before Ürbon could reach Amuliea.

The two halves of *The Pinnacle* floated away from each other and began to sink. Desperate sailors climbed the massive masts of each side to escape the sea. As the parts of the ship floated farther apart, Ürbon was forced to stop, unable to reach Amuliea. Just before he made the inevitable decision to jump, he saw something behind the ship itself, and it was approaching fast.

The crew aboard *The Swift Eel* had not been able to keep up with the sheer speed of the Maldoran vessel, but now in its chaos, they had been able to catch up. Without saying a word, the Jödmun pointed towards the ship reaching the stern of *The Pinnacle*. Nodding, Amuliea turned away and ran towards the very back of the ship, intent on making it back to her crew. With that matter settled, the stone giant looked around himself for any other way to escape.

The ship itself was doomed, there was no doubt about it, but there had been two smaller ships escorting it. One of these had been sunk after smashing into the Maldoran vessel, but the other was still presumably afloat. Quickly scanning the area, ignoring yet another shriek from the beast below, he saw the ship near the port side of the doomed vessel.

Breaking into a sprint, his heavy feet thundering against the wooden deck even as it crumbled behind him, he shouted to the men around him to board the other vessel. Those not maddened by their own fear recognized his intent so they too began to sprint towards the vessel, even as the hull cracked and split beneath the leviathan's onslaught. Those who did not notice the Jödmun's escape met their demise aboard the sinking ship, and many a man vanished into the maw of the invading creature.

As Ürbon reached the smaller ship, he turned around and saw *The Swift Eel* across the scene of chaos and destruction. As he watched, Amuliea raised a red cloth high above her head, and waved it several times at the duo; she had made it back to her ship. Even Tlupic could understand that it was some sort of farewell on the high seas.

However, their farewell was stopped short by the groaning sound of wood. Both watched as *The Pinnacle* disappeared under a sea of tentacles. They continued to watch the brutal spectacle as their ships drifted away from one another. Each sailed in an opposite direction, neither dared to cross the Leviathan's path.

***

The ship Ürbon and Tlupic commandeered sliced its way through the waters. The men steering her relaxed, collapsing in exhaustion from the raw terror they had experienced. Ürbon stood at the raised stern of the ship, his stone hands on the wheel and Tlupic sleeping on his shoulder. Absent-mindedly, he pulled the small leatherbound book and began to write his memoir of the day.

Suddenly, Tlupic twitched and jerked awake, standing straight up on his rocky shoulder. Ürbon could barely hear him utter a single word, "Magic." Almost immediately after this premonition, the air seemed to surge and rip and tear itself apart. Sleeping men were woken abruptly as the sudden wind buffeted them, cracking and snapping like whips. The air stank with magic, and soon the boat was encircled by several twisters of varying magnitudes. Ürbon let out a roar of defiance as the whirling maelstrom swallowed them whole.

Chapter 3:
The Sands of Death

Standing atop a sand dune, a lone figure stared at a train of white-clothed peoples traversing the desert dunes.

"Looks like the pilgrims are out. Must be that time of the year again," He chuckled.

Send a dust storm on them!

"That's not nearly as fun as what I have in mind!" He said.

Appear in front of them and call them your servants, then make them do funny things like eat sa-

"Shhhh!" He said, drowning out the voice inside his head. He watched as the white-clothed pilgrims walked unwittingly closer to the raider camp a few miles ahead. Just a little bit longer and they'd walk right into them. Now that would indeed be interesting. It had been incredibly boring so far flying over the desert from the sea. Though he wondered what would wash up after the instability he'd caused from arriving in this realm.

He stretched his wings and mentally checked to make sure that the spell of invisibility he wrapped around himself was perfect.

Finding it to be, he launched himself over to a dune farther ahead of the travelers, but closer to the bandit camp. Idly, he sent a gust of swirling sand into their camp and watched as they stumbled out of their tents, scurrying like insects to recover the tents that had blown away, their eyes immediately stung by the sand. It was amusing, but doing the same thing over and over tended to be less entertaining the more it was performed.

So he stopped the wind to allow them to regain their tents. It wouldn't do to have their ambush revealed to the pilgrims. Once more stretching his wings, the sound of metal on metal familiar to him, he laid his golden form to rest on the sand dune, excited to see how everything played out. Playing the part of god was fun, but it was annoying when the pieces didn't want to play their part. So Hydrulian waited, anticipating the opportunity where he could allow his sword to claim more petty lives.

***

On the coastline of the great Savarrah desert, the waves gently lapped against the sands, trying in vain to touch lands far beyond their reach, always to fall short of its goals. Yet still they try again, as they have for time immemorial. The harsh sun was beating down upon the sands with wave upon wave of heat, basking the grains in a golden light. The sands were thankful for this kind gift but had received several similar gifts throughout their lifetime, and so they sent it back, releasing their stored heat back into the air, where it shimmered and danced in the light, distorting the ground behind it. The only things marring this sight were the masses of wood and rigging left on the beach, the wood already being bleached by the light of the sun.

Beneath this great mound of broken flotsam, a massive hulking shape emerged. The form of Ürbon the Wanderer made itself separate from the broken wreck of the ship he travelled on before a storm of magic threw it to land. Cradled in his arms, he held Tlupic. The reptile took several hits and his chest was still sucking the heat aside in an attempt to mitigate the magical cold which was implanted there.

Ürbon took one last look at the ruin of their ship, the corpses already rotting under the intense glare of the sun, even though it had yet to fully rise. He set about looking for valuables to keep his unconscious friend alive, even if he himself did not need to eat or sleep. Making a mental check that his leather-bound book was still secure, and finding it was, the Jödmun used his mighty strength to search through the wreck.

He found a few measly scraps of food, and luckily, several containers of freshwater, somehow unbroken by the sheer force of the storm. Seeing no further essentials, he picked up Bjarl with one hand, still cradling Tlupic in the other, and he walked south along the coastline, hoping to find civilization soon. He knew that there was a city to the south of him; he was through the area once before. Looking towards the sky, he saw the sun reached just above the horizon so he began to walk down the beach.

The giant walked for several hours along the coast, shielding his reptilian friend from the brutal rays of the sun. A few hours after the sun began its descent, he felt a twitch in his arms. The Geck'tek finally woke from his slumber, and slowly pulled himself upright. He was unwell, his legs unsteady as he raised himself, and his eyes seemed unfocused.

He slowly processed the world around him before asking his stone companion. "Where are we?"

"On the western coast of the Savarrah Desert," replied Ürbon, making sure the lizard was out of the way of the sun. "Our ship crashed on the shore."

Tlupic blinked quietly in confusion, as if he didn't understand the words that came out of Ürbon's mouth, until realization dawned on his face a few seconds later. But he still didn't fully understand the situation. Nodding his head as if in agreement, he settled back down to rest. Checking once more that his reptilian friend was secure, the Jödmun continued his march.

***

After several more hours of walking, the sweltering heat of the day had passed, and now the night sky twinkled with bright stars. Though the sun's light had long gone, the sand still radiated warmth as the giant's stone feet sunk into the golden grains, bathed white in the starlight. Tlupic shivered in his hands as the air grew colder. Ürbon was beginning to get worried about his friend's wellbeing against the cold. Temperatures in desert regions were brutally harsh, with it being sweltering during the day then dropping to freezing cold during the night.

As he marched down the coastline, he saw a red glow from farther inland. The light was most likely from a fire. Taking another glance at the still unconscious body in his arms, Ürbon set off towards the light. Hopefully, the one who started the fire would be willing to share.

Ürbon marched unfalteringly, the warm sand parting around his feet, even as the air grew colder. The stars twinkled, distant, uncaring of the affairs of mortals that happened beneath their watchful gaze. Slowly, inexorably, the red glow began to grow closer. When he crested another dune, he was greeted by the sight of the campsite.

Upon the sea of sand was a single campfire, alone against the dark of night. The fire was tiny, barely sustaining itself against the cold. There was a single tent next to the fire, although not close enough to accidentally catch fire. Sitting cross-legged next to the fire was a man with a scimitar on his hip, a staff laying on the sand on his other side, and he had his hands clasped together in some kind of prayer.

Just as the Jödmun crested the hill, the man looked up from his ritual, spotted them from the glow of Bjarl, and was predictably shocked at their appearance. However, he beckoned him over, offering him a seat by the fire. Ürbon began the trek down the dune, reached the man and bowed formally as an introduction.

The man was a Sonasian and seemed to be barely twenty winters old. With dark skin, a pair of brown eyes and dark hair, he was clad in pristine white robes that looked as if they had been in the desert for far too long. The man smiled before standing and bowing himself. After sitting back down, he gestured for Ürbon to do the same. Ürbon complied, and sat down cross-legged, setting Bjarl down on the sand, and laying Tlupic in his lap.

The man spoke to him, first in the Sonasian language, and then in the Common Tongue. "Hello, friend! How may Askia, son of Samir, be of service to you?"

"I am Ürbon, and this is my companion Tlupic. He is in need of aid. He has been injured by a magical blast and crushed during a storm." Ürbon had replied in the Sonasian language, and Askia seemed pleasantly surprised by this revelation.

"Give him here my friend, I may be able to help."

Ürbon, having experienced their culture before, knew that this Askia was no threat to Tlupic or himself, as they prided themselves on their honesty and good intentions. Without hesitation, Ürbon lifted Tlupic and set him down in front of Askia, who lifted a staff from the sands at his side. As he brought it over Tlupic, the Geck'tek squirmed and writhed beneath its proximity, startling Askia. The man did not realize that the reptile was magically sensitive and that the power of the staff was discomforting to him.

Nevertheless, the man continued his efforts. The staff was soon surrounded by a blue light, which grew brighter the closer it came to the Geck'tek chest where the magical bolt had hit him a day before. Closing his eyes in concentration, sweat began to bead and fall down the man's face until they snapped open, and the light faded altogether from his staff.

With shaking hands, Askia put down the staff, before setting his gaze upon the Jödmun once again. His expression was grave.

"I'm sorry, there was nothing I could do. The magic is too strong." The man said this between breaths, clearly drained from the effort of his sorcery.

"It is alright. You did your best, friend," replied Ürbon, smoothly. "Is there any other way to heal him?"

Askia glanced around at the dunes, nervous, contemplating his answer before formulating a response.

"I suggest coming with me, on my pilgrimage. If you complete the passage, I am sure that Gow will restore your friend to health. If he is fickle, and does not bestow his blessing, then there is a town farther down the coast, where I am sure you will find aid, and it doesn't stray far from our path."

Ürbon contemplated these words, knowing that they were meant in good faith. In truth, the nomad's path was similar to the one he had been taking originally, and he could always simply stray from their path if the need arose. The Jödmun had heard of several godly miracles in his travels, he saw no harm in this course of action, so Ürbon decided to accompany the traveling pilgrim.

The Jödmun nodded his approval, and Askia smiled before springing into action. He kicked sand over the fire to put it out and began to take down his tent for the long walk. It was safer for him to walk during the night, he explained. Soon the party began to trek down the coast, walking through the inhospitable desert. Unbeknownst to them, they were being watched.

***

As the trio continued along their path, Hydrulian watched them from atop a distant dune, cloaked in an invisibility spell. Usually, such spells that needed to be constantly fueled by magic would drain their users extraordinarily fast, but Hydrulian was anything but a normal mage.

Hydrulian was a Sentriel, a member of a long-forgotten race that was believed to be extinct. They used to be a great race, one of the ancient species of Faladon, along with the elves and dwarves, and several others. They could manipulate magic to a degree that the elves could only dream of, and the Sentriel radiated light from every surface of their body. Seated upon his back was a massive set of metallic wings, currently folded against his body.

Hydrulian had ruled over this desert from a distance, changing and directing its course from the shadows, toying with its mortals and playing with their lives like toys. The pilgrim used to be part of a much larger group, consisting of hundreds of men, and Hydrulian had thought of sending a calamity towards them to entertain himself. But he had been interrupted by a tremendous blast of magic from the north. This caused an immense sandstorm which decimated the ranks of the pilgrims, much to his annoyance.

Shaking himself of these thoughts, he refocused on the group in front of him and was shocked to see that they were several more dunes ahead of him than anticipated. This was something that troubled him only in the last few centuries, where he would become lost in his thoughts for periods of time, far longer than he was comfortable with, and they had been increasing in frequency over the years.

Shaking these thoughts once more, he snapped his wings open, the sound of metal on metal slicing through the air, only to meet the soundproofing spell he encompassed around himself, and launched up into the night sky, climbing high above the desert.

When he was sufficiently high to see everything in the surrounding area, he focused on the small dot that was his target, the trio of adventurers. Casting his gaze to the surrounding landscape, he searched for something he could use to make their journey a bit more eventful. The self-proclaimed king of the desert would not let them leave without at least entertaining him first.

After several sweeping glances, he finally found something nearby that he could manipulate to intercept the travelers. Smiling sadistically, the golden being began to concoct a plan that would amuse him for a bit and began setting his plan in motion.

***

As the trio walked through the desert, they remained quiet, intent on reaching their destination. However, hours of silence obviously grated on their guide.

"So," started Askia, "what brings you two to the desert?"

"We were on our way towards the Shattered Isles, but our ship was intercepted by pirates," Ürbon replied smoothly, not acknowledging how the man struggled to keep quiet for as long as he did. Clearly, he was the chatty type.

"I see. Well, how did you manage to escape?"

Ürbon was quiet for a moment, as if trying to formulate a proper response.

"That," Ürbon replied, "is a much larger tale."

"Well, we aren't getting anywhere anytime soon, so we have nothing but time."

Ürbon took his first real look towards the man, before nodding and refocusing on the trek.

"Very well."

The Jödmun then told him his story, and the tale of how he met Tlupic and found his axe. The man listened in rapt attention as the stone giant told of his long journey. During his tale he was surprised by a familiar sentiment of peace and joy that he only felt when he and his crew would dock at a port and boast of their grand adventures to the onlooking tavern dwellers. He found the easy laugh of the Sonasian to be comfortingly familiar, and as he continued his tale, he tried not to think of his lost companions that were still prisoners of the elves. He looked down at his sleeping friend and a grim determination set over him, so he chased the phantoms of his shield-brothers from his mind, readjusted Tlupic from where he laid still unconscious, and continued telling his journey to the young man.

"I had no idea you were so travelled, friend," said Askia, his voice barely above a whisper, so awestruck was he by his companion's deeds.

"Not as well traveled as I would like, as there are yet things I have not seen, and bounties yet to claim." The Jödmun trailed off, remembering the elves that captured his crew, "And scores yet to settle." Ürbon seemed lost in thought for a moment, as the two trekked along the hot sand, Tlupic in his hands. He looked at Askia beside him, a lone pilgrim in this harsh environment.

"So tell me," he asked. "What brings you to this desert?"

Askia smiled as he looked up to the tall Jödmun, happy to break the silence with more conversation.

"My journey started in the pilgrim city of Ouatagouna. As per tradition, a group of pilgrims, including myself, began our long trek to the shrine of Tuct. We walked for days and nights, keeping close to pools of precious water. Walking through the desert was like walking through fire itself. I would've perished multiple times if it were not for the Bedbaddins."

"Bedbaddins? I've never heard of such people," said Ürbon. Though he had travelled far and wide, life in the desert was strange and mysterious to him.

"They're a tribe of camel warriors," Askia explained. "They often laugh at us Sonasian pilgrims, believing themselves the only ones able to brave the harsh desert climate. But for all their bantering, they do care for others. A hospitable folk, though ferocious."

Askia took a small sip from his flask and continued his story. "I come from a family of farmers. My father and I grew dye plants on the outskirts of the city. I lived a life of hard work, but it was comfortable and safe. That is, until scarabites killed my father."

Ürbon looked at Askia. The Sonasian leaned on a mahogany staff as he walked and had a scimitar strapped to his waist.

"You don't look like a farmer to me," The Jödmun remarked. He felt sorry for the Sonasian's misfortunes, yet he hesitated to trust his words. He wondered how a farmer got his hands on a magical staff and a beautifully crafted scimitar.

"During the pilgrimage, after we left the Bedbaddin camp, we were attacked again by scarabites. They killed all the pilgrims. It was only because I fell behind that I survived the massacre. It was then the whispers led me to Tuct's shrine, where I found this staff and scimitar. They told me I was a holy warrior and so, here I am now."

"The god whispered to you?" Ürbon asked, confused.

"I cannot say for sure, but I believe it to be so," he replied, with an air of pride.

It was at that moment the sands began to writhe and coil beneath their feet. The earth shook beneath the pair as Tlupic writhed within Ürbon's grasp. The Jödmun fought to keep him under control as the two stumbled. Askia lost his balance and fell to the sandy ground. Just as quickly as it started, the ground grew still and the sands stopped shifting.

"What the blazes was that?"

Askia was understandably concerned by the whole scenario, but all Ürbon did was check that Tlupic was still secure in his grip, and raise a hand for silence. As the man chafed under the order, the giant checked the surrounding area. He could have sworn he saw a flash of golden light on a distant sand dune, but he couldn't see anything now. Finally settling, as he saw nothing out of the ordinary, Ürbon gestured with his hand, beckoning Askia back towards him.

He was just in time for a high pitch trill to burst through the air, as the sands to the east surged with sudden activity. As the two turned towards the origins of the sound, they saw the sands before them surge upwards and burst as though made of boiling water. The sand fell back down to reveal dozens of enormous desert-dwelling insects skittering across the dunes.

The creatures were massive, several were the size of a man, some even larger. The larger ones had sets of serrated mandibles attached to their heads, and they gnashed them together in discomfort. Clearly, they were as unsettled by the earthquake as the three of them had been, and displayed their irritation by fighting amongst each other. With swift movements they'd get a hold of other members of their swarm and crush them between their mandibles, leaving them to be finished off by a smaller species which had appeared with them. These smaller insects were much different to their larger counterparts. With oddly mismatched bodies and hairy legs they looked like a sad joke of creation. Nevertheless they were equally as violent as the larger creatures, and swarmed over whatever was left dead in the sand.

Ürbon heard Askia whisper the word *scarabites* beneath his breath. The Jödmun looked down at his terrified companion and quietly asked how good he was with his scimitar. Askia just looked at him gravely, a shadow appearing to descend over his face.

"I've only just received it at the start of the pilgrimage, same with my staff."

The giant snorted, but saw that there was a glint in the man's eyes, a spark of anger and vengeance. Ürbon could dimly relate; he had been in several scenarios against insurmountable odds. However, he gave no reassurance and readied himself for battle.

Ürbon knew that he would be able to win an engagement with the insects, but he also knew that his companions could not say the same. Knowing this, he decided to attempt to sneak around the insects first, trying to avoid detection. Although he was a massive giant, he may be able to avoid their baleful gaze, if he could just keep a sand dune between them.

However, even as he moved behind a dune, Ürbon saw that the insects were beginning to spread out in all directions across the desert. That is, when they were not busy fighting each other. They crawled their way atop the sands like disgusting worms. Several were even burrowing back into the golden ocean, disappearing from view.

As the group moved silently from behind the dunes, a pack order seemed to have established itself between the so-called scrabites. The largest and biggest of the red breed clawed at the night sky in triumph, as its challenger's cooling corpse was beset upon by its fellows. This winner seemed to gain control over the other insects, as if it had earned their respect. After a few shrill calls, the gathering disbanded, and the red insectoids joined their cousins in scouring the desert.

All had been going well for Ürbon and Askia, as they crept behind another dune, when suddenly they were showered in a cloud of sand from above. A few seconds later there was a sound of frenzied chittering from above the trio, which was quickly silenced as Ürbon used Bjarl to smash the offending insect's head in two. As the dust settled, it was clear that the scarabite had tunneled through the dune. Hearing the shrill cries of other nearby scarabites, the two began to run.

They sprinted through the sand, Askia in front, Ürbon behind, as the chittering hordes followed suit. Soon several insects were chasing alongside them on adjacent dunes and popping out of the sand. One of the red breeds managed to get into striking distance of the massive Jödmun, only for its face to be slashed with the blade of Bjarl, Ürbon barely breaking his stride. The chase continued in similar fashion as the insects continued their pursuit. However, Ürbon could see his human friend beginning to tire, while the scarabites drew in closer.

Ürbon knew that he would be able to survive the attack, but he wouldn't be able to protect his friends from death at the hands of the insectoids. Sprinting up to the desert man, Ürbon saw his face was flushed, and covered in sweat. Without explanation, Ürbon quickly placed Tlupic into Askia's arms, the man almost stumbling from the unexpected weight, before he immediately slowed his pace.

The man looked back once, before continuing on, sprinting. The insects took the bait and began to encircle the trapped Jödmun. Much to his annoyance, a few scarabites still followed Askia, but there was nothing he could do about that now. All he could do was hope for the man's safety, as the insects closed in.

As the scarabites approached, one of the large red bugs tried to leap at the giant, but found only death in the form of the axe, Bjarl, as it came crashing down, chopping off the offenders head, but this did not stop the insect tide. More of the insects tried to attack the Jödmun, but he swatted them away with his axe, ripping and tearing through them like the insects that they were. Smashing Bjarl into the thorax of another one, he split it in two. And still they came. Ürbon sighed, this would take a while.

Askia kept running, trying to put as much distance between him and Ürbon's distraction as possible. It wasn't easy with the burden he was carrying, however, and Tlupic refused to wake. He wanted to keep running, but he was only a human, and he had his limits. He could feel them rapidly approaching. With a few more labored breaths, the man came to a shuddering halt, his legs feeling as though they had fallen off somewhere on the journey. Putting his unconscious companion down on the sand, Askia refused to sit down, as he knew he wouldn't be able to bring himself to get back up for a long time.

As he rested, however, the ground in between him and the Geck'tek was disturbed, creating a shower of sand which exploded outward. Askia drew his scimitar, his eyes burning from the onslaught of sand. The scarabite that had followed him flew out of the dust cloud. It's mandibles clamped shut, narrowly missing Askia's face as he stumbled backwards in horror of the scarabite revealed by the settling sand.

The insect launched itself at Askia, ready to tear him to pieces. Intercepting the insect with his sword, its mandibles caught onto the curved blade. The insect, momentarily foiled, shot its jaws out, attempting to bite the man's head off. Leaping back once again,

Askia pulled his sword free of the scarabite's grasp and tried to think of a strategy to defeat this abomination of nature. However, the bug left him no time to think as it lunged once more, heading face-first at the man's chest. Instinctually, he used one of the very few moves he knew and parried the creature's huge jaw. The move resulted in a high-pitched shriek from his insect foe as he lobbed off a small piece of its chitinous maw.

Recoiling in pain, the insect flew back, its partitioned body attempting to coil about itself, as if to defend its head. Then, it dove into the sand, throwing grains in every direction. Raising an arm to shield himself from the sand, Askia turned back to find the insect gone. Quickly, he scanned the area for the scarabite, finding no sign of it. Even so he held his ground, continuing to glance around himself in an attempt to find the burrowing insect. For several seconds, the sands were calm. Then Askia felt the ground beneath him tremble and threw himself clear, just as the insect burst forth from the sand. As it exploded up, Askia couldn't move fast enough, and his leg was scraped by the maw of the scarabite.

Landing in the sand, his leg on fire from the pain, he raised his sword to defend himself. He knew that he wouldn't last much longer. He could feel his strength slipping away, even as the scarabite recovered from its attack and began moving towards him. It reared back, as it prepared for another strike, and Askia readied himself to counterattack. Shocked, he realized he didn't need to, as a spear suddenly sprouted from the insect's body.

Not wasting the opportunity, Askia lunged forward and planted his sword firmly into the insect's head, careful not to get into its range. As the sword bit through the chitinous head, it's dreadful cries fell silent, and it slowly fell to the ground, dead. After staring at the corpse of his fallen foe for a while longer, a little in shock after surviving the battle, he turned his head towards the source of the thrown spear. He was greeted with the sight of Tlupic, shuddering, as he took a step forward and collapsed into the sand.

Askia rushed towards him, picked him up in his arms, and shivered at the cold which radiated off of the Geck'tek's body, it seemed to suck away all the heat nearby. After making sure he was secure, he limped towards his staff, discarded on the ground. As he picked it up, he felt an agonizing pain in his leg. He felt the energy contained in the staff and asked for its assistance. Bringing it to his wound, the staff seemed to stop the gushing flow of blood, but not before Askia lost consciousness. The last thing he saw was the Jödmun approaching, the telltale blue glow of his axe by his side.

The Jödmun stared at the unconscious man, before casting a glance at the nearby corpse of the insect. Grabbing Askia, he slung him over his shoulder, before grabbing Tlupic and cradling him in his arms, and continued the march through the night.

As the journey continued, Ürbon shared the few rations that he had saved for Tlupic with Askia. After a few nights of marching they arrived at a massive rock formation, and they did not need Tlupic's magical senses to know that dark magic was afoot. The mountain stones were a dark grey, almost a sickly green and the sand was black as ash. Even the air felt wrong.

Eventually, the mountainside opened to reveal two titanic statues, much taller than Ürbon and made out of the same dread stone. The twin figures depicted two warriors with skull masks, and two long curved swords forming a cross over each of their chests. The one to the right had a royal cobra circling its head, while the left one had a large scorpion. Beyond that, the travelers could see what appeared to be the ruins of a city.

The group hesitated to enter, but Askia could feel a pull from his staff, and it was leading them into the dead city. This could only mean that the temple of Gow was within the ruined settlement. Telling Ürbon as much, the group continued on into the depths of the city.

***

Hydrulian cackled as he watched the group enter the ruins.

Those scarabites really got 'em good!

"We've got other things to do now. I've already got another plan for our new playthings."

Wait, didn't we have something important to do?

"Shut up!" Hydrulian said as he lifted off the ground and flew towards his chambers, awaiting his guests.

***

Entering the city, the three were met with the sight of ruins stretching far ahead. The dark mountains formed a wall of jagged rock around the necropolis, with the only obvious entrance being the one that they had used. The ancient city seemed completely abandoned, and their cautious footsteps echoed across the vast expanse. Moving further in, they walked down a deserted street lined with grey-stone houses covered in black dust. The city had been deserted for quite some time, as some of the structures had crumbling walls, or caved in roofs. Every now and then they'd pass an obelisk-like structure, decorated with carved skulls and hieroglyphs. It would've been quite a sight to see the city before it was abandoned, especially as they came further towards its center. As they moved forward they could see a gigantic black pyramid ahead, casting a long shadow over the ruins and emanating an eerie green fog.

Tlupic was shaking uncontrollably in his sleep, and even Ürbon was slightly unnerved by the sight of this dead ruin. Askia looked ready to turn around and run, but the soft blue light emanating from his staff served as a beacon of light and hope in this sea of darkness and dread. As they continued following the light that Askia carried, moving even deeper into the dark land, they could finally see what had drawn them there. Carved into the very mountain wall stood the temple of Gow. It was Constructed into the mountain-wall, and they looked up at its entrance the feet above them, with no stairs or rope to reach it. Before they could move forward, they were interrupted by the sound of movement coming from within one of the abandoned houses to their right.

Out of the crumbling ruin came a lone figure, draped in the remnants of torn clothing and wielding a rusty dagger. As the figure slowly stepped out of the shadows, it was revealed as a walking, blackened skeleton. It took three agonizingly slow steps before Ürbon smashed it to dust with a solid kick. Upon contact, it cracked apart, its bones, brittle with age, crumbling beneath the force of the blow.

As the bones were dropping to the ground, whatever dark spirit had taken the skeleton fled. After a second of silence, the group heard a chorus of rattling bones and noticed movement from all around them. From every possible crevice, legions of charred and brittle skeletons holding various weapons crawled out, and one of the undead let out a piercing, chattering cry as they began to march menacingly towards the group.

Ürbon has seen many things in his life, having been to so many places over so many years, but *never* has he seen the dead walk. So Ürbon, seeing that he was surrounded by undead monstrosities, did the only thing possible; he grabbed Askia, hoisted him over his shoulder and simply walked towards the temple. Ürbon closed the distance between him and the holy building, charging through the brittle skeletons like an unstoppable force, hacking at the more stubborn ones with Bjarl. He leaned up to put Askia and Tlupic atop the rock wall, as the skeletons uselessly slashed at him with their rusty weapons. With his companions safe and out of danger, he hoisted himself up. Opening the temple-doors he slammed them shut once they were all inside, leaving the rattle of bones and sea of skeletons behind them.

The Jödmun gazed around the temple, the architecture was old, so old that Ürbon didn't recognize it. The walls, floor and ceiling were all made of marble, but were inlaid and gilded with gold, enough for any man to live the rest of his life in comfort, and three of his children past that. There were several glyphs also embedded in the wall, similarly made of gold, although they couldn't read them. Having gained no new information, the group walked down the hall of the temple.

They walked through the corridor of the temple, unable to talk about what they had witnessed behind the temple doors, maintaining silence until they arrived at the main chamber. The chamber was hexagonal, the walls all made of marble and covered in gold and silver carvings. In front of the walls was a sanctuary, ravaged by time, the statues and stone carvings of Gow and his followers having cracks covering their surfaces. They no longer felt the same horrible *wrongness* that permeated the rest of the necropolis. Perhaps it was the sky above them, for there was a perfectly circular hole in the roof that allowed the room to be bathed in sunlight, and it shined down onto a shrine directly in front of the team.

It was a small shrine, similarly made out of marble, but with some granite as well. It was very lightly gilded with a small smooth space parallel to the floor, apparently for offerings, while a small statue of Gow himself looked down on them from above. As the travelers observed the old temple, Askia told the Jödmun to put Tlupic on the altar. Ürbon complied, and gently rested his friend upon the marble slab. At the same time, the pilgrim fell to his knees in worship and began to pray to Gow. Askia recited several prayers of praise and worship to attract the gods notice, but the god did not answer. The pilgrim tried harder, speaking even more of his religious ways, and asked the god to heal Tlupic, but nothing happened. It was clear that, for one reason or another, the god would not heal the Geck'tek.

While the man asked for his god's assistance, Ürbon paced around the room, anxious for news. As Askia's chanting filled the room, Ürbon glanced behind the shrine and saw something intriguing. Behind the shrine of Gow was a door, which seemed to meld almost flawlessly with the wall. As he approached it, the outline grew in strength until it became apparent there was a door.

Before he could push it open, there was a horrifically loud screech of metal on metal and a flash of light from behind the shrine. Hurrying back, Ürbon saw Askia, his back to Tlupic, staring at the figure in the center of the chamber. The light shifted, and

Tlupic writhed upon the marble surface as the sun's rays refocused on the figure before them. It was a creature of bright light, so bright under the sun's glare that it hurt to look upon it. The dust swirled around it as it landed on the tiled floor. It was humanoid, and from its back sprouted two massive wings, that looked as if they were made of pure gold. It slowly approached Askia, its heavy footfalls echoing through the chamber as it towered over the Sonasian.

"You are trespassing here, travelers." Its voice was almost as radiant as its body, a choir of different speeches and tongues. "Leave now or face the consequences."

As the thing spoke, Tlupic's shudders grew frantic, and he started to twitch uncontrollably on the dais. Askia looked visibly shaken at the creature's arrival, seemingly in response to his prayers.

"M-my apologies, my lord!" started Askia, deciding that this was indeed a servant of his god, sent down to answer his pleas for help. "Please, heal my friend here! He is in desperate need!"

"Careful, Askia," interrupted Ürbon, wary of the newcomer. "This is no servant of Gow."

"Oh? So what am I then?"

"Part of an ancient race long thought dead."

The radiant being looked at Ürbon curiously, "And what might the name of that race be, if everyone one seems to have forgotten?"

Ürbon hesitated for a moment, though he knew the name. Clearly it wanted to provoke him, though for what reason he did not know.

"They were called the Sentriel, and they are still spoken of in all sorts of myths and legends, the celestials of the north, the first to die off in The Old War."

Suddenly the creature doubled over, and burst out laughing, the cacophony of voices making it sound utterly horrific in nature. Recovering rapidly, he waved his hand, and the voices stopped echoing. He started clapping, a smile on his radiant face.

"Correct, my good sir! You win!" The voices had stopped when he waved his hand, so now his voice was alone, and he spoke with a patronizing tone, as if to a child.

"Now, I would help you for how damn entertaining you have been so far, but...that's not really good enough is it?" He turned towards Ürbon, his grin sliding off his face as easily as it had come, and his eyes filled with malice. "Your name. Now!" he demanded.

"Not until you give us yours."

The Sentriel snarled, then smiled, although it looked as if it had pained him to do so.

"Very well. My name is Hydrulian," his face seemed to clear of all emotion, and he looked calm, before continuing, "and I can help your friend there."

Before the others could ask, he continued, "But, it comes at a cost." Turning his head, Hydrulian gestured towards Ürbon, "You. Give me your fealty, and I shall heal your friend."

Ürbon knew he shouldn't do it, but he knew that he didn't have much of a choice. Moving to step forward, he was stopped by Askia, who put a hand in front of him.

"Don't do it," the pilgrim whispered, "he's up to something, and it's not good."

"I know, but we don't have a choice."

He continued walking up, and when he reached the grinning Sentriel, sank down on one knee.

"From here on out," he started, forcing himself to speak the words, "I, Ürbon the Wanderer, swear fealty to Hydrulian, and offer him my axe, and my service as long as I am able. I swear to uphold this vow until the day I die, and to take my foes with me to the grave." Standing back up, he looked down on the smiling Sentriel. "Good enough for you?"

"Oh, quite." The Sentriel walked past the glaring stone golem, and shoved Askia out of the way, as he continued on his path towards Tlupic. As he neared, the Geck'tek writhed and squirmed, as the Sentriel's magic drew closer.

"Oh, keep still." Hydrulian stretched out a hand, and suddenly Tlupic started floating, his arms pinned to his sides, as his mouth opened in a hiss of pure hatred and agony. The Sentriel finally reached the squirming Geck'tek, and placed a hand upon his chest, closed his eyes and began to chant. His words echoed across the room and down the halls, as Tlupic struggled harder against his magical bonds. Ürbon and Askia watched with muted anger, having no other option than to observe the torment their friend was going through.

Hydrulian's voice kept growing in strength until it reached a crescendo, and abruptly the chanting stopped, and Tlupic fell back onto the shrine, coughing. Hydrulian turned his back on the now healed reptile, and began walking out the exit.

"Now, back to business!" he called on his way out. "Follow me, I have a task for you, Ürbon the Wanderer!"

As the Sentriel left, cackling to himself, Ürbon rushed to Tlupic, quickly followed by Askia, who helped him to his feet. Despite the severity of his previous injuries, the Geck'tek was visibly furious at his savior, and he tried to grab one of the spears on his back, only for Ürbon to hold his hand back, preventing him from drawing his weapon. Tlupic snarled at him but made no further attempts to attack.

"Come on! I have places to be and things for you to do!" shouted Hydrulian from down the hallway. Turning back to the sound of his voice, he put Tlupic on his shoulder, and then, feeling utter resignation, Ürbon followed suit.

***

"You guys are going to love what I've got planned for you!" shouted Hydrulian, elated by the fact that he had company for the first time in centuries. The group had finally reached the barred entrance to the temple, and without further ado, the Sentriel waved his hand, and the doors slowly opened, giving them a view of the hordes of the undead still gathered around the temple. Upon seeing the gathered army of skeletons, Hydrulian snarled like a wild animal, and snapped his fingers, and the assembled skeletons crumbled to the ground like marionettes. He turned back to the astonished group behind him with a grin, and when he realized that no one was laughing, he frowned.

"Come on, I've been around for more years than I care to remember. One would have to learn a bit about necromancy in that time, yeah?"

As the group continued to stare, Hydrulian just sighed, and turned back to their destination; the massive black pyramid in the center of the city. To those who knew its actual name, it was *The Pyramid of a Thousand Damned Souls*, but to Hydrulian, it was called the pretty black light. He told himself to shut up, declaring that was a stupid name for a pyramid. He chastised himself by replying that pyramids shouldn't have names in the first place. After a short mental debate with himself, he turned back to the group.

"What? Don't you see I'm busy?"

When no one responded, the Sentriel shrugged, spread his wings and took to the sky, veiling himself in a soundproof cloud. When he checked to make sure his invisibility spell was also in place he found it was not. He did a flip to hide the fact that he was far more exposed than he preferred and rapidly performed the spell. He then realized that he probably shouldn't do that, because he was with company, and so he dispelled the invisibility. Then again, he was a god and could do what he wanted, so he recast it. He did this a couple of times before he accidentally undid the soundproof spell, and finally decided he didn't like flying very much anyway.

Realizing where he was, he landed directly in front of the black pyramid and patiently waited for the rest of his company.

"Alright, I've been looking for some help with this one for a while." He said as the others caught up to him.

"Within this pyramid is an artifact, one I have been seeking for quite a while. I am going to use you to help me receive it." The aforementioned group began casting looks about themselves, as if silently discussing what he meant by "help". Hydrulian smiled, "I assume there are no objections? Good!"

With a slight effort of concentration, he willed the doors on the pyramid to open and was blasted with a gust of old, dusty air. He breathed it in deeply; it helped remind him that he was still alive. He exhaled.

"Well, best go on about it. Go on then!"

Reluctantly, the group went through the doors and entered the black pyramid. He almost cackled madly when the one he had saved cast a hateful glare at him, but he caught himself. He entered after them deciding he would cast his invisibility at some crucial point to play a trick on them. That time, he let out a weak chuckle.

***

Askia was definitely not having a good day. It had started alright before they had entered the dread city, but it had started to rapidly go downhill the further they progressed into the ruin.

First, he learned that there really were some dreadful things in the world. Something had destroyed the city, and he certainly did not want to meet whatever that was. After that, they had been introduced to the reality of the living dead as they were swarmed by charred and gruesome skeletons. Then, as if to mock him, his prayers were answered by some creature masquerading as a servant of his god. A creature who sought to trick him for its own entertainment! Not only that, but it used his pleas as a sick bargaining chip to force his friends to swear fealty to the accursed thing! It then trivialized all of their recent troubles by calling them nothing more than tiny annoyances. He was reaching the end of his patience when it sent them into that place of pure *wrongness*, all on his friend's oath of loyalty to do its bidding!

Well, nothing to be done about it, he supposed. The entire situation was out of his control, and he suspected that the creature, which named itself Hydrulian, would not take kindly to him attempting to leave. So, he endured the darkness of the pyramid as he led the group deeper with the faint blue light of his staff. Hydrulian was staying at the back of the group, humming a merry tune while lighting the entire area around him in a bright golden glow. Why the thing wouldn't lead was beyond him, but once again, he couldn't do anything about it.

The air on the inside of the mysterious structure was hot, fetid and smelled so disgustingly rancid he felt as if it was coating his skin. The walls were made of some strange black material, but like the temple earlier, it was also covered in gold and silver gilt, much of this forming strange runes or images. He attempted to read one of the pictures with the light of his staff so that they might learn more about the place, but he was tapped on the shoulder by Ürbon, whose rumbling voice whispered in his ear.

"It's best if we don't stop," the Jödmun said, his voice calm and reassuring. "He's madder than a raging Viilkin."

Askia turned towards the stone giant, "what in the blazing hell is a Viilkin?"

"They are the sacred creatures of my people, similar in appearance to a wild bear, but much bigger and with horns."

"What in the blazing hell is a bear?"

"Just get moving, the Sentriel isn't right in the mind."

"I'm with you on that front, friend. To be honest, I don't trust him either." Askia turned around and cast a glance at Hydrulian, who cheerfully smiled back.

"Correction, I hate him. With everything I have."

"I understand. Keep an eye on him. He's unpredictable."

With that, the giant continued forward, leaving Askia to wonder how he had gotten into this situation.

Chapter 4: Deserted Plans

As they walked along by the dim light of Askia's staff, the corridor slowly widened, meaning they could walk side by side. The silence in the corridor was palpable. Askia disliked having to search through tightly cramped corridors. Tlupic didn't like the thought of even being around Hydrulian, whom he despised for his ability to use magic. Ürbon may have been uncomfortable with the situation, but was more concerned by it being yet another detour on his quest to rescue his crew. As the corridor widened farther and Askia's staff continued to radiate its blue light, they encountered the first obstacle in the pyramid. What lay ahead of them were six stone sculptures of humans, each raised upon a pedestal that was guarding the path to the other side of the room. Each one wore what looked to be ancient armor sculpted onto their stone bodies, and a mask resembling a skull. Each also held a long spear pointed straight up. In between the six statues was a pathway, and beyond the statues on either side was darkness.

As the group took in the room, a series of torches lining the walls unexpectedly lit up, revealing the full chamber. With the abrupt torchlight, the statues started to shift. Dust fell from their ancient bodies as they lowered their spears towards the group, looking ready to push the invaders out of the pyramid.

As the statues descended upon the group, Tlupic acted first and drew one of his spears. He ran towards the closest statue and dropped beneath it, stabbing it with his weapon. The statue barely had time to draw a sword before the stone crumbled away from its wound. The stone was so ancient that the blow rendered it to dust. Oddly, it clutched the new hole in its chest as though in pain before crumbling away. Soon the other two acted as well, with Ürbon in the lead. Their spears cracked and broke against his stone skin. He slammed Bjarl straight into one statue, and while it disintegrated, he swung it into the side of another causing that one to crumble as well.

In rapid succession, Tlupic threw one spear into the side of a distant statue and a second spear into the head of another one who came closer, causing both to crumble to the ground.

"Oh my, I made a great decision making you swear fealty to me!" said Hydrulian as he surveyed the ruined statues. "Shall we?" he asked, pointing toward the door that would lead them out. Nodding, Ürbon kicked the door, grunting with satisfaction as it crumbled under his strength.

Tlupic didn't even bother acknowledging Hydrulian as they followed the giant deeper into the structure.

As they walked onwards, the walls started to give off a green glow, lighting their way, but it was a warning that they were not welcome, and they knew it. They entered another chamber with statues on either side, but these were different. They seemed decorative and, though larger than the others, didn't look like they would come to life. What drew their attention the most, was at the far end of the room. It appeared to be a raised grave made of stone and completely covered in dust, with a sword lying on top of it.

Standing above the grave was a large metal statue holding a sword in the ground. Tlupic walked towards it, only to be stopped by Hydrulian.

"Yes, finally! My prize! We're so close. I can almost feel it!" The excited Sentriel flew straight to the grave with several beats of his wings. Hydrulian seemed excited as he grabbed hold of the dust-covered sword and waved it in the air victoriously. As he did that, the room began to shake. Behind Hydrulian, the statue's eyes turned green as it came to life and picked up the sword half-buried in the ground.

Ürbon, Tlupic, and Askia saw this change and Tlupic immediately threw his spear, which merely bounced off the metal statue, barely making a dent.

"What was that for, lizardman? You almost hit me!" Hydrulian said right before the statue slammed its sword into his side, knocking him off his feet and slamming him into a wall. When the dust cleared, the Sentriel's golden form was covered in rubble and dust. Hydrulian was dazed from the force of the attack leaving Ürbon to charge the metal statue with his axe. He struck as hard as he could but Bjarl was intercepted by the statue's own blade.

Tlupic pulled out his second spear and hurled it at the statue's head, doing nothing except causing the giant to stagger back from the force of the blow. Ürbon took this opportunity and slashed at the massive metal man. However, despite the force of the blow, all it did was cause a dent in the giant's chest. Tlupic grabbed his spear from the ground and threw it into the dent, creating a small hole, but also trapping the spear's head in the body of the metal statue. Seeing his spear was now out of reach, the Geck'tek scrambled for the other, having lost track of where it fell.

Askia drew his sword, but he had no idea how he was even supposed to fight the metal giant. He heard the sound of marching behind him and turned around, only to see smaller stone statues blocking the corridor where they entered. Ürbon blocked a blow from the metal statue and quickly struck back creating another dent in its side.

Tlupic saw the statues blocking the hall as well and ran towards them, throwing his spear straight into one's head. Askia watched as the statue crumbled from the blow and — seeing that he was going to have to fight — ran with Tlupic towards the enemy. Reaching the statues, he slashed at one and parried a jab from another. But as soon as he felt confident of his fighting ability, he lost his footing and was knocked off balance while attempting another parry. As Askia tried to regain his balance, another statue stabbed it's spear into his side. He fell back, wounded yet still trying to defend himself with his sword, but the statues were just too many. Seeing his friend in peril, Tlupic quickly ran up to Askia, hurling another spear directly into the back of one of the attackers, giving the Sonasian a window to withdraw from the fight.

As Hydrulian recovered from being knocked to near unconsciousness, he decided that he was mad. Unbelievably mad. He thought about what may have hit him, and how badly he was going to hurt it. After a good amount of time lying on the floor, he had come to a conclusion. The only being he knew of that could hit him that hard was Ürbon, seeing as he had hit him that hard before when he knocked him through a door. With this thought, his mind united itself, and he charged out of the rubble, seething with the need for revenge.

Ürbon was still fighting the giant statue, blocking blow after blow, and striking when an opening presented itself. Clearly the spirit controlling it wasn't a trained warrior, and as a result, it was swinging wildly, without the finesse of a swordsmen. Ürbon had managed to cause several dents in the metal that made up his foe. Just as he blocked another attack from the odd metallic statue, he suddenly felt as if his back was on fire. This might be expected of a human, or one of the other mortal races, but the Jödmun do not feel fire the same as mortals. They would bathe in lava pools as their stone skin didn't allow the heat to hurt them.

The cut from Conflagration, Hydrulian's sword, didn't cut as deep as he would have liked, as he was still a bit dazed, but it did hurt. It hurt a lot.

Meanwhile, on the other side of the room, Tlupic dodged back and forth between the stone creations, stabbing back each time they attempted to hit him. Leading with his spear, he jumped from the head of one to the shoulder of another, disintegrating his targets as he continued the cycle. Carefully avoiding the weapons of the statues, Tlupic's distraction was enough to allow Askia to escape from the fighting and give him time to use his staff to heal his wound somewhat.

Tlupic jumped onto yet another statue. As he raised his spear to strike, a flash of lightning cracked around the room, and the statue beneath him stopped moving. Turning towards the flash, he saw Bjarl glowing a blue so bright it was almost blinding. Tlupic flinched as yet another loud *crack* echoed across the chamber. He saw a great nexus of lightning arced from the tip of Bjarl into the metal statue's chest, destroying it in a huge flash. As the metal statue fell, the others crumbled to the ground. They could almost see spectral forms leaving the statues and retreating into the roof.

Ürbon fell to the ground after this show of strength, and once everyone had recovered from the awe of what had happened, they rushed to his side. Hydrulian quickly sheathed his sword, hiding it from view so as to avoid suspicion. He told himself that he was right in the end. Askia knelt next to the fallen giant to use his staff to stop the icy blood flow. The legends about the Jödmun were true, their blood was pure as water and cold as ice. His staff froze the water coming from the giant, beginning to close the wound. He saw how the cut had been made.

"What happened, Hydrulian?" He said.

"I wouldn't know" Hydrulian responded calmly.

A bit of icy water still leaked from the cut as Askia attempted to heal the wound. He could not repair the stone flesh, but he could prevent the ice-blood from leaking out. He knew that the Sentriel had been the cause of this, for only his blade was able to make a cut as clean and precise as this, not to mention leave such blatant heat damage marks. He also knew that if he pressed the issue he would likely die, along with Tlupic and Ürbon, so he ignored Hydrulian for the time being.

Hydrulian was inwardly stunned, for he acted out of rage. He didn't give himself any time to realize that the metal statue had been the one that had hit him. He also didn't expect the reaction from Ürbon to be so powerful. Nevertheless, Hydrulian cared not. He had acted accordingly and as he saw fit, and there was no fault in that, not for him at least. Besides, it all turned out well in the end; he was one step closer to his prize.

Casting a spell of invisibility he flew to a far corner of the room. Once he had landed, his great metallic wings folding behind him, he sat down. Holding the sword he had taken from upon the grave, he held the blade in one hand and the hilt in the other. With a forceful twist the hilt clicked and gave way. He threw the blade to the side — he had no use for it. What he was looking for was within a hollow space inside the hilt, from which he shook out an old tattered map. As he unraveled it he found that it was still legible, and showed him the way to what he sought.

Coming back to his senses, Ürbon awoke to the patter of feet as Tlupic walked about the rubble, searching for his spears. Raising his head, he saw Askia by his side, staff in hand.

"Is it dead?" he asked.

"Yes, it's dead," replied Askia.

Lifting himself up from the floor, Ürbon looked around the debris. All he remembered was the sudden searing pain on his back, loud cracks of lightning, and falling over. He saw the shattered and broken body of the metal statue, lying on the ground beside them. The stone statues were also destroyed, yet had crumbled to the ground in front of the exit, blocking their only way out.

The Sentriel was also nowhere to be seen, but the closed up exit meant that he was still trapped inside with them. Ürbon called out as politely as he could.

"Well, would you mind telling us what we came here for?"

From behind the Jödmun came the sound of metal screeching against metal, and the Sentriel appeared.

"Not to worry, we have what we came for," Hydrulian stated, waving the map in the air.

"And what," questioned Ürbon, "might that be?"

"A map to my great prize. Now come! We have work to do!"

"And how do you propose we do that?" said Ürbon "There's no way out of here, it would take us days to move that rubble."

Their reactions were interrupted by a hiss of triumph coming from Tlupic. Walking over to the Geck'tek, Ürbon saw what he had found. Tlupic had moved the remnants of the metal statue, revealing a stairwell underneath. At that same moment he saw that the mysterious green mist had started to seep in from the cracks. Without missing a moment, Ürbon called over the others, he didn't want to spend any more time in that room than he had to. Together they moved the broken statue further away, and with a final glance between them, descended into the depths.

***

Atop the desert sands strode a golden figure, her dark brown skin accented with the gold markings embedded in her clothing. Against the wind, her dark braids whistled behind her head, tugged and pulled by the air around her. Sitting queenly upon the saddle of her horse, Stixerio, a gift by the priesthood for her journey. She scanned the horizon with eyes flecked with gold and she spotted her destination. The city of the dead god Dedpheker, where it was said her great journey would begin. With a swift kick to the flanks, she urged Stixerio onward towards her destiny.

Chapter 5:
Deal With Death

As the team descended further into the depths, Askia at their head, the black limestone of the pyramid began to glow with a dim green tint, nearly identical to the mist outside the structure. The hieroglyphs on the wall seemed to be glowing with the same sickly green light. Ürbon slowed his pace so he might talk with Tlupic. The Geck'tek was incredibly tense, both because of the mysterious location, but also because of their golden companion. The Geck'tek's ability to sense magic was going haywire around the Sentriel.

"We need to keep an eye on him." Ürbon said, nodded towards the Sentriel, who pretended not to notice.

The Geck'tek barely responded, nodding slightly, his eyes fixed on Hydrulian's radiant figure. Ürbon could sense something was amiss, though he didn't know what. He had a horrible feeling that something was going to go awry. However, the group walked on, though he couldn't shake the feeling from his mind.

They continued down the stairwell, the black reflecting the growing green light off of the inscriptions, which now glowed with enough light to make Askia's staff unnecessary. Even still he kept his staff out, shining its blue aura, which seemed to be keeping the mysterious mist at bay.

His companions seemed to feel similarly as they cast nervous glances about themselves. Their feet trod on grounds undisturbed for hundreds of years, causing dust to waft around their feet. The silence was deafening. The dust was muffling the sounds of their feet hitting the floor, making it sound as if the noise came from far off in some distant chamber.

Without warning, the walls which had guided the four down the stairwell were gone, opening up into a massive chamber. The walls were made of the same black stone, but there were no runes covering them like in the hall. There were, however, small runes on the high ceiling, and these radiated light downwards, throughout the length of the room. They were spaced evenly apart, revealing the contents of the floor.

Lying upon the cold stone floor were several skeletons, some partial, many whole and often with rusted weapons beside them. They had been there for a very long time, and appeared to be of several varying species. Ürbon thought he could see the remains of a Zuut and beside it its Haikosun master. The Haikosun were a race of tiger folk that resided to the far east and dwelt within the aptly named "Divine Haikosun Empire," where they ruled over the other races they had conquered. One of these conquered peoples were the Zuut, a race of massive, two-headed hyenas that, despite their great strength, lacked intelligence, and were trained from birth to serve the Haikosun as slaves.

They could have been fellow adventurers, but they were most likely the deceased builders, buried within what they had given their lives to create. If this was the case, then they were definitely desecrating their tomb, a statement which was emphasized when Tlupic slipped on a skull at the room's entrance.

The resounding thud of the Geck'tek hitting the ground, and the *crack* of the skull echoing across the room, brought a change to the atmosphere. The air seemed to hum with power, and the group's unease doubled. Their wariness was validated as the bones upon the ground began to twitch. The skeletons began to rise off the ground with agonizing slowness. Arms which had fallen out of their sockets clicked back into place, and legs which had previously been broken, became whole again. In the space of a moment, two dozen skeletal horrors had arisen from the floor, all different species and sizes. The skeletons stood there unmoving as a vibration resounded through the room, and shards of bone gathered in the center, merging together to form a skull.

The head was that of a human, complete with a full set of teeth, and it let loose a piercing, insane laughter. The sounds of bone smacking against bone echoed alongside the laughter, creating a chilling effect. Then the skeletal creatures also threw open their jaws and joined in the cacophony of laughter. After several seconds of this bloodcurdling laughter, the skeletons cracked teeth clattered shut, now only letting out the occasional chuckle, and the floating skull spoke, what it uttered was chilling.

"Ah, visitors!" the thing's high-pitched voice cutting through the air, feeling as if it filled the entire room. "Join us, forever!"

After the skull finished its speech, it burst into another fit of laughter, inciting the other skeletons to laugh as well. Its mad giggling was cut short by a wooden spear to its eye socket, breaking through its brittle bones, dropping it to the ground, lifeless. Suddenly all the laughter stopped, and the skeletons stared at the motionless head on the floor, slowly rolling to a stop. The silence was total, and the group readied their weapons. All at once, the skeletons looked up, uttered a shriek of anger and charged forward, their rusted weapons raised in challenge.

The group responded in kind, raised their weapons and charged. Ürbon hefted Bjarl, raising the axe above his head. Tlupic, having already thrown a spear, drew the other and flipped himself into battle. Askia, having already drawn his scimitar, offered a quick prayer for his delivery from danger, before charging behind Ürbon. Hydrulian rested his head on his hands and began an intense debate on whether or not to contribute to the fight.

The groups smashed into each other with incredible ferocity. Ürbon smashed the skeleton of a dwarf clear across the room, where it shattered into several pieces. Tlupic's frantic spinning resulted in his spear slashing straight through a human skeleton's head and coming back out of their chin. When his foe didn't go down, he used the spear and his momentum to lever the skeleton's head off of its spine.

Askia was having a harder time than those two, since his training was little to none. He was facing off against another human skeleton, and this foe seemed to remember its combat training from before its demise and easily parried Askia's inexperienced blows. Barely able to block in return, Askia was going to need more than brute force to best his foe. Thinking quickly, he used his staff to throw water at his foe's eye sockets. Despite it having no eyes with which to sting, it reacted as if it did, and the skeleton stumbled as if blinded. Askia took his opportunity, and his sword sliced through his enemy's chest. The skeleton fell back to the ground, devoid of the magic that had powered it.

Taking a moment's rest, Askia saw that Ürbon had already destroyed three monsters of his own and was currently facing off against a huge skeletal Zuut and its Haikosun master.

The Jödmun was circling his enemies, his feet pulverizing bone as he stepped. The two skeletons were working in tandem to take him down, in a parody of their relationship in life. With the way the smaller skeleton stood, and the way the giant followed it, there was no doubt that they were a Haikosun and his Zuut slave.

The Haikosun skeleton charged, its fists held in front of it, the same fighting style as its living counterparts. The feline fossil threw a punch, which became enveloped in a glowing blue light. Ürbon had spent time in their land, and he knew the power of the attack that the skeleton launched. Quickly intercepting the blow with Bjarl, there was a loud crackle of released magic, and a cloud of smoke emerged. The skeleton flipped backward out of the cloud, landing squarely on its feet.

Ürbon took the offensive, now knowing the strength of his opponent. His foe did likewise, charging forward, its arms thrown behind his back, chest low to the ground, and the massive lumbering shape of the Zuut following behind. Ürbon opened with a sideways slash of Bjarl, which would have smashed through his foe if the Zuut had not caught the blow with its forearm, and while it sliced through its bones, it halted the momentum of the blow. The Haikosun used this opportunity to jump into the air, launching a kick at the Jödmun's face. The giant grabbed the feline's outstretched leg, and threw it into the ground behind him, scattering its bones along the floor.

Meanwhile, Tlupic was facing off against a group of skeletons clad in ancient and desiccated armor. Although their armor and weapons were covered with verdigris, in some spots, the original orange of the bronze showed through. Tlupic eyed his target and sprang towards the group, spear in hand. The enemy raised their weapons in an attempt to block him, but he dodged them all and took the head off of one before landing on the ground behind another.

However, as he prepared to leap again, a spear swung down towards him, aimed straight for his head. He reacted fast, and instead of throwing his spear into an enemy skull, he parried. The weapons met with incredible force, and Tlupic winced from the pain vibrating in his hands. Luckily his spear had held against the blow, but as he leaped away from the skeleton it came apart in his hands, broken to pieces. Angered at the loss of his spear, he drew his dagger and furiously struck at the skeleton, and it crumbled to dust. The ease with which he slayed his foe only angered him further, and he dashed into the fray, taking off another head.

As Askia dispatched another skeleton, he spared a glance towards the others. Tlupic seemed to be in the middle of several skeletal spearmen and swordsmen, and one of his spears was broken. Ürbon was wrestling for control over Bjarl with a massive, two-headed, skeletal giant, while the previously destroyed skeleton behind him was re-assembling itself and seemed to be gearing up for a strike. He could not see Hydrulian anywhere, but he had to get busy defending himself from another skeletal swordsman that had launched a stab for his torso. He parried and attacked in return.

Ürbon tried to regain control of Bjarl, but the massive Zuut's strength held firm, and he would not relinquish his hold. Frustrated with this development, he urged Bjarl to shock his foe to bits, hoping to once again gain control. However, the axe did not respond to his command in any way. Out of nowhere, he felt a pain in his back, and a cloud of dust flew outward from behind him. Turning his head to look, he realized he couldn't see anything through the cloud until a blue light suddenly came flying toward his face. Releasing the axe to roll out of the way caused the Haikosun skeleton to miss its attack, so it flew towards its Zuut, landing nimbly on its shoulder.

He snarled, and charged at the two, annoyed at the Haikosun having recovered, and at the theft of Bjarl. The smaller skeleton leapt ahead of the Zuut, and its fists once more glowed with a blue light. Before the feline could reach him however, the entire room began to shake. Dust fell from the ceiling, and the skeletons looked as confused as their opponents as to what was happening. Suddenly a massive crack was heard, and the black and polished surface making up the ceiling split into two.

The skeletons suddenly burst into panic, running amok as if out of control. Ürbon delivered a punch to the back of the Zuut's head as it looked around in mute fear, and grasped Bjarl from its skeletal hands. The Haikosun saw its friend fall and found himself launched at the Jödmun, his limbs fully enveloped in the glowing blue light. His charge was cut short by Ürbon's axe, splitting the entire skeleton in two, causing the two halves to fall to the floor, where it didn't move again.

Looking around through the chaos, he spotted Askia running towards Tlupic, who was covered in shattered bones and chunks of stone. He moved to help, but then he saw Hydrulian, his face a mask of chaos and insanity. His arms were raised in front of him, and the dust and chunks of stone swirled around them like halos of destruction. His lips moved endlessly, powering a spell that was tearing the room itself apart. Seeing the threat, Ürbon charged towards the Sentriel, his stone skin being battered by windblown pebbles and falling chunks of stone.

Maddened laughter spilled across the room as Askia rushed to Tlupic's side. Though exhausted, he heaved at the objects piled on top of his companion. Luckily the skeletons which had fallen on top of him had lessened the impact of the stones, but Tlupic was clearly unconscious. As he pulled at the biggest chunk of stone that had trapped his friend, he found that he could not move it. He couldn't even remotely shift it from its position.

Ürbon reached the Sentriel, whose insane laughter was echoing throughout the room. His brilliant radiance was hard to look at, and as he flared out his wings, the screech of metal on metal was barely heard over the tumult of violence spreading throughout the room. "Stop this!" he shouted, barely hearing his own voice over the sound of falling rock.

His voice was not heard, or if it was, it was not heeded, as Hydrulian's laughter continued, and his arms never faltered. Feeling the room shudder, he knew he had to act fast.

As Askia pushed and pulled at the massive weight, he was joined by one of the skeletons, who helped to move the stone. The skeleton was covered from head to toe in ancient red armor and looked to have had some rank in life, judging from the helmet upon his head. Staring, shocked at the turn of allegiance, he went back to trying to move the stone. With both their efforts, it shifted, but not enough to retrieve Tlupic. The skeleton turned around and seemed to bark at the nearby skeletons, not needing words for communication. Skulls nodded in resolve and the skeletons rushed to help the Sonasian. With their combined effort, they pushed the stone away and off the Geck'tek.

Reaching down to pick up his friend, he saw the skeletons staring blankly at him, and they were standing straight, unmoving. Askia looked around uneasily but was quickly reminded of his situation as the room shuddered again, much stronger than before. He turned to run, but was stopped by a skeletal hand on his shoulder. Whipping around to face them, he saw that it was the skeleton in the red armor. It pointed to his staff, and then pointed at itself.

"What are you trying to say?" Askia shouted, trying to be heard over the massive crashes of stone around him.

The skeleton did nothing more so Askia turned back around, only to hear a tremendous cracking from above. He looked up and saw a chunk of black stone falling fast towards his head. At that moment, he knew he was about to die. Before he could come to accept that fact however, he was launched forward, and everything went dark.

***

Ürbon bodily tackled the Sentriel, hoping to shake some sense into the clearly maddened immortal.

"Snap out of it before I make you!"

His threat seemed to have no effect, as Hydrulian's maddened laughter kept spilling from his lips. Snarling in anger, he saw he was out of time as the roof was coming down. With little time to think, he picked up the giggling Sentriel and threw him against the far wall, before diving that way himself.

***

Askia awoke on the cold stone floor. His head was pounding and his whole body ached. He tried to remember what had happened, but was having trouble getting his bearings. After a bit he began to remember how the room had shaken, and how he had tried to rescue Tlupic from his fate. Tlupic! He had to find out where his friend was, and if he had survived the cave-in. But each time he tried to get to his feet, his legs buckled, and he would fall back down again. Determined not to give up, he kept trying to regain his footing, but after the third time, he was starting to lose hope.

As his knees crashed to the stone floor once more, a metal covered arm reached down from in front of him, offering its assistance. Raising his head, Askia saw the skeleton who had helped him move the rubble off of Tlupic. Its crimson armor was more ruined than before, covered in more scratches and dents with some pieces missing altogether, but now he could see that it had pale, dead skin still attached to its body. The creature's blank gaze looked down upon him, its fangs of pure ivory reflecting the light from Askia's staff, its hand remaining outstretched. Without any other options, Askia took the skeletal hand into his own, and the strange skeleton's surprising strength pulled him to his feet effortlessly.

Nodding a quick thanks to his skeletal savior, Askia took a moment to examine his new surroundings. The room was utterly destroyed from the tremors, with cracks running down every surface. Dust fell from the cracks in the roof, along with pebbles and small stones. Everywhere lay shattered bones and weapons, split into pieces by falling stone in the madness of the quake.

What drew the eye most was a massive wall of rubble, which had cut the room almost directly in half. The wall seemed several feet thick and was composed of gigantic piles of debris and boulders. Askia knew without a doubt that there was no way to get to the other side. After first looking back to his silent skeletal companion, he went off to search for the rest of the group.

Walking carefully, so as not to trip and break a bone, he searched the rubble by the fading light from the runes above, and by the light of his staff. The rubble was everywhere, and he wasn't sure where exactly to look. He knew that he had been carrying the Geck'tek before the roof had caved in, so he figured to start looking around where he had been. He walked around piles of rubble, finding no trace of Tlupic. He dug through larger piles, praying to Tuct and Gow in equal measure that his friend hadn't suffocated under the piles of rock.

As his hands sifted through the gravel, the red armored skeleton followed him around, and though the thing's eyes were blank, Askia could feel his gaze on the back of his neck. Frankly, it was distracting, and he had to find Tlupic before his panic overtook him. After several minutes, he was considering telling the thing to leave him alone, but before he could act, he realized that the skeleton was already gone, leaving him to his own business.

After sifting through more rubble in the dark, and coughing from the dust settling down and rising up from his movements, he suddenly heard footsteps approaching. Turning around, he was almost consumed by joy when he saw Tlupic alongside his crimson companion. Before he could celebrate the reunion, a flash of golden light exploded from the other side of the room, and the group ran to find the source, although Askia had a good feeling of who it was.

***

"Would you calm down already?" asked Ürbon.

His annoyance heightened when the golden being in front of him launched another golden bolt of magic into the wall, releasing a flare of exceptionally bright light, and leaving the black stone wall blackened further with ash.

"I command you to shut up!" shouted Hydrulian, his eyes filled with hatred for the being attempting to soothe him. He was the one at fault here!

Ürbon stomped towards the enraged Sentriel, attempting to utilize his massive size to intimidate the Sentriel into reason.

"Stop it. You're draining your energy pointlessly, we'll need it to get out of this mess you've created."

"I told you to shut up!" Hydrulian, enraged by the giant's arrogance, drew his sword, Conflagration.

The stone giant responded sensibly, by grabbing the Sentriel's sword arm, and when he tried to squirm out of his grip, proceeded to throw him into the wall. What came out of the dust cloud that the impact created was a very, very incensed Hydrulian.

"You swore a vow to me to obey my every command! And I told you to shut up!"

Ürbon, seeing perhaps he should give up trying to make the Sentriel stop acting like an overly powerful toddler, shut his mouth so that the golden figure before him would calm down. As the Sentriel climbed out of the rubble, he heard the sound of footsteps from behind the massive rock wall. Leaving an infuriated Hydrulian behind him, he found a spot near the bottom of the wall where he had a small view to the other side, just in time for a certain human to reach the same spot.

Askia's face seemed to light up with joy at seeing the Jödmun, and he looked as if he was about to launch into questioning when a large golden form shoved the Jödmun aside, making room to find out what was so interesting. Upon seeing the face of his fellow companion, or 'slave', as he liked to call them, he turned back around and stalked away, having lost all interest. After watching him retreat, Askia turned back to Ürbon, about to blast into a flurry of questions but was stopped as the Jödmun raised his hand, gesturing for silence.

"First off, we have to figure out how to get through this rubble," he said, in reference to the massive wall of stone between the two groups. "We can't take it down by hand, and I doubt that Golden Boy over there will be of much help."

"I HEARD THAT!"

"Anyway, I don't think that..." Ürbon froze, as he saw a skeleton clad in crimson armor appear behind the man, steadily getting closer.

"Watch out, behind you!"

Askia tensed, and turned his head, but relaxed once he saw that it was only the skeleton.

"Oh, don't worry, he is friendly."

"Askia, we were just fighting them. You can't trust them." Ürbon worried for his friend, not understanding how he could trust one of them.

"He saved me and Tlupic during the cave-in. I'm not sure if I fully trust him yet, but he has proved his worth."

"You need to listen to me, he's not trustworthy..."

"Sorry to interrupt, but I have a strange sense of déjà vu." Hydrulian pointed to the original entrance to the room, and as had happened before, the green mist continued to drift down into the lower chambers.

"We have to get out of here. Stay safe, Ürbon." Askia said his farewells before making as if to leave, but Ürbon's voice gave him pause.

"Don't trust it! There's something evil down here, dark and corrupting. We need to be careful. Just find an exit, and meet us outside." Askia nodded before dashing away.

Ürbon sighed. He was stuck with the Sentriel again.

***

Hydrulian seethed in rage. He had been kicked, punched, and thrown through doors, walls, and enemies. And when he had attempted to save his slaves from a horrifying demise of being crushed under thousands of tons of rock, (ignoring of course that he created that scenario) he was promptly tackled and thrown to the side like a ragdoll.

Checking his spells of soundproofing and invisibility, he launched himself into the air using his metallic wings. Avoiding clouds of green mist which had begun to seep down. The green gas, pretty though it was, was radiating something he would describe as malicious intent. Rising up all the way to whatever remained of the ceiling he scanned the room for the exit.

He had truly leveled the room, as several portions of everything were in pieces, including the floor, wall and ceiling. Taking in the sweet destruction, he returned to his goal of finding an exit. After several seconds of running his eyes over the ruined walls, he finally spotted a doorway on the far side of the room. He was almost happy about his find, until he saw that the Jödmun had found the door first, and was currently walking toward it.

The absurdity of what he was seeing from across the room spurred him to action. He flew as fast as he could towards the doorway in hopes of overtaking Ürbon, who was only just a few steps away from it. The race was futile; Hydrulian knew he couldn't reach the door first. But he was unwilling to accept such blatant defeat, so he surged forward with all his energy, cackling as the wind whistling through his wings.

Ürbon saw the Sentriel rush over the rubble straight towards the door, his wings folded inwards like a swooping hawk. Taking the rational option, the Jödmun took no further steps towards the door. He preferred not to have a chunk carved out of his side from the oncoming collision.

Hydrulian continued to sail towards the open doorway; he knew he had to slow down somehow. Thinking fast, he cut off the magic surging through his wings, hoping to stop himself from gaining speed. This worked, but not well enough and he knew that he had no other choice but to slow himself down physically. He opened his wings and let his toe scrape the floor, hoping for the friction to slow him down.

This proved an impractical strategy. Instead of gently rolling to a stop as planned, he found himself rolling over shards of rock and piles of gravel. It was not pleasant. Eventually, and thankfully, he slowed down, and ended up — bruised and scraped — right at the Jödmun's feet.

Lying in rubble, Hydrulian finally gathered the courage to look up. Ürbon was laughing at the Sentriel's embarrassing landing.

Shouting in outrage, he threw a bolt of pure light directly into the Jödmun's chest, knocking him back.

"That makes us even, Stone-Skull!"

Ürbon glared bitterly at his rival, there was no more laughter in his eyes, but before he could fire back a retort, Hydrulian darted through the door frame and out of sight. Muttering some choice words under his breath, he followed after the Sentriel, who's giggling could be heard even from the top of the hall.

***

Tlupic was livid. Stuck in this damned dead city, the stench of evil magic everywhere, fighting for some golden magic-wielding heretic, and now traveling next to a walking corpse. It didn't help that he was stuck with yet another heretic. Though they had fought side by side, he still wasn't too sure about Askia. The fact that the Sonasian had rescued him from being buried alive twice didn't help with his hatred for magic thieves.

They were trapped, lost and separated from Ürbon, the only mercy being that the gold-feathered lunatic was also far away. The Sentriel represented everything he had been raised to despise, and one day he would bring retribution onto him.

The corpse was eerily silent, but there seemed a sort of awareness to it, a sharpness in its movement, like that of a jungle predator. It disturbed Tlupic, for the magic that permeated it was so similar yet so different from the magic that he felt from this cursed land, he could feel it. Tlupic was confused that the thing had helped them, this abomination, a walking corpse made from stolen magic. Such creatures weren't meant to exist, and why the human trusted it so completely was beyond him. But for now Tlupic followed and waited for the right time, holding his spear and his dagger, his eyes on the enemy's neck, waiting for the opportunity.

***

As Hydrulian continued to skip down the stairs, currently enjoying the fact that he had indeed gotten to the staircase first, he continued to dwell in the deep spaces of his mind. In one corner was a burning forest, from which came the crackles and pops of burning wood. In another corner, he saw a scarabite arguing about coral reefs with a separate copy of himself. Before he could prove to the scarabite why it's facts were so easily disputable, he found that his foot had dropped into open air.

Falling forward, he snapped open his metallic wings and gazed down at the massive pit below him. It was rectangular, going farther down than he could see. He looked around and saw that there were no other doorways, and the pit was the only way to continue forward. Checking to make sure that the Jödmun was still in sight, he slowly descended into the depths. At least, he *was* descending slowly, until something slammed into his back and caused him to lose control. He was only able to let out a shout of alarm before he plummeted downwards, into the depths.

Hearing Hydrulians alarming shout, Ürbon ran forward and found the massive pit. All he saw was the shadow of a many-legged form scurrying against the wall, and the golden light of the Sentriel fading as he plummeted farther away from him.

***

Askia was once again leading the group, his staff keeping the darkness and green mist at bay. Curiously, the skeleton remained close to the staff at all times, as if its life depended on it. He could not deny he was beginning to feel nervous: first there was Ürbon's warning, and now Tlupic looked ready to pounce upon the skeleton. But why would it betray them, there was nothing to be gained from killing them on the spot.

"There is no need to worry, young ones." The voice was raspy, like sand being scraped over stone, both Askia and Tlupic froze.

"I can feel both of your heartbeats quicken. Do not worry, I no longer possess The Hunger."

Askia glanced at Tlupic to see that he was equally confused by the skeleton's words. The undead stood silent for a moment like he was waiting for a response before he continued, "You don't know what I am referring to? Not even you, Sonasian? I know your people are familiar with our...kind."

Askia felt a cold shiver run down his spine as recognition set in. He could barely utter the words from the fear rising from the depths of his soul. "Night Demon," he sputtered, as the being before them removed his helmet and revealed his face.

It was now easy to see that it was not a skeleton at all, but something much, much worse. Its pale, dry skin revealed a once-human face, now resembling the corpse of a desiccated man. Its nose had long since rotted away, leaving only two slits surrounded by dry blood. It's ears were long and bat-like, and from its long missing lips, two ivory fangs could easily be seen. Its bony eye sockets held a pair of glowing red orbs, with pupils resembling the slits of predatory animals such as lions or snakes. All of these pointed to what it truly was, a Night Demon in Askia's tongue; a blood-sucker; a creature of the night; a terror of the desert nights. It has been named all of these and more. Askia's hand subconsciously reached for his sword, and Tlupic followed him by grabbing his spear.

"Now, now, young ones, there is no need for violence," the creature said, its dry voice alike to crackling parchment, "but yes, I am what your people call a Night Demon, or, in the Common Tongue, a vampire."

The admission did nothing to calm the living.

"Truly, children, I mean no harm, and even if I wanted to, your blood is too...pure. It is protected, and even if it weren't, I don't like the taste of lizard," the vampire could see that his reassurances were for nothing so he explained again,

"Children, listen to me, I no longer crave blood and I am no longer under that foul creature's spell." He pointed at Askia's staff. "I should thank you for that, as your staff managed to break the corruption of the mist. And for that, I shall help you escape this dreaded place."

Askia was about to speak when the creature said something startling.

"Though, I must admit your friend's spell also contributed to freeing me."

Askia stood, somewhat confused at the vampire's words.

"You mean that the Sentriel's spell freed you?"

"Not entirely, but it helped considerably with the massive wave of magical interference that was released." However, before the Sonasian could delve into a silent rage about Hydrulian trying to kill everyone, he was interrupted by the vampire once more.

"For the freedom you have given me, I will continue to accompany you, and aid you in getting out of this accursed place..."

"No."

This simple word seemed to bring pause to the entire room, even the mist seemed to falter in its attack.

"First we must rejoin the rest of our group, and only then can we leave." The words that came out of Askia's mouth had a sense of finality and command that sounded very foreign to him, but he did not stop and wonder from where it came from, or why both his sword and staff glowed for a second.

The vampire was silent for a while, but eventually it bowed down, and put a hand over its heart "I am Asherai, Knight of the order of the Blood Serpent. I am at your service. Now come. If your companions are hell-bent on facing death, then they would have gone this way."

***

Climbing down to Hydrulian was easier said than done. Ürbon found himself losing his footing more than once, only saved from plummeting to his death by Bjarl. He hacked his axe into the rocky surface, carefully placing his footing lower down. Making progress inch by inch he wondered why he was even trying. Hydrulian didn't mean much to him, and so far only brought more trouble. Yet he felt compelled to rescue the Sentriel. The shame of abandoning someone he was sworn to protect would taint him forever, even if that someone was an absolute ass.

He took another step down, but his footing felt different this time. It sank into the surface, almost like stepping into mud or sludge. He looked down and saw the surface was covered in some white, silky material. The bottom of the pit was visible now as well, and he saw the silvery sheen of a silky web stretching across the floor. In the middle was Hydrulian, covered in it, his golden form illuminating the strands.

Who knows what monsters lurk here, whatever it was must be arachnid. Clearly they had already trapped Hydrulian, which meant that the creatures were nearby. Ürbon continued his slow descent down, his feet and hands coming away covered in cobwebs.

As he finally made it to the bottom, he heard the sound of scattering feet moving away. He walked amongst the dead bodies of their prey up to the cocooned Hydrulian, but by getting a closer look it was clear the Sentriel was just lying there comfortably.

"Get up, Golden Boy," said Ürbon, noticeably annoyed.

"Oh, shut up," the Sentriel replied, waving Ürbon away, though this arm was considerably restricted by the webs. "These are real servants. They even made a nice bed for me here, more than you ever did."

"Just shut it for once and come with me."

"You dare argue with me? Servants, dispose of him!"

Though not at the Sentriel's command, the spiders had been gathering in numbers around the two. All at once, dozens of the eight-legged monsters came running at the giant, skittering across the webbed floor. With barely a sigh, the giant answered them with the roar of thunder.

***

After a while Askia could no longer endure the silence. Asherai had taken them through several rooms now. They had faced yet another room full of skeletons, but before Askia or Tlupic could react, the Asherai killed them all in the blink of an eye, its movements simple and effective. Their guide even helped them avoid traps and puzzles, but despite this they still could not fully trust the vampire. It was a terror of the night, and legends revolved around their cruelty and unnatural hunger.

"It is true, my people are infamous for the carnage left in their wake." Asherai said in reaction to another nervous glance.

"And if we had met a few centuries ago" he continued. "I would have drained every single drop of blood from your body, but like I said, I no longer possess the Hunger."

The next to break the silence was Tlupic, surprisingly.

"What do you mean by the Hunger?"

Asherai looked pensive before explaining.

"I am a vampire, a creature of the night. There are many types of us, but I won't bore you with the details. I came here to find a possible cure for the Hunger that enslaves my kind, for I knew that this ancient necropolis held many secrets of death and the arcane.

"And I was correct. As I descended down to the depths of this pyramid, I eventually encountered the Priest-King, the ancient undead overlord of these realms. He overwhelmed me, caught me, and forced me to bend to his will. He cured me of my hunger for blood, for down here there is no blood for me to consume, but now, thanks to you, I am free, and he will pay for the many centuries of enslavement."

They walked through the maze-like corridors as Asherai told his tale. The vampire's words relieved Askia and Tlupic; if he truly had lost his unnatural hunger for blood and violence, then it was possible he was a true ally. But their relief was short-lived as they heard a clicking sound echoing across the room.

Suddenly the floor beneath them fell away, dipping downwards as if on hinges with a loud crash. Unable to grab hold of anything, the three plummeted down the pit beneath them.

Ürbon continued down the path, Bjarl in one hand and a cocooned Hydrulian in the other. The spiders had been little more than a nuisance. A single powerful blast of lightning and they scurried away, back to their hiding hole. But that was not the end to their problems. As Ürbon walked further along, the green mist became unavoidable.

***

Ürbon continued down the path, Bjarl in one hand and a cocooned Hydrulian in the other. The spiders had been little more than a nuisance. A single powerful blast of lightning and they scurried away, back to their hiding hole. But that was not the end to their problems. As Ürbon walked further along, the green mist was close behind him. Its tendrils seemed to stretch out, as if trying to catch him as he quickened his pace.

But try as he might he couldn't outrun it, and for a split-second he was forced to breathe it in. To his surprise it didn't do any harm. In truth it almost felt pleasant, like a heavy burden lifting from his shoulders. The green mist seemed to draw back as he inhaled, as if losing interest.

Shrugging away a bit of stray webbing on his shoulder, he heard a dull thud come from somewhere on the path in front of them. Anxious to investigate, he checked his grip on Bjarl and Hydrulian and set off to find the source of the sound.

He found the answer when he entered the next room. It was somewhat similar to the one with the spiders, but without the webbing. Above them, in the center of the room, was a square shaft, leading far up to another chamber. The area around the hole was supported by engraved pillars, in the same glowing green script that had provided the light that had led them throughout the pyramid.

Littered all around the rubble were ancient statues, like those they had fought in the beginning of the maze. He could also see skeletons lying in a pile in the center of the room, right below the square shaft above.

He watched as three skeletons rose up from the pile. One of them turned its head towards Ürbon and screeched in an inhuman voice. With no time to waste, Ürbon set down Hydrulian and charged the skeletons.

***

Groaning, Askia picked himself up off the floor and saw that his companions were also slowly recovering from the fall. Scanning the rubble, he saw that this was not the first time something had fallen there. Bits of rubble and cracked bones littered the area, it seemed they were one of the lucky ones to survive the fall.

But their luck did not end there, and Askia was overjoyed to see Ürbon on the other side of the room. The Jödmun looked content, almost peaceful, and was carrying Hydrulian in some sort of white shawl.

Askia shouted a greeting, gaining the giant's attention. But realized that something was wrong when he noticed the green mist circling around the Jödmun. Ürbon did not reply, but instead threw Hydrulian to the floor, hefted Bjarl, and charged towards Askia and his group. Not knowing what to do, Askia stood in place, even as he saw the hatred in Ürbon's eyes draw closer and the mystical axe come hurtling down towards him.

Chapter 6:
Bury The Dead

Bjarl descended towards Askia, seemingly in slow motion, as the mystical blade left a trail of blue particles in its wake. Frozen in disbelief, Askia could only watch as the blade came ever closer.

However, instead of the expected blow to his skull, he felt a sharp pain in his side as he was thrown to the floor. Bjarl sunk into the stone floor several yards away, and Asherai lay beside him.

Once more the vampire had pushed the Sonasian out of harm's way. As the man recovered from his encounter with certain death, Asherai pushed himself to his feet and turned to face Ürbon as he pulled his axe from the stone.

The two clashed and sparks flew as Asherai's blade locked into a deadly embrace with Bjarl. The Jödmun pushed his blade down towards the crimson-clad warrior. Snarling in effort, the vampire proved to be no match for the raw power of the giant, and he leapt back, his speed letting him reach safety without harm. The giant lumbered towards him, his face devoid of all expression, the green mist trailing behind him.

He launched himself back at the Jödmun, his sword in front of him in a stabbing motion. However, as he got into range to strike, Ürbon backhanded him and sent him smashing into a wall. The pain was total, he tumbled to the ground.

Even while his opponent was knocked to the ground, the giant kept coming. With a final effort Asherai pushed himself to his feet, raised his sword and waited for the Jödmun to come to him. However, it turned out he need not wait, as Tlupic leapt onto the golem's shoulder. Ürbon made to grab the Geck'tek and throw him off, but suddenly he froze, his hand halfway towards the lizardman.

Ürbon stared at the skeleton upon his shoulder. It looked exactly like Tlupic, but if he had been stripped clean of flesh. His skeletal frame sat upon his shoulder, just like Tlupic had before they had been separated. It even had a spear, in imitation of Tlupic's own weapon. Was it possible that Tlupic had fallen? And now his remains were re-animated by whatever curse was upon this place?

Then he noticed that the skeleton's image seemed to be flickering. It appeared as if the living body of Tlupic was surrounding the skeleton, as if this was all merely an illusion.

With an effort of will, the Jödmun reached his hand out, knowing it would be the only way to tell if it was real or not. However, he was interrupted by a pain in his leg. The skeletal swordsman had slashed at his stone frame with its glowing crimson red sword. Ürbon lashed back at the skeleton, but roared as it tugged out its blade and dodged back. Furious, he stomped towards the swordsman, intent on destroying it utterly. The fact that it had survived his first hit was impressive, but its bones were cracked, and its elegant movements were marred by a slight limp.

At that moment he saw that the skeletal Geck'tek had jumped off his shoulder and landed in front of the skeletal swordsman. They seemed to be talking to each other, their bare jaws hanging open in a mockery of true speech.

***

"Why did you attack?" Tlupic hissed at the vampire.

"He was about to kill you! You should thank me!" shouted Asherai, wincing in pain.

"He's under a spell, we have to break it."

"How do you think we're going to do that with no mage?"

"Run!" Tlupic managed to hiss out before Bjarl came crashing down, destroying the spot where Asherai had been standing. The giant reached out, and grabbed Tlupic and put him onto his shoulder. Tlupic could not do anything about it, so he remained still, trying to seem as unthreatening as possible.

***

The Sentriel watched the duel progress with a bored expression on his face. However, he did turn to acknowledge the Sonasian running towards him.

"Is this your doing?" Askia was livid with the Sentriel, the only being he knew of that could potentially manipulate things in this way.

"As always," Hydrulian responded, "as soon as something goes wrong, you all blame me. No, this was not my doing."

"Then who did this?"

The Sentriel chuckled lightly, before responding. "Though I do wish I came up with this idea myself, unfortunately, someone else did. And I'm not going to go spoiling someone else's fun, that's just bad sportsmanship."

"Come on, just be useful for once!"

The golden figure laughed and refocused on the battle, saying nothing more. Askia turned back to the fight as well, enraged at the Sentriel's unwillingness to help them. Looking down at his weaponry, a plan came to his mind. Though he knew it was a bad plan, at least it was *a* plan, which was better than no plan at all. Knowing this, he ran towards the deadly duel between the giant and the vampire.

Asherai was struggling against the might of Ürbon, his vampiric strength simply not a match for the Jödmun's raw power. Instead of trying to match the giant in a test of strength, like he had in the beginning of the fight, he was now dodging and evading the giant's attacks. Ürbon attempted to hit the vampire with an overhead swing of Bjarl. Asherai avoided the blow by rolling between the giant's legs and stabbed him with his enchanted sword. The Jödmun responded with a wide swing of Bjarl, which Asherai leapt away from with ease.

Ürbon was relentless in his assault, smashing Bjarl down but narrowly missing Asherai. Enraged, he lashed out with the axe's pommel, striking the vampire in the chest. Luckily, the vampire's crimson armor protected him from the icy spike, but he was still launched back by the sheer force of the blow.

Seeing the vampire thrown against the wall, Askia ran to help him.

"We can't win here!" said Asherai, his breath labored and pained.

"Don't worry, I've got a plan."

"What have you come up with?"

"Just keep him busy a while longer."

Asherai nodded to Askia, and charged towards the Jödmun, his footsteps limp and his arms heavy. Askia also charged but shifted so that he would be attacking from a different angle. He needed to get closer for his plan to work. As they had predicted, Ürbon attacked Asherai, who rolled beneath the blow and attacked from the opposite side. Ürbon turned to face him, ignoring Askia in favor of the more powerful vampire. Askia pulled out his staff. This would work. It had too.

Asherai struggled to hold against the might of the Jödmun. The power of Ürbon and Bjarl was proving to be too much for the vampire to handle. He was barely able to parry Ürbon's attacks, and every hit knocked him farther off balance. Inevitably, he faltered and stumbled. Ürbon didn't waste the opportunity and slammed Bjarl directly into the Asherai's chest. The force of the blow launched him across the room, and smashed him through a supporting column. Fortunately, the vampire's distraction had allowed Askia to close the distance.

With the vampire finished, Ürbon turned towards Askia. The man had already rushed up to the Jödmun and reached out with his staff, the tip glowing blue as it made contact. The blue light spread over Ürbon's body, burning away the green mist clinging to his rocky frame. Suddenly, as if in protest, his eyes turned bright red. He swung Bjarl straight down with all his might, a blow to cleave the Sonasian in two. Askia closed his eyes, awaiting the inevitable. However, the blow never came, and Askia opened his eyes to see Bjarl a hair's breadth away from his head.

The blue glow from Askia's staff had completely engulfed the Jödmun, encasing him in a brilliant blue light. The light seemed to burn, flickering like an open flame caught in a light breeze. Tlupic jumped off the giant's shoulder before the same fate befell him, and rushed over to where Asherai lay. Before Askia could join them, a remarkable change occurred to the light before his eyes. The blue of the light seemed to harden and condense until it appeared to be a crystalline outer shell. As soon as the light had stabilized itself, it started to crack all over, fissures appearing in the previously smooth surface. Suddenly the crystalline cage crumbled away, the stone form of Ürbon crashed to the ground, and lay there, unmoving.

Having dealt with the Jödmun, Askia saw Tlupic race towards the fallen vampire. The blow from Ürbon had launched Asherai through a three feet thick pillar supporting the roof, burying him under rubble. The vampire was lying very still, though it was clear he was still alive from the way his eyes flitted about. As Tlupic advanced closer, about to speak to him, the warrior's fanged mouth opened in a shriek of pure, unbridled pain and agony. Tlupic covered his reptilian ears as the scream continued on, piercing through the nearby area and echoing around the room.

After several seconds of non-stop screaming, Asherai's shrieks of agony finally died down and he sat up. Bits of rubble fell off his crimson armor, revealing a massive crack in the meta stretching across his whole body.

"I swear I'm going to tear the giant's heart out!" yelled Asherai, as he slowly pushed himself to his feet. "By the Serpent, that hurt!"

Across the room Askia was trying to rouse Ürbon, doing everything he could think of, but to no avail. He was about to give up when Ürbon began to stir. Askia backed up as the giant pushed himself up off the ground, his eyes were clouded with confusion as he looked at the people clustered around him.

"What happened?"

***

Askia told Ürbon what had happened since the time they had split up, and how they had ended up fighting with him. He described how he had come to realize that Ürbon was under a spell caused by the green mist. He also explained how he realized that his staff somehow repelled corruption, since the mist appeared unable to get anywhere near him and his party as they advanced through the ruined halls of the pyramid. Ürbon took it all in with grim determination.

"My friend, I am ashamed to have fallen under such a spell," proclaimed Ürbon, "I'm in your debt."

"Nonsense," responded Askia, waving his hand in a dismissive gesture. "I'm just glad to have you back."

"As am I, but for now we must go on."

***

The next chamber was huge, gargantuan even. The ceiling resembled a small inverted pyramid made of green crystal. It illuminated the entire room with the same pale green lights that came from the hieroglyphs in the pyramid. Directly underneath the crystal, in the center of the room, stood an imposing coffin made from the same dark stone and decorated with obsidian. It was partially open, and from its crack spilled out the dreaded green mist. Hydrulian carelessly walked into the room, even as the inverted pyramid on the roof began to glow and a hundred green glyphs lit up, their lights snaking down towards the coffin. As they reached their mark, a shockwave of ancient dust and power throughout the room and the sarcophagus exploded open.

When the dust settled, a long-dead corpse rose up from the interior of the sarcophagus. It was clothed in ornate robes and wore a golden funerary skull mask, more decorated than any other they had seen so far. Its gaze swept across intruders, pausing at Asherai, and it let loose a broken cackle.

"So, you're finally here, I saw you stumble your way through my mighty palace. Behold, mortals, for I am Hankedrish the Third, the High Priest of Dedpheker, and Priest-King of Necrophantis. I see that you also brought my pet. When he first came here he was a blood-hungry mongrel, so I fixed him. But now look at how he has thanked me, his master. But I suppose it doesn't matter, you will all be my servants soon."

As the Priest-King finished his speech, twenty statues rose out of the ground. They came to life as they emerged, drawing their weapons. Along with them rose twenty golden armored skeletons. Both groups were decorated with the typically curved blades and funerary skull masks that they found on most foes in the pyramid.

Asherai lunged forward, trying to hit one of the skeletons with his blade, but instead was forced to dodge a blast of dark magic that came his way.

"Be careful, anything that that spell touches turns to dust as if millions of years had passed." He said to the others.

Ürbon was unimpressed by the spell, for he was immune to such simple things as the passage of time. Seeing this turn of events,

Hydrulian cast a spell of invisibility and disappeared to observe how the scene would unfold. Ürbon charged towards the decrepit king with Bjarl in hand. Asherai flanked him while Tlupic and Askia stood their ground and prepared for the oncoming soldiers. Ürbon saw that a blast of magic was barreling his way and blocked the strike with Bjarl, the mighty axe unaffected by the evil magic. The undead master angrily summoned a torrent of blue flames and unleashed it upon the giant.

Tlupic resembled a living tornado. Spinning and leaping around with his spear and dagger, he destroyed skeletons and statues alike while Askia made sure he was never surrounded. He cut at his foes with his blessed scimitar, even managing to fell a few of them. The battle was fierce, anytime Ürbon got close a blast of blue flames would stop his advance.

Asherai tried to find an opening while he avoided the deadly blasts. Exhausted from his previous fight with Ürbon he struggled in his duel with three statues. What was worse, though he was ashamed to admit it, was that even though he had been cured of the Hunger, he still needed blood to survive. Centuries without had left him weak. Even so, he had to push himself further, and with one hand he made a sweeping motion and chopped both statues in half. With a predatory gaze, he launched himself upon the Priest-King who quickly turned around and caught him in a crushing grip.

The Priest-King held both of Asherai's wrists in a vice-like grip.

"Even after so many centuries, you still lack the strength to defeat me?" He cackled. "You're pathetic. Nothing more than the starving animal that descended into my palace with hollow bravado."

With an effort Asherai managed to kick the corpse in the chest, making the Priest-King release its grip and stumble back. Free to move once more, Asherai reached out for his blade and lunged, but once again his foe turned out the faster. Quick as a striking snake, it caught the blade in its mummified hands which glowed with necrotic energy. Asherai refused to release his hold on the blade, and the two undead struggled for dominance, swaying back and forth in an effort to shake off the other. As they continued to wrestle, and becoming more desperate by the second, the blade began to crack and crumble away. Too engrossed in their effort to defeat the other, neither noticed as the blade's metal folded and crumpled like paper. With a burst of energy the sword finally broke apart entirely, leaving behind thousands of blood-red shards, glowing like the dying embers of a campfire.

Asherai was launched across the room, unable to withstand the outpour of magical energy. The only thing to remain in his hand was its encrusted hilt, its mighty blade reduced to a simple red shard, alike more to a dagger than anything else.

Hydrulian was tired of this constant fighting. It had been non-stop since they entered the crypt, and was especially annoying now that he could feel his prize calling for him. He looked up at the green inverted crystalline pyramid from where he stood, hidden from the others. He felt the souls swirling around it, there were thousands of them, and it gave him an idea.

Spreading his wings and launching himself upwards, he flew to the top of the pyramid. Aiming his sword, Conflagration, he stabbed the green crystal, causing it to shatter and fall to the floor like thousands of emeralds. With a shudder the statues and skeletons below fell to the ground lifeless and the pyramid shook violently.

The glyphs decorating the walls lost their glow, and the Priest-King paused to look around in disbelief.

As Hydrulian was shooting towards the pyramid's apex, Ürbon was busy fighting five re-animated statues. Two had already fallen to his axe when, from the corner of his eye, he saw Asherai get launched into a wall. He sparred with the remaining three opponents, parrying their lumbering strikes and dispatching them with wide sweeps of Bjarl. He hacked at the last statue, but his axe met with open air. For some reason it had crumbled to the ground of its own accord.

At that same moment the pyramid began to shake, rocks tumbled from the ground and Ürbon raised an arm to shield himself. Looking around to find the others he saw Askia and Tlupic rush towards the Priest-King in an attempt to divert him away from Asherai, who lay slumped below a wall.

Tlupic threw his spear, yet the Priest-King didn't seem to even notice. Unwilling to give up he rushed towards the undead, grabbing hold of its robe and launching himself onto its back. In a scrambling effort Tlupic raised his dagger, stabbing at the Priest-Kings neck desperately. This certainly grabbed its attention, and with swift movements it threw Tlupic off its shoulders and onto the hard stone floor. It reached back to pull out the dagger stuck between its shoulder-blades. With a contemptuous smirk it crushed the dagger in its hand, leaving nothing but powdered obsidian to fall from its rotten palm.

Towering over Tlupics, the Priest-King seemed to be relishing the moment as it summoned a ball of swirling darkness. It was about to launch the missile, and Tlupic could do nothing but stare into the eyes of death. From across the room came a sudden roar of fury, and Ürbon rushed forth, charging at the enemy. With a mighty heave from his shoulders he knocked the Priest-King aside, ripping off a large chunk of its rotten form and launching it across the room.

As if by some stroke of luck the Priest-King landed beside Asherai, who had recovered some part of his strength. The vampire still held the crimson hilt in his hand. Seeing his chance for vengeance he lunged forth with a final effort. A horrific cry of anguish pierced the air, and the Priest-King clawed at the hilt impaled in its chest. The broken blade had struck right into its blackened heart, and with one final scream it faded away, nothing remaining of its tyranny but a pile of ash and a blackened mask.

Askia came to the aid of Asherai who lay unmoving on the floor. He tried to heal him, but his staff could not heal the undead.

"Do not worry, child. My time has come. I have lived a long life, and now it is ending, as everything must." Asherai croaked. "Once I was afraid of death, of what I would see on the other side, but now I welcome it like an old friend."

The dying vampire reached out for a piece of his armor that had broken off during the battle. He held it gently in the palm of his hand. He gave it to Askia, who saw that it was a small metal snake head.

"*All that lives may die, all that dies can dream.* Live, child, and when your time comes, welcome death like a friend."

Asherai then looked at Tlupic and handed him what remained of his sword. The lizard studied the weapon. What remained of the red metal blade looked more like a knife, and with a whetstone it could be made into a capable killing tool. The cross guard was made out of black metal and had white fangs on each end. The grip was wrapped in black leather, and the pommel resembled a black snake with ruby eyes.

Tlupic accepted the weapon and gave the vampire a weird look. "Why?"

"Because you need a new dagger, and I need to be laid to rest." Tlupic looked at the vampire's wounds and gave an understanding nod.

Tlupic held the red blade high, pausing for a moment before he plunged it into the vampire's chest. Asherai was finally at rest.

***

Hydrulian saw the corpse fall to the ground with a dull clatter, its body crumbling to dust. The engraved trappings on its clothes burned a bright green before they, too, faded. Its blackened mask was all that remained as its body became naught but ash. Confident that it was dead, Hydrulian sped across the room, while the remainder of the group caught their breath.

Ürbon looked at his beaten and battered friends. Marching over to pick up Tlupic, he saw a harsh flash of golden light from the other side of the room. A frown formed on his face, and he left to find Hydrulian with Tlupic in tow.

As the two went around to find the Sentriel, Tlupic's magical senses perked up. He hissed into the Jödmun's ear, telling him to walk straight into the ordinary wall in front of them.

"Are you sure?"

Tlupic nodded and Ürbon followed through. He trusted Tlupic, who had been with him the longest, and had survived many mishaps by his side. Despite his initial contempt towards Tlupic, he had grown to admire Geck'tek's bravery and loyalty. His small friend had stood by him through all manner of dangers. And so, trusting in his friend, he walked straight into the wall.

The wall proved to be a magical illusion, and it waved and distorted to allow the Jödmun passage through. Soon his bulky frame passed entirely through the illusionary wall, vanishing within its depths.

Emerging on the other side, Ürbon found himself in an ancient hallway with cracked walls covered in holes. He noted that they were not built of the same pure black stone as the previous rooms. Instead they seemed to be carved from the granite and native rock around them, and so were a mix of differing grays and dark sandstones. The rock was carved to form pillars, covered in light gilding which decorated the walls. It drew Ürbon's gaze down the passageway, where he saw an unsettling sight.

He saw Hydrulian at the end of the hall with his back to the pair. His golden wings were spread out behind him, almost reaching the edges of the hall. In his hands, raised high above his head in triumph, was a golden amulet with a small ruby set into its center.

As if sensing that he was being watched, a change seemed to come over the golden figure. Hydrulian's wings suddenly snapped back, and he tensed, spinning around to face the two. His eyes were clear of the insanity, but full of fear. As the Sentriel focused on the pair, he rapidly drew Conflagration, to which Ürbon readied Bjarl.

"Who are you? Where am I?"

The two stared at Hydrulian, clearly a drastic change had come over him, and they lowered their weapons.

"Answer me! Do not make me ask again!"

"My profound apologies, Hydrulian, but..." Ürbon's words were interrupted by Hydrulian.

"How do you know my name? Tell me where I am before I cut my way out of here!"

"I am trying to help you. Please, just listen to me."

"I listen to whoever I wish to listen to, now tell me where we are!"

Tlupic and Ürbon shared a brief glance, and nodded to each other, before attempting to explain.

"We are deep beneath an ancient pyramid, which we have just fought our way through," began Ürbon, attempting to tell the truth as plainly and truthfully as possible, "You told us to go down with you because you wanted to retrieve something."

"Lies!" shouted Hydrulian, angered. "I've given no such order, nor do I remember how I came to be down here, in whatever cellar this is!"

"I assure you, I speak only the truth," said Ürbon.

"I have every reason to assume that your mind was not...in its right place, when you made those orders."

"Do you mean to say that I've gone crazy?"

"No, I'm saying you were unstable before you got down here."

The Sentriel looked as if he was about to argue, but suddenly he clutched his head and fell to the floor. A loud screech ensued as his metal wings dragged across the ground. Ürbon and Tlubic rushed forward, but before they could get close enough to help, the Sentriel flung out a golden hand. The Jödmun was flung backwards by an intense blast of magic. The force of the blast was enough to throw the giant halfway across the hallway.

As Hydrulian flung out his hand to prevent the giant from reaching him, he received another brutal mental assault, from what felt deep within his psyche. Dozens of voices called out to him at once, in different languages and accents, and hundreds of images passed over his eyes. A small part of him knew what was happening as waves of memories cascaded through his mind. Memories of a sea, memories of a desert, memories of a pyramid and memories of a company bound to him by oath. Memories of a life unknown to him, but one which he had lived nonetheless. It was too much. The Sentriel screamed as he felt his mind splinter. Suddenly, a single thought emerged within his fracturing mind, perfectly clear amongst the maelstrom.

I don't want to go back there.

As those words reverberated through his entire being and his mind began to settle, the storm passed as quickly as it had come. An odd weakness spread through his limbs, his body drained as much as his mind. He opened his eyes and saw a white lizard, the same one that had been upon the giant's shoulder. It was holding the amulet.

With the amulet gone from his grasp, he could feel the memories all receding. They faded back into the depths of an insanity which gripped him for so long. His body slumped down to the cold stone floor, and he lurched out with his arms, seizing the lizard by its shoulders.

"D-don't let me go b-back there," he stammered. "Can't do it again. Not again."

He watched as the giant stood up from the rubble and stomped up to him.

"I can't, I can't. I won't make it back."

The giant, whose name he almost remembered, looked the Sentriel in the eye.

"I won't allow that. We'll get you back out, no matter what it takes."

Despite the imminent prospect of descending back into madness, Hydrulian smiled. Suddenly he felt a cold shiver down his spine, and his vision turned black as he felt himself lifted from the floor.

Ürbon gently laid the Sentriel over his shoulder and walked back to the illusionary door with Tlupic beside him.

"Well," he said as he picked up Bjarl without breaking his stride, "That was certainly an experience."

Tlupic said nothing, busy inspecting the amulet he had taken from Hydrulian. Whatever it was, it had induced Hydrulian's sudden burst of clarity. It was certainly a magical object, but he could sense nothing from it.

Reaching the illusion of the wall, they left the chamber behind and saw Askia huddled over a campfire. As soon as he heard them approaching, he raced over.

"Where were you?" asked the Sonasian, obviously distraught. "I looked all over, and I didn't know where anyone went. I thought some dark power took you!"

Ürbon placed the Sentriel by the fire as Tlupic explained what had happened. Listening to Askia's gasps of amazement, he saw a glimmer of light from the corner of his eye. Readying Bjarl, he slowly made his way over to where he had seen the flash of light.

What he found was a stone wall faded with age and ash. Yet the hint of gold beneath was unmistakable, and as Ürbon reached out a hand to brush away the soot an engraved mural was revealed.

In the center of the mural was a mask, much like the one worn by the Priest-King, but made of solid gold. Its mouth was curled upwards in a disturbing smile, mocking the viewer. Three separate engravings surrounded the mask to form a triangular shape. Each one was distinct and defined, creating a vivid contrast between the gold with which they were made, and the stone upon which they were set.

The leftmost point showed the figure of a lizard, standing upon its hindlegs. Its head was turned to the side, and its wide eye and open mouth gave a sense of it looking around in wonder. Yet there was something distinctly sinister about the engraving. A streak of obsidian much like a tendril of a shadow was coiled behind the lizard, who seemed completely unaware.

The uppermost point of the triangle showed a bird of prey. Its wings were spread upwards in flight, and its beak was ajar in triumph or agony as it reached out a taloned foot towards a golden orb above and out of reach.

It was the rightmost point that held Ürbon's interest the most. A lone golden bear rearing up, its snout grizzled and baring its long pointed fangs. A mighty paw was raised up towards the central mask, but the bear could not reach. The surrounding empty golden field made the bear small and harmless despite its size, and no matter how much it roared and snarled it could do nothing to those that threatened it.

As if by impulse Ürbon smashed his fist against the mural. The rock wall cracked and fell apart and the golden engraving fell to the floor, bent to illegibility.

"I hate prophecies" he grumbled before turning to join the group but saw Askia walking toward him, something red flashing in his hand for a moment before he put it away.

"What was it?" He asked, looking at the crumpled gold and shattered rock on the stone floor.

"Just a load of rubbish." Ürbon answered.

The Sonasian looked as if he was about to ask more questions, and Ürbon steeled himself for the oncoming verbal barrage. But they were both interrupted as they heard Hydrulian cackle loudly from across the hall.

***

Hydrulian suddenly awoke and sat up still for several seconds. He then started giggling madly, beginning as a low chuckle, and building up to a mad cackle. The Sentriel's insanity had returned.

Hydrulian's eyes flitted about the room, before coming to rest on Tlupic's closed fist. All the maddened happiness in his expression melted away and was swiftly replaced with cold, stark anger.

"Thief! Give it to me!" The Sentriel stood up and drew his blade.

Tlupic hissed in defense as Hydrulian's grin returned to his face.

Muttering a few words of power, Hydrulian gestured towards himself and then to the artifact. He felt the spell pull tight, and the amulet shot towards him. The stubborn lizard refused to let go, and the spell dragged Tlupic with it like the tail of a comet. Reaching out, Hydrulian caught the lizard's wrist. Tlupic saw the others rush towards the campfire from the other side of the hall, their weapons at the ready. This proved unnecessary, as the Sentriel stumbled when he caught the Geck'tek's arm, clearly still weakened from the amulet's effects.

Snarling, Hydrulian regained his balance, and tried to pry Tlupic's hand open.

"This amulet is rightfully mine to take," growled the Sentriel, "now give it to me!"

Tlupic hissed in response, desperately trying to resist the mage's fearsome strength. However, the Sentriel was much stronger than the Geck'tek, despite his current weakness, and he pried open his grip.

"Listen to me, lizard!" Shouted Hydrulian, as his anger spilled out of him, casting an excess light that emanated from his golden figure, as he began to glow brighter and brighter. "This amulet is our way out of here!"

As the Sentriel's grip tightened on the Geck'tek's wrist, and their companions came closer, suddenly the area began to shift and warp. Tlupic felt a strange magical surge from the amulet, and the area around him unexpectedly destabilized. All around him, the room zoomed in and out of proportion and twisted as if he was viewing it through water. When the air abruptly stabilized, Tlupic fell to the ground with a jolt. It appeared that he was just outside the entrance to the massive pyramid. The green fog which had previously surrounded it was gone, presumably with the death of its master. Tlupic saw that though Ürbon and Askia had fallen close to him, Hydrulian was nowhere in sight. Though fortunately the amulet was still in his hand.

Tlupic gazed at the man in front of him, who had appeared mid-change, his sword at the ready. The man's dark complexion was noticeably paler, and he looked like he was going to be sick, most likely a side effect of the teleportation. Ürbon was lying face-down in the sand, so he pushed himself up, looking around for the rest of the group. Seeing Tlupic, he headed towards them, as the Geck'tek picked himself up.

Suddenly Hydrulian crashed down in front of Tlupic, his wings flaring outward in a show of power as he landed. Startled, Tlupic scrambled away from the Sentriel. He dimly noticed Ürbon and Askia running towards him as the golden figure before him advanced. Tlupic felt the overwhelming sense of the magic stolen from his gods emanating from the very essence of this maddened being. The Sentriel represented everything the Geck'tek hated, everything he was born and raised to destroy. He was the chosen warrior of his clan, and yet he couldn't stand up to the monstrosity before him. It drowned him in shame that he had to rely on the one that he was charged to defend, to protect him from his greatest enemy. But he knew that if he attempted to go against the mage, he would be utterly annihilated. So he watched the Sentriel draw ever closer while awaiting the rescue of his stronger friends.

To his surprise, the Geck'tek was saved by a different force, one he never expected. As the Sentriel advanced, a new light began to glow from the entrance of the city, growing in brightness as it appeared to approach. Tlupic could sense some sort of magic coming from that direction, but it felt different somehow, more like the dull background radiation that came off of Ürbon. As Tlupic and Askia turned to the source of the light, they saw a black shape emerge from beneath the light, and as it got closer, it revealed itself to be a horse. Upon the horse's back, however, was a figure that radiated pure power.

Upon the back of the great black horse was a humanoid figure, her dark brown skin accented with golden markings. Her pure black hair was tied into several hundred individual braids, each swinging as her steed drew to a stop. She sat upon the horse's saddle like a queen upon her throne, armored in gold and silk. However, what instantly drew the attention were her eyes. They were the deepest purple, resembling the sky right when the sun was setting. They drew you in, were mesmerizing. Motes of gold seemed to drift within them, like sand drifting over the dunes, floating endlessly through their infinite depths.

Hydrulian stared blankly at her, completely entranced by her commanding beauty. The woman's eyes flickered briefly towards Tlupic, contemplating him with their endless intelligence, before returning to the Sentriel where he stood, frozen. As he felt her eyes on him, a change came over him, his lips spreading in a maniacal grin. Slowly, he swaggered towards her, his grin growing ever wider as he approached, not noticing the blank gaze of the woman. He flared his wings out to their full extent, showing off his impressive wingspan.

Hydrulian stopped in front of her horse, who snorted directly into his face, as if in disgust, but the Sentriel paid him no heed. He bowed low; a hand outstretched toward her.

"My lady," was all he said, his words coated in flattery and conceit.

The Sentriel raised his head, to gaze back into the woman's magnificent eyes, only to be met with the sharp crack of her steed's hooves, smashing directly into his face, launching him back several yards. While the woman sharply scolded her steed, Tlupic could easily see that she was suppressing a cold smirk. Tlupic was having equal difficulty keeping in his own. From the cloud of dust that arose from Hydrulian's sudden meeting with the ground came the purest form of laughter. The metallic wings of the mage emerged from the cloud of dust, and threw their owner atop one of the crumbling buildings. And still, he continued to laugh uncontrollably.

Tlupic watched as the rest of the group surrounded the newcomer, each regarding her with a reverent gaze. She dismounted from her horse, whispering something into its ear, before walking up to Ürbon, regarding him with a distant form of curiosity.

"I am Maka Rabymat," she said, her eyes directing a commanding gaze towards the Jödmun, "the Golden Lioness of the Desert, Princess of Osharis the Last Golden City, the Warden of the Nebu-Gi. Now tell me, foreigners, what are you doing in our great ancient city Necrophantis? This place is meant for the dead only, and you tread on holy ground." The woman before them spoke with such authority and confidence that Ürbon was the only one capable of answering.

"Lioness," the Jödmun said respectfully, going so far as to bow slightly, "I am Ürbon the Wanderer, son of Ongul the Wise, Slayer of the Beast of the Moon Forest, and Raider of the Western Seas. We come from far away and must travel even farther. We do not mean to belittle your people or your gods, but this land is not holy, it is cursed with death and decay. We have only just escaped its horrors and madness and, having survived, it appears I must ask your forgiveness, for we did not intend to trespass. But I do wonder what you are doing here, then. As this land holds nothing but dead, there is no room for us, the living."

There was a tense silence as the lioness stared into the giant's dark eyes. "You are a bold one, colossus. You come to the land of my deceased people, insult them and my gods, and pretend there is no harm done. I like you, you are obviously the only one here with a spine, but no matter. I am on a quest, and you must still explain yourself."

Ürbon was impressed, this human had the same spirit as many of the shield maidens of his people, and so he spoke freely. He spoke of how he and Tlupic ended up stranded, how they met Askia, of their discovery of the dead city and Hydrulian, and finally of the perils they had faced in the heart of the cursed pyramid. When he finished telling their tale, the queenly warrior looked pensive before speaking.

"*In your journey into the land of black sands you shall meet many who walk the same road as you, follow them for their path leads to doom and glory.* Those were the words of the High-Priest of Osharis, he who set me out on my quest to find salvation for my people." The woman paused in her speech, before smiling up at the golem. "If what you say is true, then there is indeed nothing for me in these ruins of old. In that case, I command that as punishment for your trespass, you must escort me with your group on your travels." She cast a glance at Hydrulian, who giggled madly at her gaze, and added, "and keep that golden-feathered fiend away from me."

Ürbon burst out in laughter, and he just knew that he would enjoy the presence of their new companion.

**

The group made their way to the exit of the ruined city with Maka at their head on her charcoal-black steed. Suddenly Hydrulian landed in front of the company, causing the sand to be blown away by the force of his descent. The group halted when the Sentriel blocked their path. His typical deranged grin upon his face, he stared directly at Maka. This was halted by a swift kick to the stomach by her steed, to the thanks of his master. Despite this, the Sentriel recovered quickly and delivered his piece.

"Now, now, I hope you don't mean to leave, my lady."

"Don't sully that title with your tongue, snake," retorted the woman, haughtily, her steed glaring at the Sentriel with clear disdain. "I will be on my way."

"Would you prefer Lioness?"

This earned Hydrulian a swift hoof to the leg, but despite this blow, he did not fall, or even flinch. If anything, his smile grew wider.

"Come on, I won't give up that easily."

Maka snarled, and her steed acted accordingly, rearing up on his hind legs, smashing the Sentriel all over with its front hooves. Despite the battering to his chest, legs, and wings, he would not fall, although he did stagger once.

"Fear not, fair Lioness, nothing shall drive me away from you."

The woman who sat as a queen upon the throne of her steed looked at the Sentriel with disgust, before retorting with a simple question.

"What do I need to do for you to let us leave?"

Hydrulian was overjoyed at the sound of submission. He knew exactly what he was going to request. She was meant for him. The way the gold was reflected in the sunlight was enough to convince him of that. The sand in her eyes, her beautiful eyes, was enough to make him certain. And he knew he would relish the time to study those features during the next few minutes, so he opened his mouth to give the command to the woman he knew he loved, that he was meant to love...

But nothing came out. He opened his mouth and found that he could not say the words. He tried again, but all that was released from his lips was a dull breath, unable to communicate the depth of feeling he wanted to convey. He slowly peered up towards the woman, who sat regally upon her steed, her expression stern, and those beautiful eyes fixed on him. That's when he realized that her eyes were fixed on *him*.

That was the moment Hydrulian knew, he was about to mess this up. He couldn't tell her, there was no way, she was too beautiful to return those feelings. His mind was instantly clouded by a million different futures of how this would go horribly wrong. He could feel the weight of a million worlds as a stream of incoherent babble spilled from his lips. He watched the woman in front of him begin to grow impatient. Realizing that he had to do something or else he would ruin his chance, he concocted a plan. Reaching behind him, his normally steady hands fumbling for the piece of paper, he pulled out the map he had found in the temple.

"I, uh, um, need you to um, to uh, help me find this thing!"

"What thing, for goodness's sake?" Maka said, shaking her head.

"I, uh, HERE!" shouted the Sentriel, throwing the map at the woman, before disappearing in a flash of golden light.

As Hydrulian recovered from his positively horrifying experience, Maka caught the map with ease and stepped down from her horse. She unrolled the map with the others watching over her shoulders. It was a map of the entire world, though without any borders of the current nations, which made sense because the relic was most likely made hundreds of years ago, and her people had never been too interested in outside affairs. However, there were geographical symbols across its surface, such as mountains and rivers. Tlupic stared in awe at the map, he never knew the world was so big.

Across the length of ancient parchment, was a series of ancient numbers, each in different locations across the world. There was also a great line from their current location, which formed an arrow pointed to the right. In the bottom right of the scroll of paper was a compass, also written in the ancient script. What was more important, however, was that Maka could understand its language, as it was her own, though of a more ancient dialect. Perhaps, she thought, the golden fool wasn't so useless after all. This could be part of her quest.

"So, where are we headed?" rumbled Ürbon, forced to wait on Hydrulian's orders, but Sentriel hadn't reappeared.

Closing the map, the Warden of the Nebu-Gi had only one response.

"East."

***

As Hydrulian watched the others left the cursed city, his eyes never left the golden woman. He was only just recovering from whatever strange spell she had bound him with, and was just now beginning to catch his breath. He couldn't recognize the kind of magic she used, how effortlessly she was able to manipulate his breathing, his words and his mind. She made him look like a fool, unable to speak or think clearly.

But it did not matter. He would make her his, no matter the cost. No matter what, she would be his. Eventually.

Chapter 7:
A Long Way to Go

East, that was the way they were going. Ürbon thought about his original goal, it was far off, and was going to be even farther off once they headed east.

He longed to get back on track and find his way home, yet to break his oath to follow Hydrulian would bring him even greater shame than leaving his crew on that forsaken island. He thought about all he had gone through so far, the loss of his crew, the gaining of Bjarl, the ship being blown off course, the temple, and now, eastward, further away from his goal. He knew he must go east, for that was where Hydrulian wanted to go, for whatever reason. Ürbon reflected on all of this where he stood, settling on a decision that he must get away from Hydrulian, if ever a chance to do so presented itself, but for now, he must follow the Sentriel.

They started out, Hydrulian a bit behind them until he caught up the short distance they travelled. They continued eastward, through the desert, the sand, and the sun.

"So where does this map lead?" Ürbon asked Maka.

"It will lead to the first of ten great artifacts," responded the Nebu-Gi.

"And what may they do?" asked Ürbon who was wondering what he was going to be doing in the near future.

"I cannot say, but you will learn soon enough," said Maka.

They continued to walk across the desert, the path ahead either a flat unending sea of sand, or a dune looming high above them. It was the latter which lay ahead when Hydrulian barreled into Ürbon mid-flight, knocking them both off balance.

"What in Yanvild's name is wrong with you?" Ürbon yelled furiously, pushing himself off the sand though his hands sunk down into the ground.

The Sentriel appeared before him, giggling madly. Ürbon charged at him, knocking Hydrulian back down into the sand.

"Why are you like this?" He said.

Ürbon remembered the sane Sentriel he and Tlupic had found holding the amulet. It was a glimpse of the real Hydrulian free from whatever it was that tormented him, and had turned him into such a moronic fool. He almost felt sorry for him.

As if sensing Ürbon's sympathy, instead of launching himself off the sands, Hydrulian rose up slowly. His mad cackle had fallen away, and what was left was a dark silence.

"I don't know." Was all the Sentriels said; as he shook his wings free of sand.

"What do you mean you don't know?"

"Years of existing in this desert, alone and with no company. You'd have voices in your head too." Hydrulian said defensively.

"Why did you end up in this desert all alone?"

"All I remember is that there used to be more of us... I wonder where they ended up; I can't even recall their names. But the things we built, now that I can remember, they were so beautiful. Nothing else in the entire world can surpass them."

"What happened to them?"

"They were destroyed," the Sentriel replied, his voice getting darker.

"No, I mean, the others." Ürbon said. Though the Sentriels — like the Jödmun — were one of the ancient races, none of the historical texts Ürbon had read discussed their disappearance, much less their survival.

"I don't know, maybe they went through portals like me..."

"Portals?"

"Was at... city of Werdenhof... and portal took me... to desert..."

"What portal, answer me!"

"Ürbon! Come here, quick!" came a voice from behind the dune, interrupting Ürbon's questions, much to Hydrulian's relief.

With heavy steps he walked up the sand dune towards the shout, leaving Hydrulian behind him. At the top he found the others standing over large forms in the sand. As he got closer he saw what had once been living creatures. They had precisely the fair features of elves; the only difference was that their lower bodies were chitinous like an insect; with many legs and a long scorpion tail stinger. Ürbon noticed that a few of the mutated elves were already semi-covered in sand, which meant that at least some of them had been here for long.

"What are these creatures?" Askia asked, directing his question to Ürbon. But to everyone's surprise he was not the one to answer, instead it was Maka.

"They're called Teshar" said Maka. "They are elves who went through a magical transformation long ago, now they bear the lower forms of scorpions and despise magic. They're little more than beasts, killing everything they could find across the sands, including my people." She paused and frowned, before continuing.

"They're led by a bloodthirsty warmonger called Gles, a vile brute with a hideous scar across his chest. Many years ago he and his army came and attacked one of our settlements, and killed everyone there, burning it to the ground."

"How dare they do such things to one as fair as you!" came a shout as Hydrulian hurtled towards the group. Dropping onto the ground he raised a burning-white hand towards the still Teshar on the ground. "You shall be avenged!" he said as a golden beam shot out from his palm.

At the same moment the beam made impact, the Teshar jolted awake, raising a horrified face to Hydrulian.

"Deciever!" it screamed, before its head fell back to the sand, this time certainly dead.

"You fool!" said Maka furiously.

"What did he call me?" Hydrulian said, ignoring Maka's anger.

"The deceiver is the embodiment of the magic that created their current form, they'll go to any lengths to destroy it. And now, because of you, every Teshar within hearing range will be gathering to attack us, thinking that their chance has arrived to get revenge."

"Well, we better get out of this desert before it comes to that then." Said Ürbon and resumed his march across the sands.

***

The group of five had walked a good deal farther since the Teshar attack, and didn't have much trouble while moving along. So far there were no other sightings of the mutated elves, and the group was beginning to feel as if they might get out of the desert with no issue.

That changed when Tlupic spotted a group of scarabites ahead, fighting each other. None of them seemed to notice the watchers.

"So what do we do?" asked Askia. He knew that they could easily take the beasts on, but he was not sure if that was the best option.

"I say that I just blas–" said Hydrulian, right before being cut off by a scarabite that had suddenly rumbled up from the ground.

It came out of nowhere, but the sound of its appearance caught the other scarabite's attention. They all turned toward the high dune where the group was watching from, and saw Hydrulian getting knocked off the hill towards them. They immediately sprang into action and started to run towards the falling Sentriel. Hydrulian finally landed after tumbling down the hill, and spotted the charging scarabites.

Maka, Ürbon, Tlupic, and Askia all got up from their position in response to the sudden attack. Then another scarabite appeared right where Ürbon used to be, then one right where Tlupic, and another where Askia was, and a final one where Maka had been. Ürbon quickly brought Bjarl to hand and slashed the monster with it as soon as it got close. The axe cut deep, and the scarabite quickly retreated back beneath the sands it had come from.

Tlupic drew his spear and chucked it straight up the mouth of the one that was now in front him. It went through the open mouth, through the top of it, making it drop backwards and crashed into the scarabite that had hit Hydrulian. He quickly pulled the spear out of its head.

Maka drew her two golden khopeshes, and slashed at the scarabite from atop Stixerio, but it bit into the blade, stopping it before it could reach its body. The other blade wasn't caught, though, and it banged off the scarabite's head. The blow caused it to let go of the first blade, which was promptly stabbed into the scarabites mandible, causing half of it to break.

Askia pulled his scimitar just in time to block a blow to his chest. The force knocked him backwards onto the ground, leaving him defenseless, but Tlupic jumped onto the scarabite, catching it by surprise. Knocking it off balance, Tlupic stabbed at it with his new dagger multiple times. Askia got up and moved toward the distracted scarabite and stabbed it straight through the head. The scarabite that Ürbon had forced to retreat returned behind Askia right as he plunged his scimitar into the first beast's head. Tlupic looked up and threw his spear at the scarabite, but it missed. It did distract it as it turned to look where the spear went. Tlupic jumped across to meet it with his dagger.

Ürbon ran to where Maka was fighting a large scarabite, and cut a massive gash into its side. Maka took advantage of this and cut two more wounds into it as it recoiled from Ürbon's attack. The scarabite started to back off, but then it reversed direction and leaped toward Maka, grasping at her with its remaining mandible. The lunge was blocked, and the two curved blades quickly chopped through the mandible. It reared up and slashed with its talon-like claws, but this, too, was blocked, and it lost its balance when Maka kept pressure on the talon. Ürbon ran towards the scarabite that hit Hydrulian off the hill, it was knocked over by another scarabite which had been dealt with, and he quickly cut off its head. Ürbon started to run down the hill after doing this, towards where Hydrulian was fighting the scarabites alone.

Hydrulian had gotten up as soon as he stopped rolling, and he quickly cast a spell that outright evaporated a scarabite. He then cast another spell which caused a thin beam of golden light to cut through the head of the beast. Then, just before he would be forced to use Conflagration, he cast a spell that crushed a scarabite up into a ball. He drew Conflagration and cut straight through the nearest scarabite. Another one attempted to flank Hydrulian, but he used his metal wings to block and stab in defense. The sharp metal "feathers" had cut multiple holes into the creature, but it still lived until Hydrulian used his wing to stab it again. He continued to cut them down, one after another. There were so many of them, each coming one by one, only to be cut down.

At this point, Ürbon arrived and he bowled straight through three scarabites. Each one was knocked to a side of him. He came up with Bjarl at the ready, which he used to cut down the nearest scarabite. One of the scarabites that was knocked over got up and bit his back, only to be smashed into pieces by a round strike from Bjarl. Another jumped on Ürbon's back and the weight arched his back forward. It was quickly dispatched when Ürbon grabbed it from between his shoulders, threw it onto the ground and punched it with his fists.

As the Jödmun and Sentriel fought side by side, the rest of the Scarabites seemed to sense that they were unmatched. In a second they had fled or burrowed into the sand and out of view.

It was then they realized the smell, and the disgusting rotten pus that coated Ürbon's hand.

"This will take forever to clean off," said Ürbon.

Hydrulian walked up to Ürbon. "Thank you for the help in clearing them out, even though I didn't need it."

"We should regroup with the others," was all he said in response, before turning to walk back up the hill.

Upon the hill, Tlupic and Askia coordinated an attack on another scarabite. Tlupic lunged at it with his spear, knocking it back a bit. Askia followed this up by landing a swing from above. Tlupic jumped off, pushing it to the ground, towards where his spear had landed. Askia executed another hit while it was stunned from being knocked to the ground. At that moment, Maka rushed in and finished it off with her golden blades. Finishing with their scarabites, they waited for Tlupic to get back with his spear. At about the same time, Ürbon and Hydrulian came back up the hill.

"What is that smell?" said Askia as soon Ürbon had started to get close.

"I squashed a bug. I suppose it caused the others to flee because of the smell," Ürbon said as he showed his hand to the other three.

Maka recoiled from the sight and sudden smell of it, Tlupic shifted where he stood, and Askia outright turned away and walked a few paces to distance himself. Hydrulian didn't care that much.

"Well, it sounds like these creatures won't want to get close to us now," said Hydrulian.

"Still, Ürbon would you please stay a bit away from us?" asked Askia, not wanting to offend Ürbon, but also not wanting to stay close to him.

"Yes, please." Maka added.

"Alright, we will get this cleaned off once we hit water," replied Ürbon.

"Well, let's get going," said Maka.

So they started off eastward, Ürbon isolating himself from the group and Maka in the lead. Hydrulian let her be in charge in an attempt to get her to have a better opinion of him. They walked past a dune, trudged over sand, and made it through a sandstorm. Night passed with Ürbon on guard for the group. No scarabite dared come close, as the ripe smell of Ürbon's hand scared them off.

The trip was fairly uneventful, that was until they heard a loud war cry in the distance, the thundering of steps on sand, and the sound of horns blowing. They came from over the hill like a swarm, each one yelling to kill the Great Deciever. One shouted louder than all the rest, a large Teshar with a long scar across his chest.

They came from the opposite direction of Ürbon, meaning that Ürbon was farther away from the charging Teshar horde. Suddenly he saw about fifteen archers branch off to the side. They readied their arrows and shot at Ürbon as he started to turn to face the horde.

The arrows, as one might expect, bounced off the stone skin of the giant. He immediately turned to face the archers. A sudden thought went through his head. These are elves, or at least some bastardization of elves. He thought back to his crew and how they were either dead or still in elvish hands. This enraged him, it made him angry, it made him furious.

Lightning cracked from Bjarl, weak at first, then stronger, and stronger, until a bolt of lightning shot out and hit the ground. Then another, and finally a bolt shot straight towards an archer. The bolt went straight through the Teshar, and it fell over on the spot. As Bjarl let loose another bolt of lightning, they began to fall one by one, then two fell at once, then four, then the remaining five were shocked in one bolt.

As this happened, Hydrulian shot out a massive fireball at the approaching horde. It incinerated many of the Teshar, then he shot out another fireball killing even more.

Maka turned Stixerio around to face the charging force.

She charged Stixerio forward to the leading creature that was at the head of the horde, the scar across his chest meant only one thing, it was Gles, the bloodthirsty warmonger. She shouted out a direct challenge to Gles in what she knew of elvish. Gles understood, generally, that it was a challenge, and ordered his men to not attack the Warden of Nebu-Gi.

They charged towards each other, each with their twin blades, each with their ancestral hate of the other's kind, and each with something to prove. Gles wanted to prove his might, Maka wanted to avenge her race by defeating one of its greatest enemies. Stixerio and the scorpion lower half of the Teshar leader collided. The twin blades of the two warriors locked in parry and strike. Maka attempted to use both blades to push one of her opponent's blades out of his hand in a risky move. It didn't pay off, as Gles noticed Maka's side was left unprotected, and swung at it. Luckily, her armor absorbed the blow, but she was knocked off Stixerio. The horse gave Gles a swift kick to keep him from attacking Maka while she was vulnerable.

It worked. He was pushed through the sand from the force of the kick. Maka got up and prepared to fight the Teshar once more. Stixerio turned towards her and she got on while Gles was still a little winded from the strong kick. She got up right as Gles recovered, and she charged at him once again. The force of the charge and its determination pushed Gles back even more, and Maka got in multiple cuts as he was recovering yet again. He tried to block the attacks with weak attempts. Mostly it didn't work and her strikes still landed. More slices appeared over the slaughterer's body as Maka continued her relentless assault. Gles was forced backwards to escape the onslaught, stumbling faster and faster until they were in full retreat. Maka thought herself victorious and started to turn to help her friends.

She wasn't prepared for the unexpected stab to her back. Golden blood trickled down from where the attack came. Gles had feigned the retreat and had attacked when she had let her guard down. This proved to be her second mistake. Maka vowed not to make a third as she quickly buried the pain, turned around and chopped off the arm that had stabbed her. Gles recoiled in pain. Maka turned fully and charged Gles, and she easily forced his sword out of his hand. Then she chopped that hand off as well. Maka finished him with twin blades to the gut. He slumped over the golden blades that were now stained with blood.

***

As Maka had broken off from the group, The Teshar horde charged towards the others. Hydrulian cast one last fireball just as the horde reached them and drew his sword, ready to meet them. A bolt of lightning appeared to his right and struck the flanking Teshar. Another whizzed right past him and hit another Teshar in front of him. The first Teshar managed to reach him, swinging its axe only to be melted by Conflagration. The Teshar was down in a matter of seconds. Another approached but was cut down quicker than the previous.

Askia and Tlupic fought desperately against the horde, blocking and stabbing when possible. Some had managed to get behind them, meaning they had to give ground to keep from getting cut down from both sides. Then Ürbon charged straight into the fray, lightning crackling from Bjarl. The bolts of electricity shot out at all that were close enough to the stone giant. Several fell from the sudden shocks of electricity, and others went down from Bjarl slicing massive tears in their body. Askia and Tlupic continued attacking the Teshar thanks to the breathing room Ürbon had given them.

In the midst of the battle, a shout shot across the fray.

"GLES IS DEAD!"

Most turned back, only to see a corpse and Maka, weakly astride Stixerio. The remaining Teshar scattered. The separate clans routed, each going their own way, and with a new reason to hate the Nebu-Gi and the Great Deceiver.

Ürbon, Tlupic, Askia and Hydrulian started off toward Maka. It looked like she was hurt and wasn't able to move just then. Hydrulian got to her first, while the others arrived close behind. The wound on her back was large and needed immediate attention. Askia quickly took out his staff to aid him in healing her wound.

"Will she be okay?" Hydrulian asked. "We will stay the night here, and only continue once she has healed."

"Why do you care so much about her, anyway?" said Askia, tired from the fighting and drained from healing Maka's wound.

"The Sentriel is right, the sun is already going down. We'll continue in the morning." Ürbon said before the conversation could escalate. Clearly everyone's patience and nerves had worn thin, and though Jödmun didn't tire, he felt the need for peace and quiet.

Not only that, but they needed to be rested for what was to come. Because tomorrow they'd be reaching the Titan Divide, a treacherous river not by its nature but by its location. For to the East of it lay vampire territory.

.

Chapter 8:
The Titan Divide

The rushing white waters of the Titan Divide surged before him, its roaring almost deafening the party of five standing upon its banks. The river swept southwards, purportedly splitting the continent all the way from the north to the south. The Divide had allegedly been created by an ancient Titan, hence the name, which had hailed from the city-state of Venova. The city was located upon an island in the middle of the lake situated up river, called the Inner Sea. The Inner Sea was indeed a lake where two halves of The Divide met. Water poured down from the river into the lake from the north, before continuing its course southwards to the ocean. It was to this lake they would have to continue towards, walking beside the river shrouded in legend.

Other legends told of an ancient race, bigger even than the Jödmun, carving out the river before being pushed out by the orcs further north. In the many years since the fissure was created, water rushed in from the northern and southern seas to join with the previously disconnected Inner Sea and create the large river that they gazed upon.

Ürbon took a moment to take in the large surge of water. He had seen the river before, but every time the enormity of it took his breath away. Reaching the Divide meant that they must've crossed the land of the Daz Wera, the southern dwarves, called Dhueyra by its inhabitants, without meeting any sign of civilization. That worried him slightly, but looking at the waters relaxed him. The crashing water against the rocks made a soothing sound that eased his worn nerves.

His dark eyes turned away from the rushing waters and focused on the rest of the group. Tlupic was gazing in muted wonder, his eyes transfixed by the white waters, and the occasional spray in the air where the water hit the rock. Askia was also entranced by the waters, most likely because he had lived in a desert his whole life, at least to Ürbon's knowledge. The fact that there could be that much water in one place must have been astounding.

His gaze leaving his mortal companions, he turned to check on the immortals of the group. He turned to Hydrulian, the golden Sentriel idly flying through the air, seemingly uninterested in the river below him. His metallic wings continued to take him higher into the sky, as he did small acrobatic stunts in the air above the company. He caught Ürbon's gaze, and waved at him as he folded his wings and began to dive at an incredible speed. Before hitting the water, with the screech of metal on metal, he shot them open and coasted across the width of the river. From there he shot back up ignoring the discomfort of the group at his insane flying antics.

Frowning at Sentriel with distaste, Ürbon turned to the final member of their group, Maka Rabymat, Golden Lioness of the Desert, the Warden of Nebu-Gi, to name a few of her many titles, with her horse, Stixerio, at her side, who calmly observed the waters.

She had turned away from the river, her face creased in annoyance and disgust, most likely because of the Sentriel's actions. It was quite obvious how Hydrulian was obsessed with the golden woman, but the interest was clearly not reciprocated. The Lioness detested the Sentriel and everything he stood for. She saw him as a servant to their god of wealth, who had cursed her race to become what they were now and destroyed her old nation. Catching the Jödmun's calculating gaze, she held it for several seconds, before turning away, using the movement to toss a strand of her dark braided hair out of her sight, and focusing her glare downstream.

Despite the fact that they had gotten to the river itself, their destination — according to the map that Maka now carried — was upriver on the Isle of Venova, and they needed a way to get there. Even if they walked all the way north, they would be stopped at the lake, and the nations around there weren't exactly friendly.

Ürbon shifted Bjarl on his back, he remembered how he had gotten to the island once before. Turning his gaze away from the roaring waters, he walked up to Maka, who looked back at him as he approached.

"What is it, stone-spawn?" she asked.

"First, you may want to cease with the name calling. Second, I know a way we can get up to Venova," replied the Jödmun calmly, as first a look of disgust, then a look of confusion swept across the woman's face, if only for a second.

"Venova?" inquired Maka, obviously ignoring Ürbon's comment, before a look of realization flashed across her face. "Ah yes, that is the name of the isle, is it not?"

"Indeed," rumbled Ürbon, "and it is our destination, according to the map."

The woman said nothing, but instead took out the map, which had been 'gifted' to her by Hydrulian, and checked their destination. Indeed, there was a circle around the island, indicating that it was the destination. Rolling up the scroll, she turned back to the Jödmun.

'So then, how do you propose we get there?"

"There is a town south of here that has friendly relations with the Venovans," the giant answered, "and they have a port where we can acquire a vessel to go upriver."

Instead of arguing like Ürbon thought she would, Maka simply nodded her head.

"Very well," she stated plainly. "We will begin to march at once."

"Give them a moment," interjected Ürbon, receiving a dark glare from the Lioness for doing so. "Let them enjoy the river for a while longer."

Though Maka looked as if she was about to argue, ultimately she conceded. "Fine, give them as long as they need."

"Thank you, my lady."

As the woman turned away, seemingly indifferent to the idea, the Jödmun turned and stoically marched to where Tlupic sat cross-legged on the sandy banks. The Geck'tek seemed just as enthralled by the river as Ürbon had been the first time he had seen it. As the stone golem approached, the lizard turned his head away from the raging waters to speak to him. A sort of reverence and excitement glittered in his eyes.

"I have never seen water this beautiful before." Tlupic spoke in his own language, his forked tongue flicking out as he spoke. "It sparkles like starlight."

It was true, the water from the river was pure, clearer and cleaner than the ocean they had crossed to get to the desert. Despite being deep enough to allow ships to pass through, you could see directly through to the rocks below, where the water wasn't frothing white.

"Indeed," replied the Jödmun, turning to gaze at the river himself. "It struck me with it's beauty the first time I saw it as well."

"It was sights like these I wished to see when I left the burrow to join you on your adventure, that and my duty to the clan. Though I miss them dearly, I am glad I came."

The two waited there for several moments, each regarding the river with their own unique appreciation and respect. Tlupic stirred soon, however.

"May we revisit this place another time?" questioned the lizard, his eyes never leaving the water. The Jödmun responded accordingly.

"Of course, once our business is done."

At that, the two waited there for several more moments, regarding the sparkling waters, before Ürbon stood up, leaving the Geck'tek to the river and his thoughts. Looking around the river, he spotted Askia, who also was staring at the waters. He looked awestruck by the sheer size of the river, it being so big he could barely make out the other side of the bank.

"Amazing, isn't it?" said Ürbon, startling the man in front of him, who had been so intent on the river he hadn't noticed the giant's approach.

"I-I've just never seen this much water before," stammered out Askia, whose dark face was noticeably paler than usual, "I've heard of oceans and large bodies of water, but..." The man trailed off, unable to express how impressed he was by the width of the river. You could just barely see the other side of it but if you looked up or down its length, it merged into the horizon.

Askia finally turned towards Ürbon, looking up at the cheerful grin on the golem's face. However, the Jödmun turned back to the waters, and the Sonasian followed suit.

Ürbon had reached a decision, now that he had gathered the thoughts of his companions, so he turned his head from the sparkling waters to the north. While he and Hydrulian were the only ones who could see it, that was their destination.

Their destination was the island location in the center of that crystal lake. The island was a center of trade and culture and — according to Hydrulian's map — it had a magical artifact on it. Ürbon had been there once before, the city-state of Venova. The city was a point of riches and culture due to its location and history, and Ürbon looked forward to revisiting its grand halls and its many marble temples and statues. However, that brought up the topic of getting there.

Ürbon headed back to where the Princess of Osharis stood, patiently gazing at the waters like the rest of the group, occasionally shooting glares of disdain up at Hydrulian where he flew around the sky. She turned her eyes to the Jödmun as he approached.

"It's time to go," Ürbon said.

"Took you long enough," responded the woman. "So, where to?"

"South," he responded, "there is a town not that far away with boats that can take us to the city."

"Well, let's get a move on then." This concluded their conversation, and the woman pulled herself onto her horse's back, who huffed in annoyance at the sudden weight. However, after a seemingly brief argument with Maka, Stixerio walked her towards the others. With that, the group would continue their journey towards the island.

From a spot in the distance, a dark figure was watching them, preparing to follow from the shadows.

***

The group followed the river southwards, looking for the town that Ürbon had promised. The traveling conditions weren't exactly equal, however. Maka rode Stixerio down the sandy coast, the horse was seemingly distressed about his lack of say in his circumstances. Hydrulian flew through the air, but didn't really feel like doing too much on the traveling front, so he flew far ahead of the group, and relaxed on the ground as he waited for them to catch up. Tlupic sat atop Ürbon's shoulder, observing the flying Sentriel with a constant scowl of hatred. Askia walked alongside the Jödmun, despite Ürbon's many offers for him to rest on his other shoulder. The man seemed to count it as a point of pride that he could keep up with the giant.

"Are we there yet?" questioned Hydrulian, whom they found reclining on the ground, which had turned into a mix of sand and dirt as the climate changed.

The group regarded the Sentriel with varying levels of dislike as they passed him. Ürbon was the only one who bothered giving an answer.

"You should be able to see the town from up there, Golden Boy." Askia and Tlupic both chuckled quietly at the mention of the Sentriel's nickname. Even Maka smiled for a moment, as Hydrulian's eye twitched slightly.

"Alright then, servant," replied Hydrulian, a smile growing on his face. "Well it might serve you better to know that we've been followed for quite a while, so the joke's on you!"

As the Sentriel began to cackle madly, his hands clutching his stomach, the others of the group were thrust into instant alarm. Tlupic jumped off of Ürbon, landing on the giant's outstretched hand before reaching the ground. Askia turned to Ürbon next to him for clarification of this information. Ürbon, however, remained silent.

Maka reacted differently. She stopped before turning to the giggling Sentriel, drawing one of her swords from her back. Tlupic and Askia watched from the sidelines, conflicted. From the way it looked, it seemed that the Lioness of the Desert was finally fed up with Hydrulian's antics. They both loathed the Sentriel, but his power was undeniable. Tlupic was especially conflicted with his hatred for the Sentriel because he could be useful to Ürbon and the quest he now had to serve. However, before they had time to act, the woman, who sat regally upon Stixerio, pointed her sword towards the mage, who was currently rolling around in the dirt in hysterics.

"I don't have the time or patience for your antics, you halfwit." At her words, the mage immediately stood upright, appearing to leap into a position of perfect attention, his grin sliding from his face.

Even Maka was taken aback by the speed of the action, while Askia and Tlupic were barely able to register it.

"My apologies, m'lady," said the Sentriel, a smile growing on his face, not a maddened one, but that of a cultured nobleman, formal and polite. Maka was thrown by the sudden shift in personality. "Actually, I can do better than tell you."

The Sentriel turned and pointed a finger out into the desert. From his outstretched hand shot a beam of light, which shined directly on a squat figure, crouched upon a hill in the distance. It seemed to be a dwarf, as wide as it was tall, and holding a strange tool in its hand. The dwarf seemed to scramble where he stood as the light found him, and he turned around and fled in the opposite direction. As Hydrulian turned around, a smug grin plastered onto his face, the others looked at him in surprise.

"What? I know I'm great."

Ürbon stared at the Sentriel in shock and said: "Do you have any idea of what you have done?"

"Now they will come for us, an entire clan of angry dwarves! You better pray for your own sake that it was only a small clan and not the one from the port town that we are heading to, or by Yanvild, I will bash your head in."

Hydrulian looked more surprised than threatened. "Wait, there are dwarves this far south? Well. I guess you learn something new every day." Seeing the anger on Ürbon's face, he chided, "Oh, you worry too much, stone man. What will they do to us, stab our ankles, throw beer at us?"

Ürbon shook his head in disbelief. He could already feel a headache forming as the Sentriel descended into another fit of wild cackling at his own joke. He decided that the only thing they could do now was to put as much distance from where they were as possible. With that, he gathered the group and they quickly left.

Eventually, Ürbon allowed the group to rest for the night, and they kept a watch to make sure those scouts didn't return. With the numbers of immortals growing within the group, there were now three people constantly keeping watch over the three who actually got tired, that being Askia, Tlupic, and Stixerio. Despite the beast being unique among horses, he was still an animal who constantly had to carry someone on his back. As such, the three of them slept under the watch of Ürbon, Hydrulian, and Maka.

Ürbon and Maka stood on guard for any more scouts, with Ürbon having the advantage due to his height. Hydrulian constantly fidgeted where he stood, turning and pacing the area, and constantly turning invisible, then becoming visible in another location, which irritated Maka to no end, and she let him know it.

"Would you stop that already?" she yelled, fed up with the Sentriel, who ignored her request and turned invisible again.

"I wouldn't try it," soothed Ürbon, trying to diffuse the situation, as useless as it may have seemed. "I doubt he will listen even if he hears you."

"Then I'll have to make him listen!" she responded, clearly agitated.

"I don't think that's the best course of action here," replied the Jödmun, still trying to calm the woman down, but to no avail.

"To hell with what you think!" retorted Maka. "I am the Princess of Osharis, the Last Golden City, and I will do as I please!"

Suddenly a voice came from behind her; "So royalty, too? Yes, indeed." The voice that was clearly Hydrulian's, though he remained invisible, started to mumble to himself under his breath. His voice was quickly silenced by an elbow from the woman in front of him. She knew she had hit her target by the whoosh of air that was pushed out of his lungs.

The Sentriel's hiss of pain slowly turned to maniacal giggling, as his form reappeared on the ground, writhing about in the dirt.

Just as the heir of the Golden City was about to stomp on the mage's face, a sudden noise there came from all around; great and powerful, a single clear note echoing across the lands. It could be nothing less than several horns, used to signal something. The group soon found out exactly what, as suddenly dozens, maybe even hundreds of dwarves came rushing towards the party from all angles, except from the rear as their backs were fortunately against the river. Ürbon quickly found Askia and Tlupic and regrouped with Maka and Hydrulian, each preparing for the onslaught despite their earlier animosity towards each other.

"We're surrounded!" yelled Askia, his sword in one hand, his staff in the other, each radiating a faint blue glow.

"Tell me something more obvious" retorted Maka, her twin khopeshes drawn and held out in front of her, and Stixerio at her side.

"I assume we have a plan here?" rumbled Ürbon, his deep voice full of stoic determination, Bjarl gripped in both his stone hands.

"Can we change the subject to something a bit less dreary?" exclaimed Hydrulian, who was now lounging on the air above the group, Conflagration drawn in an attempt to fit in with the dramatic poses the rest of the group were striking. "Perhaps to something like when we get to have a nice cooked meal?"

Tlupic responded by hissing something along the lines of "Shut up, hellspawn," but his verbal assault was completely ignored due to the language barrier. His remaining spear in one hand and Asherai's old sword in the other, he turned to whisper in Ürbon's ear, "What's the plan?"

Ürbon responded with a grunt, before turning to Maka.

"What's the plan?" He prompted, seeing that the woman was ignoring him, he turned back to Tlupic. "Guess that answers that, buddy."

While the group was conversing between themselves, the dwarves had closed in around them, forming a semicircle around the party, with more joining the encirclement all the time. Soon almost two hundred dwarves had surrounded the group, forming different rows based on their weapons and equipment. All of them had sigils on various places, like their shoulders and arms, as well as on their weapons.

The first circle was a rank of poleaxe wielding dwarves, and in front of them came a row of dwarves carrying large shields, positioned before the polearms, protecting them. Both rank's faces were nearly entirely hidden away by chainmail masks, and they were clad nearly head to toe in metal plate. The shields seemed to be organized in some way, dependent on the symbols on each shield. There were two different signs on them, one with a red background displaying a raging bull, its head raised proudly and holding a whip in its mouth. The other flag had a blue background with a lantern at its center, and a pickaxe and gemstone crossed over it.

Past the row of poles however was another rank, filled to the brim with warriors wielding axes, hammers, and maces, some even carrying spiked morningstars in their hands. However, a few carried only a pickaxe or shovel, and wore a mining helmet, complete with a hook that was intended to hold light sources as they worked. Those with actual weapons had plate armor, but these apparent miners had only leather and that same mask of chainmail over their faces. Their symbols didn't seem to matter within the rank though, as the miners were mixed in with the soldiers at random.

Behind this rank of melee, there was a row of armed crossbowmen. These dwarves had the same chainmail mask over their faces, but their armor was made of dried leather and other softer, lighter material. Their weapons were held out in front of them, pointed directly at various members of the group. Their left shoulders were adorned by the symbols on the shields, and they were again forming two distinct lines based on them.

As the lines formed and stabilized, however, two figures emerged from the encirclement. Both of them were distinguishable by the amount of gold and precious metals engraved in their armor. One of the pair's helmets had a great crest atop it, made of some sort of fiber, while the others resembled something akin to a piece of rock, embedded with crystals and carved out to fit the shape of a helmet.

The two of them seemed to be from two different factions, as one of them had the raging bull inscribed on his chest plate, which was also tinted red, while the other modestly had the lantern, pick and gem on his left shoulder, tinted blue. There seemed to be some level of distrust between the two. Because as the one with the plumed helmet began to speak, the one with the stone helmet glared at him with some level of wariness.

"Well, well, look what we've got here," said the one wearing the bull. He spoke in dwarvish, unaware that the Jödmun could understand him perfectly, "these here will sell for enough to feed our clans for a whole year!"

"Be wary, Eldruid," cautioned the other. "They are more powerful than they seem."

"Ha!" Bellowed the now revealed Eldruid, as he took steps towards the group. "You are too cautious, Caligerius," the aforementioned dwarf frowned at the use of his name, "we have them surrounded by our best."

"It doesn't hurt to be safe, Eldruid," responded Caligerius, glaring at Ürbon and Hydrulian from the corner of his eye, "They are obviously powerful."

"Another reason to capture them!"

"Sorry, but we aren't for sale." Spoke Ürbon in their language. The dwarves recoiled from the giant as he took a step in front of the others. "And we don't want trouble, so let us go before there's any pointless dea-"

"Did I hear the word trouble?!" Interrupted Hydrulian, flying next to Ürbon, Conflagration drawn, before being halted by a stone arm.

Regaining his composure, Eldruid rose to meet the giant's challenge. "If you haven't noticed, we have you surrounded and outnumbered, so you'll be coming with us!"

"This is your last warning, dwarf. We don't want any trouble."

"Speak for yourself," interjected Hydrulian, a maniac grin plastered onto his face. "I can destroy them all at a whim."

Nearly all the dwarves recoiled at the Sentriel's words, except for Eldruid. Ürbon once more put an arm in front of Hydrulian, cutting him off from the opposing encirclement.

"Big talk for a glowing piece of metal!" Eldruid said, steadfast in his goal to take them as slaves.

"Big talk for such an itty-bitty child in armor," retorted Hydrulian, despite the fact he couldn't fully understand them. He hadn't spoken dwarvish in a very long time and the southern dialect was slightly different. He climbed over the stone appendage blocking his path. Ürbon could feel the hatred emanating from Eldruid, and so he took another step forward to continue to try and negotiate. He stopped, however, when the dwarves began arguing among themselves.

"I'm not sure about them, Eldruid," said Caligerius.

"I don't care what you think!" shouted the red-clad dwarf. "We will take them in and sell them for enough to make us both into the greatest clans."

"This is too big a risk," comforted Caligerius, as he put a hand on Eldruid's shoulder.

"Get your hands off me!" Eldruid shouted, jumping away from the other dwarf, "You should know who is funding this expedition and your clan." Turning away from the lesser clan leader, the red-clad warrior pointed back to the group. "They are coming with us."

Ürbon was now starting to see that peace wasn't necessarily an option anymore. He hefted Bjarl in readiness for the coming conflict. However, the dwarves were smarter than they appear.

"I wouldn't resist if I were you," said Eldruid, "because we've got every single crossbow here trained on those two."

Following the dwarf's stubby hand, Ürbon saw who he was talking about. He was pointing at both Askia and Tlupic, who readied their weapons in defiance. Ürbon knew exactly what game he was playing now. He wasn't about to lose either of them, but even if he interposed himself between the hail of crossbow bolts, the other would still be exposed from another angle. Tlupic might be able to dodge at least one volley, but Ürbon couldn't block every single arrow.

Knowing he couldn't protect them alone, the Jödmun realized he would need help. And so he turned to the only one powerful enough to aid in stopping the arrow fire, Hydrulian. However, when he shifted his gaze to where the Sentriel had been. He found that Hydrulian was nowhere to be found. Quickly, he turned to Maka, who only stared back in cold determination, before nodding her head to confirm it. Hydrulian had completely disappeared.

"Oh, so I see the group is now uncertain?" probed Eldruid, noting the missing Sentriel. "A shame to have been deserted in such a manner. You'll be coming with us!"

Ürbon's mind was racing as he tried to concoct a plan so that they could all escape, but without Hydrulian's magical might, there wasn't one that could get them all away safely. Except for one, though he was sure no one else would agree.

"Fine," rumbled the Jödmun, his gaze burning with anger, which he calmly directed towards the dwarf, "we surrender."

***

Hydrulian was enjoying the spectacle below him. He was slightly intrigued when his puppet Ürbon willingly surrendered to the metal toys in front of him, though he was clearly upset about it. But no matter how interesting that engagement was, he couldn't keep his eyes off Maka.

Some strange form of magic kept pulling his gaze back to her, and it was incredibly difficult to look away. Not that he wanted to waste the effort of course, which was definitely the only reason he continued to stare at the woman down below.

It was such a unique form of magic that he had never heard or even seen its likeness before. It made his mind fog and his speech horrifically broken with stutters. He told himself that he would find out the secret to such power, whatever it would take, as the group below him marched southwards, with Ürbon, Tlupic, Maka, and the annoying human in tow. He would follow them, and learn as much as possible about her and her strange abilities.

***

Groaning as his sight returned to him, Arthurian clutched his head as unspeakable agony began to course through it, as if it was going to split the elven mage's head into two separate pieces.

Eventually, the pain began to ease, though after how long he couldn't tell. It was then that he was finally able to attempt to piece together where he was. He was in a bed, of that he was certain, but he couldn't remember how he had gotten here. He was determined to find out, but as he sat up straight, another explosion of pain coursed through his body, this time from his right side. It was then that he remembered what had happened. He could only remember up to when the stone golem and spear-wielding lizard came up from the bottom decks, but that was more than enough for him.

He was going to find those two and do everything in his power to make them suffer as he did now. However, revenge would have to wait, as he was beginning to feel faint. Before he fell asleep once more, he saw a figure next to the bed, one he recognized with both bitterness and gratitude.

"Mother?" was the only word he could get out before he sank back into darkness.

Chapter 9:
Schemes and Soldiers

Askia trudged along in the armored column of dwarves, his hands bound in rough iron chains that bit into his wrists with their cold metallic grip. His weapons had been taken away by the dwarves marching all around him, along with everyone else's in the group, and were currently in custody of two dwarves at the back of the marching column. While he didn't like being disarmed, it was rather funny to see them continually get small shocks of electricity whenever they tried to handle Bjarl.

That being said, he gazed into the back of the massive stone giant in front of him, who had gotten them into this situation.

Ürbon fought off his feelings of confinement and, surprisingly, shame, though he had no manacles around his arms. The dwarves didn't have any that fit. Instead, they had to bind his arms with rope, as well as his legs so that he wouldn't attempt to escape. To give the leg bindings some weight, they tied it to their supply caravan, except the one which now carried their weapons.

The Jödmun had surrendered to their captors, turning themselves in as slaves of the dwarves. Askia knew that even if the giant had been alone, he would have been able to fight them all off. Not to mention with Maka's strength and skill with a blade. He would have to find out why Ürbon made that choice later, however, because his thoughts kept being interrupted by an adjacent dwarf jabbed him with the butt of his poleaxe, a sure sign to keep moving.

When a glare back at his aggressor resulted in another jab, Askia resigned himself to keep marching. As he walked forward, he took in the positions of the rest of the group. He was in the very back of the line, with Ürbon in front of him due to him having to haul the storage wagons. Maka was directly in front of Ürbon, atop Stixerio, despite the dwarves' best efforts of getting her off. Whenever one of them approached her, the horse lashed out with its hooves and sent them sprawling across the dirt. One of the crossbowmen fired a bolt at her, but she turned and with a flash of movement drew one of her khopeshes and parried the projectile midair, knocking it away. She then fixed her rage-filled gaze onto the mask of the dwarf who had fired it. While they didn't respond audibly, they definitely shuffled in place.

Tlupic walked ahead of Maka, looking dejected and small, even among the dwarven surrounding him. His tail constantly twitched and flicked in random directions, and it was hard to look at him under the unrelenting light of the sun. He looked shaken, discouraged as he trudged through the dirt, and Askia assumed it was because of the Jödmun's surrender. The two had been the closest of friends during the time Askia had been with them.

As Askia was prodded once more by a nearby dwarf, he devoted himself to trying to figure out another way to escape from their situation. Even if Ürbon had presumably given up, that didn't mean that he would too. Even if the dwarves thought that he was powerless, he would find a way to save himself and his friends, no matter the cost.

Meanwhile, Ürbon utilized all the self-control he'd gained over centuries of travel to not lash out at the dwarves around him. If his iron grip slipped and he lost control over his anger, then his companions would pay the price in cold steel and spilt blood, and his gamble of letting the dwarves take them would have been for naught.

Even so, he did not like being taken prisoner. It brought back bad memories of his crew upon *The North Wind*. He hoped that they were still alive. It wasn't as if he was afraid of them dying in captivity anytime soon, but the elves could have simply executed them or sacrificed them for some foul purpose. He decided not to think about that for the time being, seeing as there was nothing he could do for them right now. But he had sworn that one day he would return to either save or avenge them. These thoughts weren't helping anyone, so he focused on observing details, and remembering everything he could about the dwarves around him.

He recognized the insignia of the whip and the bull as the symbol of the dwarven clan Harn Trask. They were the weakest of the four upper dwarven clans in the region. The 'Byzerions', as they called themselves, ruled over all other dwarven clans in Dhueyra. For this reason, they were commonly called the Byzerion Rulership.

Ürbon didn't know the name of the clan wearing the lantern, pickaxe, and gem, so he assumed that it was a weak and unimportant lower clan who were under the patronage of Harn Trask. What he had overheard from the argument between the two commanding officers seemed to match with this assumption. He didn't know if Harn Trask had any more clans under its patronage, but he figured it was highly unlikely. A clan's wealth could only stretch so far, especially that of Harn Trask, being the weakest of the four.

The situation was dire, but it could have been much worse. Two hundred dwarves were a small number even by dwarven standards, and even though they possessed good weapons and armor, the real threat came from their Prisms.

He remembered being told, long ago, when he had first stepped foot onto these lands, of how the southern dwarves had magical gems, mined from the mountains scattering their homeland, that were filled with raw magic. They called these gemstones Prisms, and they were encrusted into the body of nearly every dwarf.

What's more, the number of gems was directly linked to their society's hierarchy. The more gems, the higher standing that particular dwarf has. A common dwarf with either one or two gemstones was not a real threat. The gems of the lower castes were usually quite weak, but nobles in the higher echelons could have upwards of hundreds, which made them into a truly deadly force.

Even ignoring the fact that there are bound to be dwarves with even more personal Prisms within this group, it was their best hope to bide their time, and look for a moment when they could escape where his more...fragile companions would not perish. He had bet on that chance when he surrendered to their current captors. He would not allow his friends' blood to spill at the hands of his enemies, not when their lives could be saved.

Even so, he knew his chance wouldn't come for a while, that he would have to wait until nightfall before any sort of plan could be enacted. If those dwarves thought that mere rope would hold him, they were fools.

Hearing a splitting zap from behind him, he turned to see one of the dwarves standing behind the weapons cart. The dwarf was rubbing an electrified hand and frowning at Ürbon's axe. It seemed Bjarl had given the dwarf good reason to keep his hands to himself. Nevertheless, that didn't stop the dwarf from eyeing the axe longingly, and Ürbon felt a twinge of anger.

From the corner of his eye, he saw another dwarf walk behind the weapon cart. Ürbon recognized him as one of the leaders, but now he looked uneasy and doubtful.

"Tlakinger," he said to the other, his voice barely above a whisper.

"The axe, it's magical, Lord Caligerius. It zaps whoever gets too close," Tlakinger replied. Ürbon guessed he was trying to explain himself. Usually, soldiers don't go around pawing seized items without permission.

"It's too dangerous," Caligerius said. Tlakinger nodded sulkily, eyes still on Bjarl. Yet the Lord was not referring to the weapon. "We shouldn't have taken them."

"Sir?"

"Since we encountered them, I've had a horrible feeling locked in my chest," the dwarf continued, turning towards the confused soldier. "My clan is in grave danger. And I am not a dwarf who will let their clan slide into ruin without a fight."

Caligerius paused for a moment, and then reached out to the soldier, putting a heavy mail-cladded hand upon his shoulder. "I need you to follow my orders to the letter when I give them, understand?"

The soldier nodded gravely.

"Good. Now catch up. We're falling behind," Caligerius said, patting the soldier's back before Ürbon saw Tlakinger walk back into the marching columns.

It seemed Ürbon and his friends weren't the only ones in a sticky situation. After all, one dwarf's misfortune could be another Jödmun's luck.

***

Hydrulian was enjoying some time to himself, lazily flying through the air as the group marched below him. From how high up in the sky he was, they appeared no bigger than tiny insects crawling through the dirt aimlessly. He had already had his fill of watching them constantly marching through the dirt and sand, and was thoroughly bored. He could have been among them if he so chose, but he really didn't want to get involved with that mess.

Folding in his metallic wings with a loud screech (which of course was hidden from those below by a masterfully crafted silence spell) he plummeted towards the ground at breakneck speeds, before angling himself slightly so that he would fall towards the river instead. As the water rushed closer and closer, the Sentriel contemplated what he was still doing outside of his temple in the ruined city. He could blame several things: the appearance of the group, the deactivation of the green mist and acquiring its hidden artifact.

His wings shot out from his back, turning his fall into a last-second glide over the flowing waters. He determined that the reason for him being here was the golden woman Maka, before pushing down the strange feeling in his chest at her name. She had clearly implanted some form of magic into him. Making it so that he still felt the same effects at the mere thought of her.

He rationalized that he had to figure out what kind of magic it was so that he could use it himself. After all, he had never encountered this form of power before, and he would learn to use it and master it.

He steadied out his wings when he realized that he had nearly reached the water, and pulled himself higher into the air. After reaching an acceptable height, he gazed at the lands around him, searching for anything of relative interest. The train of dwarves was long behind him, and barely visible even from as high up as he was. Small towns dotted the river's edge, sustained by its ready water source and fertile lands. Finally, something managed to draw his eye.

Farther down the riverbed, there was a section where a stream of water was flowing away from the main body. Where it led might be an interesting exploration. Despite the riverbank around it remaining the color of natural sand, everywhere that was away from the water was a deep red, nearly the color of blood. While it might have unnerved others, Hydrulian thought it was an exciting discovery.

At the end of the stream was a small pool of water, almost as large as a conventional pond. Filling its waters were boats and sailboats, each with different symbols on them. There was a symbol of a large opening with bloody fangs attached to it, giving the appearance of a shark's mouth. There was a symbol of blood-red lips, with a taloned finger pressed against them, illustrating silence, or perhaps something more suggestive. There was yet another of a crimson serpent's head, which almost looked familiar to him, but he didn't care enough to figure out why.

Far more intriguing, was a massive fortress made of blood-red stone that appeared deserted and crumbling. It had strange growths on its walls in colors ranging from yellow to green to delicate hues of purple. Hydrulian knew that this place was too big for locals to have missed, but as he drew closer he felt a magical force around the place. Apparently there was a spell hiding it from the view of everyone without magical abilities.

Hydrulian looked back behind him. The group was still far away, but he could catch up to them later. He flew towards the fortress, eager to find whatever was causing that magical interference.

As Hydrulian crept through another crumbling corridor of the decrepit castle, still wrapped in his spells of invisibility and sound proofing, he tried to remember why he came into the structure in the first place. At best it would be a decent enough base to terrorize the locals. After a moment of being totally blank, he remembered that there was a strong magical presence which permeated the walls itself, and perhaps something that jogged his shattered mind to the memory. Even the candles set in the stone walls burned cold by this magic, which helped drive him onward, frantically searching.

Rounding another corner on his golden wings, he saw a flicker of movement at the end of the corridor he just entered. After being bored for some time, and being unable to locate the source of the magic, due to it permeating the entire structure, he shot off after the disturbance with renewed vigor.

He flew down the hallway, his wings beating rapidly to speed him on to his destination. When he reached the corner where he had seen the disturbance, he spotted two lean figures moving through the hall.

They were both humanoid, one a male and one a female, both quietly conversing. The man was dressed in a formal suit made of black cloth and a silk shirt. Though it appeared bare of any accessories, the golden buttons on the front gave it some color. The back of the suit was completely barren of decorations, though the bottom ended with two separate tails of cloth, each about an arm's length and coming to a point that fluttered behind him as he walked. His black trousers were made of the same material, and a pair of black leather shoes covered his feet.

The woman, on the other hand, was dressed in a vibrant crimson dress that surrounded her in a sea of silk and velvet. The clothing clung to her like a second skin, the fabric clutching greedily to her figure. The dress was cut so low and fit so snugly around her chest that it left little to the imagination. The lower half of the dress was made of silk that expanded outwards, creating a full ballroom dress, which dragged behind her as she walked and saved the rest of her from prying eyes. Between the layers of velvety crimson hung chains covered in gemstones and pearls of varying sizes and cuts, sparkling at the slightest movement, even in the faint candlelight.

Hydrulian, cloaked in invisibility, listened to their conversation while walking behind them as they continued through the corridor.

"I told you we're already late," said the man, completely oblivious to Hydrulian's presence. "We need to hurry!"

"You worry far too much, darling," said the woman, placing a hand delicately on the man's arm, as if to comfort him. "We don't have much to say to the grandmaster, anyway."

"Still, it's only polite to show up on time. We are reflecting on our order and on our Mistress."

Hydrulian already lost interest and didn't bother to listen to the woman's response. His focus was now directed on the figure approaching the pair from behind. Wanting something interesting to happen, he used a touch of magic to alert the two to this newcomer. As expected, the pair stiffened and whirled around when finally sensing its presence. However, their next action caught him a bit off guard. Instead of questioning the newcomer, they walked up and embraced him, as if they were old friends. Confused by this development, Hydrulian focused back on the conversation.

"It's been so long since we've seen each other, Galadar!" exclaimed the woman, who ran and embraced the newcomer, who hugged her back. The one called Galadar was clad in crimson metal plate armor with a red serpent engraved on the chestplate and on a pauldron. Hydrulian recognized the symbol, it was the same as the one the annoying corpse from the crypt had on his armor. But he didn't care about the markings, he was more interested in the conversation.

"Glad to see you too," Galadar said, his breath squeezed from his lungs as the two hugged.

"What brings you here, Galadar?" said the man as the trio stood in the hallway.

"Same thing as you," responded the crimson-clad warrior, his voice deep and full of authority. "All the orders were summoned, you know."

"We've been trying to figure that out ourselves," said the woman.

"Oh? Were you not informed by your superiors?"

The others shook their heads, unsure of the warrior's words.

Galadar smirked, "I forgot that your mistress is not one for telling, and more of one for taking."

"It's quite alright," replied the woman, "but, then, why are all the five vampire cults being summoned?"

Hydrulian's eyes lit up with joy as he heard the word vampire come up. He watched as the response came from the warrior's mouth, and sure enough there was a pair of fangs to meet. Now, this was getting interesting.

"There's a new raid being discussed," said Galadar excitedly, "and I want to attend, to see if I can get in on the fun."

"Well, we're already late," interjected the vampire dressed in formal attire, his eyes glaring pointedly at his female companion.

"Then we haven't time to lose! Come, friends. Let us see what the council has planned for us!" Exclaimed Galadar, before taking off at full speed down the hallway.

The two left behind glanced between each other, before sprinting after the warrior, the woman yelling after them as she tried to catch up in her dress. Hydrulian flew along behind, easily keeping pace.

Hydrulian followed the group of vampires until they finally reached their destination. After traversing a handful more corners the meeting hall appeared before them. It seemed they were already late. Hydrulian chuckled to himself as the trio burst into the room. The council had already been gathered, and Hydrulian kept himself in the shadows, watching the discussion unfold.

Hydrulian swept his gaze across the chamber. He saw representatives from all of the vampire clans gathered around the circular stone table at the center of the room. The room itself was made of stone, and it looked as if it had been carved out of a single rock instead of being laid with bricks, as the walls were smooth with no signs of construction. This design was shared with the rest of the room, except for the chairs the vampires were seated in, which were made of wood. They quickly took the open seats around the table, which was merged with the floor as if it was part of the same mass. Torches lined the walls, affixed by iron clamps set into the stone. However the main source of light came from the candles upon a massive stone chandelier hanging in the center of the room, its carefully crafted limbs a marvel to behold.

Several of the already seated diplomats glared at the latecomers. Among them were the famed slavers, or "Collectors" as they called themselves. Their leader was Perturiel the Black, named as such for the horrible things he did with those he captured. Another reason for the title was his teeth, which had long been stained black, and it was rumored it was due to the blood of those his clan collected.

The Human trade was important to the point of near necessity for the vampire clans, but the vicious horrors Perturiel inspired in the hearts of his victims was a step too far for most vampires. Sure they were slaves, but there was a limit. They were still sentient beings, after all.

Another influential face that turned towards the trio was that of Shagrath the Thrice-Blessed. He was a member of the Plaguemancers, who ruled over the fortress where they now met. Shagrath was said to have received the blessings of their lord, the one the Plaguemancers referred to as 'The Decayed'. He reflected this rather well, with his face sagging as if it were rotting away from the inside. His hair had long since fallen out, leaving nothing but a bare scalp to fully reveal the horror his head had become. His scalp was pitted at places, and some places were missing skin altogether. His skin was also full of tiny holes, as if it was being eaten by maggots, which while looking at him, might not be far from the truth. When he smiled, his lips moved far more than any humanoid creatures would have, and his dried red gums would be in full view of anyone nearby, forming a loose, fully ear-to-ear, grin. For this reason, most tried to avoid conversation of any kind with him. Receiving his notice was unfortunate, indeed.

And finally there was the representative of the magically talented Lectors of the Library, a Bloodmancer by the name of Djanter. The Lectors lived in a massive tower called the Library, where they worshipped the god of knowledge and arcane power. Djanter was no exception, and he was particularly adept in the art of utilizing blood to perform various acts, especially in the field of warfare. He was known for his prowess in battle, and his excellence as a mage. His amethyst eyes bored intently into those of Galadar, who offered a friendly smile in reply. The two had a bit of a rivalry with each other. That is to say, they had run into each other once or twice. Djanter scoffed and turned away.

Galadar, still smiling, turned back to his companions, and offered them a nod of farewell. With that, they headed to their places around the table, next to members of their respective clans. As the three rushed to their seats, Shagrath opened with the expected greeting.

"You are late," Shagrath started, his grating voice clearly not benefitting from any of his supposed blessings. "I expect there is a particular reason?"

Galadar was about to respond, before he was interrupted by the same voice.

"It does not matter!" Shouted the Plaguemancer, slamming a fist on the stone table. "You were late, and that is all that matters. I must say, we expected much better from one of the supposed best warriors of the Blood Serpent!" After he finished his exclamation, Shagrath burst into a horrid coughing fit, sounding as if his throat was near completely choked with phlegm and blood.

"With all due respect," started Perturiel, his face wearing a smug grin, "I do believe we should continue our discussion, and belittle the late ones later." At the end of his interruption he was staring at the late vampire woman with a fire born of a primal hunger burning in his eyes, barely caged by his calm, cold demeanor.

"Of course," responded Shagrath, recovered from his coughing fit. "Let us continue. Where did we leave off?"

"We've barely gotten anywhere," groaned another vampire woman that the warrior didn't recognize, sitting next to the one Galadar spoke with. "We've not even decided where it is we'll be attacking."

At that, an excited murmur took over the room. Everyone knew this was the reason that they had been summoned, even though there had been no official declaration. At once each of the representatives of each clan argued their desired targets for raiding. The woman that Galadar had spoken with was the first one to voice her own opinion.

"We, the Succubi under the Mistress of Lust vote to dedicate a slave raid to one of the nearby human kingdoms." Everyone present watched her with a keen interest as she spoke, "I propose Ravenburg, or perhaps the nomads of the Krakadian League, maybe even the Kingdom of Artaria."

Perturiel interrupted her with a bored expression on his face, "I would advise against raiding Ravenburg, it has only been a few years since our last raid, we wouldn't want to thin out the herd too much or else they might become...unproductive. The Kingdom of Artaria on the other hand, is ripe for the picking, and is a fractured and divided country with a massive population. The Collectors vote in favor of such action."

"The Lectors vote in favor of attacking the orcs to the north," interjected Djanter, his face still unaccountably calm. "Our stock of them is running quite low, and I'm sure we all agree that they make for a strong labor force as well as resilient test subjects."

Arelius, another crimson-armoured warrior shot the Lectors a pointed look before speaking. "The Order of the Blood Serpent votes to commit the raid to finally dealing with the dargoon infestation."

At this the followers of the Lord of Knowledge stopped speaking and glared at the warrior in disgust. It was well known that the horribly destructive nomadic clan of dragon-like insectoids were the invention of a Lector mage, who in his insanity created a race of monsters which were half-dragon, half-scarabite, and outfitted with stone scales and chitin. It was also common knowledge that he was killed by this new race while they were still being tested.

Djanter regained his composure unlike his brethren, and spoke for his clan when he said, "That is a truly foolish decision. I know that the Blood Serpents can only think of the next thing to kill, but we have managed to adapt to their yearly cycle of violence. During the summer they fight the orcs to the north of us, after which they migrate south into lands we have set aside for such matters, before fighting the dwarves of Kragbringer. Then they cross the Titan Divide and continue to war with our neighbors, and leave our territory in the process. Usually, the Daz Wera chase them off towards the golden desert of the Nebu-Gi, where they spend the winter fighting the Teshar Clans. By the end of their journey they go further south to the Sands of Desolation, where they replenish their numbers, before heading north along the desert back to where they started, and the cycle begins anew. All along their trail of destruction they constantly get into fights losing more and more of their numbers, and since they reproduce rather slowly, the problem will most likely deal with itself in just a short century."

Hydrulian yawned, fighting to stay awake and keep his invisibility spell from faltering. His initial expectations had completely fallen away. Instead of listening in to exciting vampire affairs, the entire thing had proven incredibly dull. For an entire hour all he had heard were names, names, locations, directions, names, directions. He couldn't care less about some draconic insectoid mad experiment he'd never seen, and if he ever did see he'd easily get rid of with a simple strike.

But the drowsiness left him as the red-armoured one called Galadar stood up, and berated the Lectors.

"I think that you are just afraid, afraid that others will discover some of the secrets of your kind!"

"Each clan is entitled to their own secrets!" Djanter replied.

"Not if they endanger the other clans!"

After this, the room descended into chaos with a cacophony of shouting. The less influential representatives tried to draw attention to themselves, and away from the argument, by proposing increasingly obscene raid targets. One non-influential member of the Collectors proposed to sail north towards the Northern Plains and raid the Free Cities, an obscure member of the Lectors proposed to sail all the way to the hidden Gataran Jungles and capture some of the creatures there for experimentation. One particularly idiotic Plaguemancer proposed to sail towards the mainland of the Kingdom of Glavier. Everybody just stopped to stare at the dimwitted vampire. This started a new round of shouting, but this time focused around berating the Plaguemancer, educating him in the fact that it was magically impossible to raise the undead on mainland Glavier, and the fact that their enormous and ever vigilant navy and army would make quick work of them should they appear there. As the poor follower of the Decayed continued to be berated, Shagrath finally lost it.

Hydrulian yawned again at the mention of more names, locations and directions. More boring conversation, lovely. He had almost had enough of it and was about to turn and leave the vampires to their dull affairs. But he was glad he had stayed a moment longer by the end.

It seemed he was not the only one who was bored of the endless and entirely fruitless argument. And the one called Shagrath slammed his fist upon the stone table, having finally lost his patience.

"ENOUGH!" Shagrath shouted, his lips spewing all manner of things as the room quieted down immediately. "You ignorant, petulant children, you have been summoned here for a specific purpose, one that will benefit our race more than any other cattle or work slave! The Plaguemancer clan votes to raid the Dwarves!"

The room was quickly filled with a surge of dull chatter as the many vampires voiced their opinions to their neighbors, discussing their options and whether or not this was even a good plan. In the end, the most prominent question was, which clan of dwarves would they be targeting.

There were the dwarves of Kragbringer, just north of their current location who, after being cut off from both the main dwarven kingdom in the north as well as their southern dwarf neighbors, became warmongers. Alone and isolated as well as being stuck between vampires to their south, orcs in the north and dargoons invading every summer, they had become adept in the art of angrily killing any non-dwarf thing that moved.

There was also the Daz Wera, west of the Bloody Sands, the Byzerion Rulership of Dhueyra, who were at any given point either allies, rivals, or trade partners. They were across the Titan Divide, which was so close that their side of the shore could be seen from the balconies of the vampire keep.

Galadar, while he wanted to go on this expedition, also wanted this meeting to be over. With the vampire nobles still talking amongst themselves that didn't seem likely to happen any time soon. In an attempt to quicken the pace of the meeting, he posed the question that had captivated a room full of allegedly wise vampires.

"Which ones, the Kragbringers, or the Byzerions?"

Shagrath responded for the Plaguemancer, for despite his earlier outburst, he was also rather bored with this assembly.

"It has come to my attention that minor dwarven clans are gathering their newly acquired slaves across the Divide, and this is where we will strike!"

A small chorus of gasps came from the Succubi and Collector parties, mostly because they traded slaves with the dwarves. While the chaos stopped momentarily, Galadar decided to interject his voice into the conversation.

"The five clans will work together to either completely capture or destroy an entire dwarven settlement," he boldly stated, shooting up from his seat, "and we will leave absolutely nothing for the dwarves to suspect it was us!" Before the warrior could continue, Djanter interrupted him with his own statement.

"Think of the possibilities! We could study the dwarven resistance to magic and the true nature of their Prisms, as well as use them as both a reliable food and workforce. I've heard they work marvelously with stone and architecture, as well as metal. Let's make them into our smiths, miners, engineers, and architects. All we have to do is act now, and we could expand our powerbase even further!"

By now the vampires were riled up, most of the clans had their goals somewhat aided by this raid. Even the warriors under the Blood Serpent and the Succubi serving the Mistress of Lust were on board. However, many among the council were still presenting arguments. Slavers who thought their supply was being threatened harshly objected, and many did not think that an attack was worth it at all. After much discussion, the representatives ended up in two separate groups, each at the other's throat.

Hydrulian watched silently as the groups tried to violently convince the other side to change their minds. He also noticed that he was not the only one quietly observing. Galadar also watched the arguments unfold, relaxing in his seat despite its stone frame. The vampire closed his eyes and waited for the debate to be over. He had done all he could, and now he could just sit back and hope no one bothered him. But as soon as he closed his eyes, the arguments seemed to stop.

The room had fallen silent, and every vampire in the room was now sitting down. It was apparent that in the end, all the clans present agreed on the raid, despite their conflicting opinions and motives.

Hydrulian let out a small spark of golden light in his excitement. Perhaps a chaotic raid in the night was precisely what was needed to give his captured companions a chance to escape. He could already picture them quietly sneaking away as the dwarves were busy getting killed. Not to mention the entertainment of observing the whole situation unfold from the heights of the sky. Oh the sweet cacophony of battle, the sound of clashing swords under the moonlight! But Hydrulian quickly collected himself as he noticed the crimson warrior swerved his gaze directly at Hydrulian. Luckily, it was apparent that the vampire did not see much, as after a moment he shrugged and looked back at his gathered comrades.

The meeting was over, and all that was left was for the vampires present to choose if they would join the raid or not. Most did not, with the exception of the majority of Blood Serpent attendees, and a handful from each of the other clans. As they filed out of the room, no one noticed Hydrulian hovering in the center of the stone table, giggling madly. This was going to be good, really good, and with a slight push it would be even better.

Chapter 10:
Now or Never

In the darkness of the tent, Askia raised his head, trying to peer through the thin fabric to gaze at the stars he knew twinkled above. He was almost successful, before a stout dwarf opened the tent flap and entered, carrying a lit candle in his hands. Without a word or even a nod of acknowledgement, the dwarf laid the candle in a metal container. Despite the man being their prisoner, he was to be kept in decent enough condition so as to be sold at a higher price. Patiently, Askia waited for the dwarf to leave, before resuming his attempted stargazing.

It had been two days since their capture, and now the slave caravan had stopped to rest on the outskirts of an aboveground dwarven village. The village rested on the side of the Titan Divide like a weary beast, being a poorer cousin to the underground dwarven communities. Though dwarves preferred to live underground, there were benefits to having dwarves stationed in these river-side residences to provide fish to the other communities. There was industrial potential with the river itself, but this village didn't seem to utilize it much, only having a pair of water wheels so as to grind wheat. This was likely due to the fact that this village was on the borders of the dwarvish territories in the area, and so clan funds weren't often directed their way, and as a result, industry suffered.

Askia wasn't alone inside his tent. There was a single dwarf guard, standing opposite the entrance, leaning on his polearm. The others had likely been taken to their own separate holdings to prevent the group from collaborating on a way to escape. Even so, Askia knew how dire the situation was, even if he didn't understand completely. He knew there were around two hundred dwarves, nearly all a match for him even if he was armed. To be able to escape with his life, he would need the help of the others.

Askia knew this, but for some reason there was a tiny spot within him that yelled otherwise. The Pilgrim knew not to trust that part of him, and he realized that it was pride working against him, telling him to take matters into his own hands. He knew he wasn't as talented as the others in the group, but that didn't mean he was without his merits. Even so he shoved that small voice of him away, and refocused on the task at hand.

His wrists had been put into rough iron manacles, each linked to metal poles which had been hammered into the ground. They had left the sands of the desert long ago, and Askia had no hope of pulling them from the dirt and rock with the guard watching. The weary pilgrim knew what he needed was a diversion, so that he might be able to eventually pull himself free of the ground. He could probably make the guard release him for a time if he said he needed to relieve himself, but even then, the guard would not entirely leave. He would have to figure out some way of taking out the armed dwarf while his hands were bound. He reasoned that he would think of something eventually and continued planning his escape.

***

Ürbon sat in the center of the dwarven camp, surrounded by dozens of armed guards, and his body weighed down by ropes and chains tied to several heavy objects scattered around the area. Things were not going as well as they should have, but the Jödmun did not give up hope. Added to that, Hydrulian had not returned from wherever he had gone. The giant could have easily escaped from the dwarves at any point during their journey, but he knew he would not be able to keep his mortal friends alive against so many enemies, though Maka could likely take care of herself. He had hinged all his plans of escape on the Sentriel returning, so that they could protect the others, but that had not happened. He needed Hydrulian's raw magical power to hold off the dwarves before they could retaliate against Askia and Tlupic.

Something else troubled him though, or in truth caught his attention. It was clear they had no intentions of executing them or forcing them into any sort of labor, instead they were being kept in good condition. Meaning they were meant for trade. However the two major officers in the caravan, Caligerius and Eldruid, seemed to be at odds. From what he had overheard, Caligerius was the leader of a lesser dwarven clan who was under the patronage of one of the major clans, that being Harn Trask. Eldruid was apparently a high-ranking member of the major clan and was keeping a watch on the lesser clan.

Ürbon remembered the Caligerius' hesitation during their capture, even going so far as to speak against Eldruid. And another factor was how nervous the lesser officer was during their march, and how clearly anxious he was of the events to have to tell his men to be prepared for anything. Perhaps something would come out of this evident conflict, maybe Caligerius could even be convinced to take action against his patron clan.

Ürbon continued to plot his course. Since they had halted, the Jödmun had kept track of where the others were being held, helped in no small part by his height and the dwarves' shorter stature. He had also been able to locate their weapons and equipment from his vantage point. He just hoped that the rest of the group didn't act out on their own and force him to hurriedly put some improvised plan into motion. If he could, he wanted to be the one to strike first and draw the dwarves' attention to himself rather than the others.

It was while he was buried deep in these thoughts that the camp erupted into action. He heard dwarves rushing about on heavy feet. It took the Jödmun some time to figure out what had stirred them up so much.

A large group of lights was approaching the camp, and seeing as the lights were in formation, it was safe to assume it was some kind of organized force, a big one at that. From where he sat, there looked to be around five times more than were present in the camp. Whatever this was, it sent the camp into a frenzy. Trapped by his responsibilities to his friends, Ürbon could do nothing but watch as the lights grew ever closer, along with the growing feeling of dread in his heart.

***

Lowering the spyglass in his hands, Galadar observed the army approaching their chosen target. The vampire council had gathered every unliving creature within the fortress. This even included the many bodyguard retinues in the service of many prominent vampiric figures on the political scene. Outsiders might have thought of the bloody sands as one unified entity, but nothing could be farther from the truth. It was true that all vampires had base similarities , but that was like saying humans all got along because they all needed to drink water. No, the vampiric orders were distinct from one another, even if they all agreed far more often than humans.

Regardless of their differences, they were now an army marching toward their raid target, with little information, and that did not bode well. It would be quite the sour start to this event if they weren't able to gather any of the slaves promised. Nevertheless, the vampires had set out, and they intended to get what they wanted, that being mainly slaves and spilt blood to drink. They had embarked on three large ships, each with a specific role. The first was for the vampires themselves, and the second was for their undead soldiers, mainly there as meat shields for their more valuable masters. The third had some of the Blood Serpents more monstrous elements on it, and they would be quite the challenge to the dwarvish clans.

The clans had been organized into separate groups, most with fifty to sixty members apiece. They idly chatted amongst themselves, awaiting the time when they would be able to spill blood.

The Blood Serpents, on the other hand, had gathered just over eighty members together, and unlike the other clans, they spread out and mingled with the others. The blood-red warriors were held in relatively high regard amongst most of the cults, and were respected for their strength and honor in combat.

The same held true for the Lectors, with their magical prowess being much higher than any other known regional power, and as such they were respected throughout vampiric society. Though, this time, the servants of the Lord of Knowledge weren't exploiting or using their influence to their advantage. Instead, they huddled together, talking hurriedly and furiously amongst themselves. Well, that's about what Galadar expected. The mages wrapped their discussion within a bubble of resonating magic, serving as both a physical and magical barrier, so the knight of the Blood Serpent could only see mouths working furiously through a translucent red divider.

Turning away from the mages, the vampire began to walk towards the Plaguemancers, looking among them for Shagrath. The knight wanted to ask them a few questions about how they were to proceed. As he approached the pox-ridden gathering, he felt a slight twinge of disgust in what was left of his gut. Galadar might not have been a man anymore, but he still valued cleanliness as he had before his transformation. As such, he didn't quite hold the Plaguemancers and their customs in high regard.

Shuffling through the diseased crowd, the knight eventually came upon Shagrath, who was in conversation with Perturiel. Shagrath was the one in command of the raid, and the fact that Perturiel was a Collector, they were more than likely discussing the numbers of slaves the Collectors were to receive by the end of it all. It was their main source of income, after all. Though none of the other leaders of the raid were there. No doubt thi meant that Perturiel had asked Shagrath by himself, not giving the raid-leader a chance to get the others involved. As per vampire law, the spoils of raids had to be shared equally amongst those involved. Keeping the other leaders out of the plan only meant more for Perturiel. A sneaky trick that many would say was dishonorable, but business was business, Galadar supposed.

It seemed he had arrived at the end of their conversation. He saw Perturiel nod his head twice and say something along the lines of 'My most generous thanks, your uncleanliness,' and walk away. The crowd of rot respectfully parted for him to make his way out. As the Collector walked away, Shagrath noticed Galadar's approach, and made to meet him halfway.

"Greetings, honorable lord," Shagraht said, bowing as he did, their disemboweled gut swaying as he moved. "What brings you here before the raid?" he asked, casting a quick glance at the retreating slaver, "Are you also here to discuss the terms?"

"I'm presuming that's why Perturiel was here a moment ago?" questioned Galadar.

The Plaguemancer nodded to confirm. "He asked an extortionate amount, but I managed to set his shares to only fifty percent. Cheap, considering their usual habits."

"I'm not here to discuss the slaves, though the other clans won't be happy about that particular deal," responded Galadar.

Shagrath waved a rotting hand dismissively. "Business is business, I say. It can't be helped. But if it is not wealth and riches you're after, then what *are* you here for?"

"I would like to discuss our tactics and strategies during the attack," said Galadar, sensing a hidden meaning behind the diseased noble.

"Ah of course, I shouldn't have expected anything less from a knight of the Blood Serpent. Please, follow me."

The Plaguemancer walked through the crowd of his diseased subordinates as they parted for him, steering clear of his decaying bulk. Galadar followed, accompanying the pungent lord through a door in the back of the ship leading to the captain's quarters.

As the pair of vampire nobles passed through the single door of the cabin, they gathered the stares of the other three vampiric presences, confined within the cramped room. Galadar surprisingly found that he recognized most of the gazes which were fixed on him, among them was Djanter and Perturiel, though there was one in the corner that he did not recognize. Their gaze felt as if it was covered in oil, filthy and pervasive, oozing down the back of his neck as he reached the table.

"Took you long enough." The Lector said before turning away from the group, seemingly disinterested.

"Greetings, your uncleanliness," Perturiel said to Shagrath, trying to restart the conversation on a lighter note.

"Greetings slave master," responded Shagrath, bowing respectfully, "I trust we all know the meaning and context of this meeting?"

Djanter waved a hand dismissively. "Yes, yes. To discuss the plan of attack and all that."

"Indeed," continued Galadar, "but first, I would like to be acquainted with the gentleman in the corner, who just so happens to be staring at me like he's up to no good."

At that, everyone in the room turned towards the shadowy figure, who true to the warrior's summary, was staring ominously at the gathered group of prominent vampires.

"Zaros." It said.

"Well, nice to meet you, Zaros," Galadar said, slightly unnerved by the vampire's short answer and cold tone. Seeing everyone staring at him, the undead knight turned back to the main group. "Well, we should move on to the topic at hand."

At this, the group began discussing strategies and tactics on how they should begin the raid, proposing idea after idea. Though in typical vampiric fashion it swiftly ended up with the nobles using thinly, if at all, veiled threats to try and get their way. Galadar noticed that while Djanter and Perturiel argued, Zaros never moved from his spot in the corner, never stirring or contributing to the discussion, if it could be called that at that point.

Eventually, the group was saved from themselves when another vampire came in through the door, interrupting the latest bout of arguments.

"My liege," he began, bowing to Shagrath before continuing. "The enemy forces are moving."

At once, the chatter ceased, and the nobles shared a look between each other, before following the messenger back out the door. Zaros remained still in the shadows, unmoving as the others left, his eyes gleaming as they faded into the darkness.

***

Tlakinger marched along with the rest of the contingent of dwarves. His hand still ached from the shock of the mysterious axe, even though that was two days ago. Two layers of armor-clad warriors surrounded the stone giant, who did not protest. The prisoner had been surprisingly calm during the entire ordeal, including his capture. He had never struggled against his captors as they tied him down to the ground, or tried to escape in any way.

Shifting his gaze again to the ground in front of him, Tlakinger continued his march and kept formation with his brethren.

After a time, he found that the group had halted. Tlakinger's feet had unconsciously stopped as well, demonstrating the discipline of these soldiers. The scout saw Eldruid step ahead of the formation, flanked by two dwarves clad in full plate mail and wielding massive warhammers, along with Caligerius.

There was a similar contingent of dwarves ahead of the trio, representing the other clan's force. From where Tlakinger stood, it looked to be almost half of the entire force back at their own camp, but the only way he could tell was by the lantern light. Another figurehead was also emerging from the dark blob of soldiers, walking to meet the leaders, accompanied by at least a dozen soldiers with varied weapons. When the two parties met, all that Tlakinger could see was two figures emerge from both sides and begin conversing. Unable to listen in to the conversation, Tlakinger waited patiently, a growing sense of dread in his heart.

***

Caligerius took a brief moment to glance back at the assembled soldiers behind him, which had accompanied him thus far, before turning back to the task ahead of him.

Caligerius and Eldruid walked side by side towards the newly arrived dwarf group. He motioned to his soldiers to stay back, this was a meeting of clan leaders, and only clan leaders may be present. The two meeting parties could see each other more clearly now. The lantern light glimmered off the polished dwarven armor, lightly illuminating the stout figures.

"Greetings, nobles of Harn Trask," Eldruid called out, bowing slightly as the three approaching dwarves stepped closer.

Caligerius looked to the largest of them, clad in bejeweled armor, his beard braided with bands of gold; he towered over the two others flanking him. Harn Trask, one of the five major dwarf clans, was ruled over by a council of nobles, yet most feared among them, was Hjalram the Axe. Infamous for his thirst for blood and cruelty, Hjalram was a fearsome sight to behold, and all dwarves knew to never cross him.

"Where are the prisoners? We'll be taking them off your hands," said one of the other nobles.

He looked out into the darkness where a large form could be seen; standing resolutely with two dwarves on either side.

Caligerius saw the dwarf looking over at the prisoner.

"Those prisoners belong to my clan just as much as yours, you cannot simply take them," he said, standing his ground. Powerful the Harn Trask clan may be, he would not simply stand by as they took for themselves what was halfly his.

"Can someone explain to me why is this fool still breathing?" Hjalram called out. Caligerius turned to where Eldruid had stood, but the dwarf was not there. A piercing pain struck Caligerius. He looked down to see the point of a blade sticking out of his chest, just before the young leader fell to the ground, dead.

***

Ürbon was brought out to where the dwarves had met, the two dwarves standing beside him were charged with guarding him, but also the to keep an eye on each other. The guards rarely spoke, Eldruid and Caligerius would not allow the other to have sole responsibility, both assigning their own dwarves to guard the prisoner. The tension was high between the two clans' forces.

Perhaps this was a good thing, reinforcing his thoughts on there being some way of manipulating the situation. He was desperate to find a means of escape, to rescue his companions from this catastrophe that he was indeed guilty of causing. He was the one who condemned them all to this fate; he had forfeited all of their freedoms. It was the situation of his still-imprisoned crew all over again. He closed his eyes, trying to escape from his thoughts. Until something made them snap back open.

Shouts and screams echoed around the camp, he heard cries calling "Murder! Treachery! We're under attack!" from all corners. Ürbon looked around him, dwarves ran to and fro, attacking members of the opposite clan. The two dwarf guards were now at their feet, hands on their weapons, trying to make sense of the scene, whether they should join the fray or continue guarding their prisoner. Ürbon knew that this moment of confusion would be the only opportunity to escape, he stood up and grabbed one of the torches stuck into the ground; it would have to do as a weapon until he could find his axe.

"Oi you!" one of the guards turned to Ürbon, brandishing a double-edged axe, he was about to swing his weapon as a figure flew out from the shadows towards the dwarf. The cloaked figure knocked the screaming dwarf off his feet, ripping out his throat with its mouth, blood spattering onto the dirt. The second guard, in a state of panic, raised his weapon to strike the monster that was ravenously ripping apart its prey; until another shadowy figure flew out, knocking the axe out of his hand. It stood in front of the dwarf.

Its red eyes stared him down hungrily and its grinning mouth revealed rows of serrated teeth, dripping with blood.

Ürbon knew these creatures. He had seen them before — vampires.

The giant himself was of no real interest to the hungering creatures, but if there were others in the camp, it would mean everyone here was a target. He took one last look at the massacre before him and ran back to the camp as fast as he could. He had to find the others quickly, before the vampires got to them first.

***

"Bloody pigs!" the dwarf exclaimed, hearing the cries from outside the tent. He threw his dagger to the floor, which he would reluctantly clean as a rule every night, and walked past the chained Askia to look outside from the tent entrance. Askia had also been woken by the noise, something was happening in the camp. He listened to the cries and screams, the noise of armor as silhouettes ran past the tent. He did not know what could have caused such a ruckus, but inside it seemed like a haven, still and silent, untouched by the chaos ensuing outside. Askia looked at the guard whose head was stuck out of the tent. He knew that the dwarf would lose interest soon, and remember his instructions to keep an eye on him.

If Askia were to escape, now would be his only chance. The moment was perfect. He saw the dagger on the ground, freshly cleaned and sharpened, glinting in the meager light. Askia wondered if he even had the nerve. If he attempted to turn on the guard and was unsuccessful, he doubted if the dwarves would care about keeping him in "fine condition." The others wouldn't make it through the madness outside to free him; they didn't even know what tent he was in. He had to take matters into his own hands.

He reached for the dagger with his leg, pulling it closer towards him. The handle was uncomfortable as he managed to grab it with his hand. This was to be expected, after all the handle was made for a dwarf. He took a long look at the guards back still peering out of the tent. Though he wore iron armor, there were weak spots where the plate overlapped. He took aim for one of these spots near the shoulder. One good thrust and he could stab through the dwarf's armor, piercing his heart and killing him instantly...but he had to get it just right. Askia took a deep breath, ready to lunge. But just as he moved to strike the dwarf jumped back from the entrance, gurgling. Askia shrieked in horror as he saw a spear sticking out of the guard's throat.

As the dwarf fell on his back, wriggling in his death throes, Askia cried out in shock yet again, as a lizard tumbled into the tent. But then as he got a moment to collect himself and take a deep breath, he realized he had nothing to fear. It was only Tlupic. He was safe.

Tlupic hissed, and flailed his tail. "Oust, oust!" he yelled, beckoning to Askia.

What on earth does that mean? Askia thought.

Tlupic looked quite the comical sight, stomping his feet on the ground hissing and snarling, typical of the Geck'tek language. Tlupic paced the room, trying to remember the words Ürbon had taught him, if only he had actually focused during his lessons. After a while he gave up, grabbed on to Askia's robes calmly but forcefully, and led him out the tent. Askia had barely enough time to grab his sword and staff. Fortunately the dwarves had left them leaning to the side of the tent and ready to sell. Weapons like that could catch a hefty price.

Tlupic led Askia out into the camp and as they moved along, the screams and shouts grew to full volume. The heat from the fires spreading onto the tents and banners blew onto Askia. Askia and Tlupic stepped into puddles of blood as they walked through the carnage. The corpses dotting the mud were not only of dwarves; human bodies also lay on the floor. But by getting a closer look they could tell that these were not ordinary humans. They had long sharp teeth that reminded Askia of Asherai, the friendly skeleton they met in the crypt. But that night demon was friendly, the rest of his brethren were notoriously not.

"Vampires? No, no, not vampires!" Askia yelled out, as a decomposed face jumped out right in front of Askia. Its mouth was hanging open and shrieking, lined with rows of long teeth. Its breath wreaked of blood and decaying bodies.

Its red eyes hungered so obsessively for Askia that it didn't notice the spear Tlupic hurled at it, striking the vampire in the chest, killing it on the spot. Tlupic retrieved his spear, and turned to reassure Askia, but the pilgrim had already run off.

Askia ran through the burning campsite, havoc and death all around him. The shrieks of dwarves dragged away by ghastly monsters rang through the night air. There were undead creatures of all forms, each one more horrifying than the other. Some had maggots crawling out of their eyes, some had organs sprawled out and dragging behind them as they walked.

Askia could see dwarves fighting back. Groups organized into ranks to properly mount a defense. They organized themselves into a shielded phalanx, polearms extending out to greet the mass of decayed bodies and bones, but there were too many undead. They seemed to be under the control of a vampire, in long dark robes standing behind the undead army, its arms raised towards the shielded wall of dwarves.

The vampire cackled as the skeletons clashed into the dwarves like a tidal wave, heedlessly stepping into the dwarven halberds and spears. Beside the cackling vampire stood another night demon, wearing crimson-red armour. He didn't seem amused by the chaos. Wielding a fiery red sword, he lazily parried and lunged at any who dared to fight him, dispatching his opponents with contemptuous ease. This vampire's sword and red armor were familiar to Askia, who stood, staring at the battle taking place. He was almost captivated by the mercilessness and complete disregard for life with which both sides fought. His mind snapped back to reality when he heard a rattle of bones approaching behind him.

Askia turned, horrified and frozen, yet, swallowing his fear and gripping his sword determinedly, struck out at the undead skeleton. Staff and sword in either hand, his movements felt unlike his own, like some external force was guiding his strikes. His weapons glowed blue like a beacon and egged him onwards, guiding him through the dark.

***

Galadar parried yet another strike from another dwarf. His movements were almost instinctive, nothing stood a chance. His speed and strength unmatched; any who had the nerve to approach him met with swift death.

Blood Serpents always had the worst time in battle. They were so dangerous and fearsome that nothing was challenging, while other vampire orders jumped gleefully into the fray. Galadar had seen the gruesome power of Bloodmancers, with a flick of the wrist they made dwarves fall to their knees. Their blood erupting from within their veins as they fell to the ground dead, bloated and purple, turned to nothing but sacks of blood. The vampires smiled as they unleashed their blood magic upon their enemies, power they had learned through centuries of studying ancient books held within their extensive libraries.

The Plaguemancer's had their own strategies; driving walls of undead forward, the sheer force of numbers overwhelming even the strongest dwarves, whose ancient tactics were of no use, their spears breaking once bodies stuck and piled onto the shaft.

Yet, for Galadar there was no amusement to be had, with lightning speed and volatile strength, a few strikes and the opponent lay dead. He scoured the field for a worthy foe, something to make the night memorable. As beside him willed another wave of undead to crash into a dwarven phalanx, a blue glow caught the Blood serpent's eye. Behind the dwarven ranks, a robed human dispatched a skeleton, his staff and sword glowing in his grasp. His movements were determined and fluid, like those of a skilled and experienced fighter. For the first time that night, Galadar smiled; cutting himself a path through the fray to get to the robed figure. He did not care what stood in his way, be it dwarf or undead. Finally, a worthy opponent was revealed, finally he had found a promising fight; something to draw out his skill in battle.

There was no end to the carnage, no matter how far Askia ran, hacking and killing as he went. All around him he could see the bloody and ruthless realities of battle. Corpses were littered around the smoldering tents, ash wafted through the air; creating a hazy mist. Creatures of different origin clashed and fought with dwarves, there was no end to the madness. Askia looked around frantically between bouts of fighting, trying to see any familiar face from the ensuing chaos. In the distance, a large figure fought a group of dwarves and undead alike.

"Ürbon! Ürbon!" Askia renewed his pace, trying to get to the Jödmun, his staff and sword paving a path before him. Askia shouted once more, but the Jödmun could not hear him over the sounds of battle. Askia whimpered as Ürbon charged away and out of sight.

Suddenly a figure jumped out before him, brandishing a fiery red sword. Askia had seen this one; it was one of the vampires who stood behind the wave of undead, standing back as their minions crashed into a dwarven phalanx. He recognized its red armor, that of the Blood Serpent order. Asherai had been one of them, so he knew what deadly skill these vampires possessed.

This was not some simple skeleton, like those Askia so easily dispatched. This was a battle-seasoned warrior, and he moved like one made for fighting, his footsteps nimble over the muddy soil. Though dwarves and undead fought around them, his red eyes were on the robed priest before him.

He moved like lightning, his sword a blur. Askia stooped back and parried, his face contorting in fear and pain as the reverberation of their blades crossing stung his fingers. Galadar saw the hesitation in his movements and frowned in disappointment; this was no swordsman.

The pain in Askia's grip subsided, and he raised his sword once more, gathering whatever confidence he could muster. He went on the offensive, attacking the vampire to the best of his ability, yet his opponent deflected his blows with ease. Askia was often leaving his defense wide open as he tried to gain the upper hand, his arms arcing wide, to and fro, his legs and body left defenseless. Galadar danced around him, parrying every blow, he had spent so much effort getting to this 'worthy opponent' he might as well make it last. Askia gave one final lunge, putting all his weight into the blow, yet at the last moment, as the two swords were about to meet, the night demon side-stepped, and Askia slipped through the mud onto the ground. Galadar looked at the pitiful sight, baring his teeth; this one can't even keep his footing.

Dazed though he was, and surprised to still be alive, Askia frantically grabbed his sword, its blue glow gone and hilt caked in mud. He fearfully stood back up, looking into the vampires red eyes. Galadar stepped forward, and Askia stepped back. He did not know what to do. Whether he ran or stood his ground, he was still about to die. Galadar sensed the fear and hesitation, and unleashed a flurry of strikes, his blade whistling in the hazy air. Askia parried what he could, and felt a jolt of pain engulf him. He saw the vampire cease his offensive and step away, disappearing from Askia's darkening vision.

The Sonasian suddenly realized how uncontrollably freezing he was in the night air. He shivered violently, looking around him; such madness, such chaos. Yet something caught his eye, something familiar. He looked down at the mud on his right and saw a hand, one he could easily recognize, for it was his own; his sword limply in its grip. As he stared down at his fallen limb, dumbfounded, a sharp pain erupted in the back of his head. He fell limply, the ground rushing up towards him, unconscious before he hit the ground.

***

With a mighty shake of his body, the undeads and skeletons fell around him. They grabbed onto the Jödmun, clawing their way up to his shoulders, trying to bring his massive bulk down. They stayed away from his front, frightful of the immense axe sweeping them away like ants. The vampire that controlled the undead willed them only to approach the Jödmun's back. Ürbon grabbed at those climbing their way up, throwing them down onto the mud, their bodies snapping and ripping apart as they crashed to the ground. The vampire was in his sights, red eyed and mouth apart in a black smile, his teeth like shards of obsidian. The Jödmun swiped to and fro whenever there were no undead weighing him down, trying to get to the vampire, Perturiel the Black. He hadn't gained much ground, the more undead he threw down, the more would appear, stabbing at his body, pricking him like bees.

Ürbon was tiring from the assault, when a familiar body jumped upon him, nimbly maneuvering upon his shoulders, kicking off the undead, securing his turf.

"My spot!" Tlupic hissed, lunging his spear into an undead's skull, its cranium shattering from the impact and scattering to the ground.

Ürbon took this chance to charge forward, only to find himself once again surrounded. Tlupic had found Ürbon earlier; they made a point not to stray too far from each other in the battle. Tlupic had the least issue with moving around, able to quickly jump and weave, rapidly avoiding harm. His size and agility were proving to be useful. Yet, he was beginning to feel the hopelessness of the battle; there was no end to the swarm of bodies, overwhelming even the Jödmun.

Ürbon knew he would eventually succumb to the weight. Tlupic, trying hard as he might, could only deal with one foe at a time. His spears were designed for fighting at a distance, not in such close quarters. The Jödmun's knees buckled, against his will, the weight dragging him down. He tried steadying himself with the hilt of his axe. For Perturiel, this was precisely what he was waiting for.

The giant dropped to the ground, unable to stand upright, his arms bracing him against the mud, making him unable to sweep the area in front of him. Ürbon saw the wave of undead surge forward, charging into the empty space, engulfing the Jödmun. They stifled his breathing, the mass of skeletons taking up every inch of space. Ürbon gasped for air, flailing wildly, trying to get them off. Tlupic seemed to be fighting on a sea of bodies; the giant's back acting as a moving island.

The Jödmun's field of vision disappeared as undead filled every gap, when out of nowhere came a stream of light. It illuminated everything around him; washing over the mass and turning them into ash. Ürbon, his vision now clear and body free, stood back up with Tlupic still upon his shoulder. Free to look up at the sky, Ürbon saw a winged stream of light soaring through the black night.

***

Stixerio thundered past like a gust of wind, ears pricked and excited, his rider leading him on. Her violet eyes glanced at Tlupic and the Jödmun, then latched onto Perturiel.

The vampire scowled at the turn of events, but he himself would not be defeated so easily. He withdrew his weapons, a small sword in his right hand and a bullwhip in his left. Maka urged Stixerio onwards, her robe billowing behind her. She raised her khopeshes towards Perturiel, the blades glowing with a magnificent light. Perturiel cracked his whip, swirling it around his head and took aim at Stixerio's leg. He cracked the whip into the striding horse, bruising its fetlock. Losing his footing from the sudden pain, Stixerio stumbled down. Perturiel assumed this sudden strike would throw Maka off her horse, yet she followed Stixerio's stumbling motion, remaining unfazed in the saddle as her steed regained his footing.

Maka aimed her sword at the vampire, a beam of light streaking out to his hand, knocking the bullwhip out of his grip. He recoiled, his arm in pain, then, gripping his short sword with both hands, rushed to the horse. Stixerio reared up and flailed his forelegs at the vampire, who dodged and swerved around. Finding himself at the horse's flank, Perturiel slashed upwards. The action was met with Maka's blade; the sword didn't strike her blade, and instead bounced off as if a force shielded the beaming weapon. Maka urged her horse forward, its strong hind legs launching off the ground, kicking out at Perturiel.

The vampire had never seen such horsemanship before, the horse not only a mount but a weapon, like a soldier defending its master. He was knocked backwards, as the two hind legs hit him with full force; he wheeled in the air but landed upright, again in fighting pose. This did not matter to Maka, she had him precisely where she wanted him. Perturiel charged towards Maka, but cried out as a winged figure flew down from above and grabbed him, throwing the vampire off into the distance.

"What, by the light of Osharis, did you just do?" Maka let out a furious scowl at Hydrulian, glaring at him with violet eyes.

"Discarded those who would dare cross you, Princess." The illuminated figure gave a slight bow, hand loosely tucked under his wings. Though this did not lighten Maka's mood, the Sentriel kept his calm demeanor, beaming with pride at the quick work he made of Perturiel.

"And now that I couldn't destroy him entirely, I suppose either tomorrow or the next he'll be back with moree vampires to slit our throats." She retorted.

"I don't believe that will happen, O' fearsome Lioness." A smirk crossed Hydrulian's lips, erupting in an uncontrollable giggle. He composed himself as Maka scowled once more.

"How can you be so sure of this?" Ürbon had slowly fought his way to Maka; reaching her once Hydrulian had swooped down and tossed Perturiel away.

This question seemed to be a wrong choice of words as Hydrulian yet again erupted in a bout of giggles; jumping up and down and hopping around as he flapped his wings erratically. "Because he won't want to tell anyone of course!" the Sentriel replied, continuing his little dance.

"What?"

"You mortals, confined to only standing on soil," he said, suddenly stopping his movements and pointing outwards of camp "There's a massive river *right there!*"

Maka wasn't the only one to have lost her patience now; Ürbon had had enough of the pointless conversation. Clearly Hydrulian had no real answer for any of their questions. "We have to get out of the camp, fast."

Though they had achieved a small window of respite, the sound of battle still reverberated around them.

"Exactly! There are boats there too, they're much faster than walking...not as fast as flying though..." Hydrulian called to Ürbon, the Jödmun had started to walk further inland, but with the promise of boats, directed the group towards the river. Hydrulian leapt into the sky, his metal wings launching him upwards. He swirled around Maka for a moment, who didn't pay him any mind, and then, he glided towards the river outside of the camp.

"We'll head there as soon as we find Askia" said Ürbon.

Tlupic shook his head, "Askia is not coming," was all he said.

"What do you mean?" Ürbon looked down at the small Geck'tek, bewildered.

"The vampires killed him." Tlupic said, "I saw him lying motionless in the mud."

At the news of Askia's death a fiery rage took over Ürbon.

"You were supposed to get him out of the tent and protect him!" He yelled down at Tlupic, who could not meet Ürbon's gaze.

"We don't have time for this." Said Maka swiftly, pointing to a nearby clash between the dwarves and vampires, close enough to splinter off and get their party involved.

Gathering his anger for another day, Ürbon roughly grabbed Tlupic, put him on his shoulder and they moved away from the scene towards the river-bed.

With the help of Hydrulian's swift cleansing and opening of a path, it did not take long for the group to reach the ships harbored on the shore.

"Right, let's get this over with," the giant said, seeing the size of the mighty ships. They were magnificent to behold, though covered in chains and having a sinister feel. Vessels this size needed an equally sizable crew, though that did not matter to the Jödmun, whose size and strength could outmatch any group of sailors. The rest of the group climbed on board, letting down a plank for Maka to bring up her horse. The Jödmun held his axe tightly, ready to sever the chain nailed deep into the sand anchoring the ship to the beach. With one hefty swing of his axe, he severed the chain.

The sound reverberated across the beach, vibrating the sand and rippling the water. Though the sand ceased vibrating, the water did not, the waves growing larger still, bubbling and frothing. It seemed the rushing waters would grow as tall as the ship itself. Yet Ürbon quickly realized that this was no wave at all, but something far, far worse.

It seemed the vampires had not left their ships unattended out of negligence; indeed they had not left them unattended at all. The monster was gigantic, its head the size of the ship's hull. Its body was covered in a metallic plate, colored red with the symbol of the Blood Serpent clan. Though the symbol could have been a representation of the monster itself, the real thing was much more terrifying. It paid no attention to those already on the boat, instead focusing on the one who severed the chain — Ürbon.

Ürbon didn't wait for the monster to fully reveal itself; he was too tired of all of this nonsense. He tightened his grip on his axe and, with a look of determination, roared and charged at the monster. He slashed and hacked at whatever part of the serpent he could reach, though he inflicted no wounds to the creature, the metallic armor encasing it deflecting all of his blows. The monster's head flailed and its mouth snapped at air trying to catch the Jödmun.

"Tlupic, throw me a spear!" Ürbon had an idea; and grabbed the spear in midair, mostly thanks to the Geck'tek's astonishing aim. The Jödmun stood on the damp sand as the serpent's head veered towards him, its mouth wide open and snarling. The monster snapped at Ürbon, and raised its head, leaving only a dent in the sand where the giant had just stood. Those on board the ship gasped and rushed to railing, but stopped in their tracks, clutching their heads as a screech reverberated through the shoreline.

The Jödmun, now inside the monster's mouth, leaned onto one of its fangs with his elbow, weapon in each hand, dearly hoping not to fall into its gullet. Its tongue was slippery and provided no stable footing; Ürbon didn't know how long he'd be able to keep from falling. He only had one chance to get this right, his aim and strike would have to be perfect, otherwise he'd be serpent-food.

He grabbed onto Tlupic's spear and looked towards the roof of the mouth; he hurled the spear, trying to get the angle straight down. As the point hit the sensitive gums, the monster let out a shrieking cry, opening its mouth wide.

Ürbon jumped out of the serpent's mouth and crashed onto the beach, he had lost Tlupic's spear, but still held his trusty axe. The beast flailed its head wildly, screeching continuously, it could not close its mouth, or even move its tongue. Ürbon looked at the creature, thrashing and screaming. Until, in its maddened agony, it crashed its head into the sand, the force closing its mouth shut, killing it instantly. It's great head lay motionless, water lapping at its coiling body that extended deep into the depths. Ürbon approached the awkwardly bent jaw, the shaft of Tlupic's spear jutting out through the tooth gaps. With a few mighty heaves, he pulled the spear out, covered in blood and bits of flesh. With one last look at the magnificent creature, previously enraged yet now peacefully at rest, he walked up to the ship to join the others.

It didn't take long for them to get underway. Ürbon was pretty much sailing the vessel by himself, he had found the rest quite useless at simple tasks and explaining things over and over again proved more exhausting than fighting multiple of those serpents would have. But the winds were kind and swept the ship swiftly out to open water, allowing the Jödmun a few moments of rest.

The sun was rising now, bringing with it a new day, finally putting the entire night's ordeal in the past, though leaving Askia behind with it.

Tlupic had taken it badly, believing the loss of his friend to be his own fault. After all, he was meant to protect Askia and lead him out of the chaotic camp. But, by the time he had found the pilgrim after he had fled, it was too late. His friend had already been killed by either a dwarf or a vampire. Seeing him lying in the mud there was only one thing left for Tlupic to do and he returned back to Ürbon as quickly as possible, to make sure he would not lose another friend.

"Look, when you come to my age, you'll realize none of that stuff matters anyway," Hydrulian attempted, crudely, to comfort the Geck'tek, but he would have none of it. Hissing aggressively, he stomped down into the cabins, seeking solitude. Hydrulian, puzzled at the response, glanced at Maka, who responded with a glare and a scoff in his direction rather than the lizard. The Sentriel ignored it and went into another bout of talking to himself, this time about the rashness of mortals.

Ürbon observed them from the quarterdeck, seeing the self absorption of Hydrulian and Maka. He looked back from behind the hull, towards the disappearing shoreline from which they had just made their escape. He hoped the vampires would not return to retrieve their stolen ship.

Chapter 11:
The Depths of Sorrow

Ürbon looked at the white waves of the Titan Divide. Where yesterday he saw wonder, he now only saw failure. He saw his ship *The North Wind* untended, he saw his shield brothers chained, he saw Askia gone. He had failed them all. He looked down at his body covered in carved runes that spoke of his great achievements and past adventures and turned to Bjarl, the mighty axe resting on the deck, knowing he was undeserving of them. He gazed at his blood-covered hands and saw his own failure reflected at him in crimson.

Ürbon would have continued his brooding if it were not for Hydrulian barging in.

"You're still thinking about that mortal? Really? We are immortals. Come on, how old are you? He would have died anyway within the blink of an eye."

Ürbon ignored the fact that Hydrulian spoke the truth. He would have outlived Askia a hundred times over, no matter the situation.

But he didn't care.

He grabbed the Sentriel by his wing and shoved him into the deck of the ship.

"Okay big guy. I'll buy you a new pet once we get to the island."

Ürbon was having none of it. He growled as he pushed the Sentriel more forcefully. "I already killed one immortal today. Would you like me to raise that number to two?"

Both of them eyed the limp body of the now-dead vampire. Seaweed was still clinging to its robe after its short dip from being thrown by Hydrulian into the river.

Hydrulian's only answer was a strained laugh, so Ürbon launched him towards the water, allowing himself a brief, satisfied grunt as he disappeared below the surface. The Sentriel remained submerged for a few seconds before he eventually rose up, cackling madly before disappearing into the sky.

***

Tlupic observed the exchange with mild annoyance that Ürbon hadn't punished the Sentriel for that snide remark. He was in a sour mood. He had grown attached to Askia, even if he was a magic-using heretic. He had also failed in his promise to Asherai; he had failed to protect him. Tlupic mourned his loss at the hands of the despicable night creatures, but from what the black-fanged monster had told them, they would not see their companion again. Though the vampire was now dead, at the hands of Ürbon, he could still hear the night demon's cocky voice in his mind.

***

Tlupic was still running on adrenaline from the battle when it happened. The battlefield was already behind them and he could see the fading smoke dissipating against the rising sun. It was during this moment of quiet when Hydrulian flew down below the ship's railing, towards the water and to everyone's surprise brought up the same vampire he had flung across camp. The night demon was flailing madly, trying to break free. Hydrulian dumped him onto the deck with a shove, the monster tripping over his seaweed covered robe and onto the wood.

"I may have misjudged our violent friend's stupidity. He's been trying to climb up onto our ship for some time now."

Ürbon wasted no time grabbing the fiend and tying him to the mast with whatever rope was lying around.

"You're going to answer my questions, or die a painful death." He grumbled. Though he said these words calmly, his voice dripped with hatred.

"If you kill me, my clan will destroy all of you," the vampire said.

"A risk we'll have to take." Ürbon said, "There was a human with us, with a staff and scimitar, what happened to him?"

"The one with the blue glow?" the vampire asked and then added mockingly. "Galadar made quick work of him. He almost looked disappointed with how easily your friend was defeated. Perhaps the taste of him won't be so unfortunate."

"He still lives?" Tlupic said, bounding across the deck to the vampire.

"I saw him being dragged out of camp with the other slaves." The vampire cackled. "We only take those who are still alive after a raid. Only savages would eat rotten meat and drink soured blood."

Tlupic turned towards Ürbon, "We have to go back and rescue him!"

At this the vampires cackle rose in volume, "He's probably already dead, after losing his hand, he'll be the first pick from the cattle to reach the table."

"Not if you help us do so." Ürbon growled, "And if you don't, we'll make sure you wish you did," with a fierce grip he took hold of Bjarl.

"I will never betray my brethren." The vampire's cackle died down, and he spat blood onto the wooden deck. "Do what you want to me, it will get you nowhere. My only regret in my life is that I will not be there to savor the taste of your weak and pitiful friend."

The vampire burst out in another fit of mad cackles, only rising higher as Ürbon raised Bjarl in a rage. He was barely thinking straight as he struck at the vampire's neck with a mighty stroke. Its hideous laughter dying down as its head rolled across the blood soaked wooden floor.

Tlupic knew his friend was not well. He often spoke of his imprisoned brothers and how he missed them, but he had never seen him like this. He knew something had to be done.

He began climbing the mast of the ship so as to be at eye level with the giant. "Azmekui, we need to talk."

After a brief moment of pure nothingness, Ürbon spoke. "What is it?" His voice was colder than normal, as if he was not fully in this world.

"You are not well. You cannot continue like this. You have the Snake Madness like many of my clanmates that lose somebody close to them."

Now Ürbon turned to look at him with confusion written across his stone face.

"You are silent and unpredictable, ready to attack indiscriminately at any moment." Tlupic continued. "Perhaps if we had a funeral for Askia, it would help you."

"Funeral..." Ürbon scoffed. "I have not lost anybody truly close to me in at least four centuries..."

The following silence was interrupted by Maka. "When one of us dies, their organs are removed and put in jars. Their body is then covered in sacred bandages. Then they are given a golden funerary mask and put in a sarcophagus. It is then put in the tomb of their family or in a pyramid if they are important enough."

Tlupic felt a pang of homesickness. "We too wrap our dead in bandages. They are then given bone funeral armor and put in the Cave of the Ancestors."

Ürbon silently stared at the foamy water for a moment before speaking. "In my home, each clan had its own traditions. Well, they did before the Mountain Birth. I do not know if any of us has been lost ever since. In our clan, we would build a burial boat for the dead and place one item of great importance to the deceased and a token of their enemies, be it from a great hunt or a rival, and send him out to sea to be burned.

"I remember when I was young, they put a door in the burial boat of my great-uncle Hardran the Stubborn. He made that door as a gift for his wife. No matter how many times he fixed it, the damned thing always got stuck again. It infuriated him to no end. Fortunately for him, grand-aunt Anma was always amused by it. That stupid door was both his greatest enemy and one of his most personal items...but I do not know any Sonasian funerary customs. Maka do you?"

The Princess of Oshiris was startled for a second before wrestling her features back into an impenetrable mask. "I do not. We do not care about the customs of trespassers. I only know that the Teshars make small mounds of bones and put their dead inside of them. They sometimes color them with paint made of sulfur and blood or tie strips of cloth to the bones, but the people of the far sands never venture deep enough in our lands to die and still have the luxury of a proper burial."

"So we have no idea how to honor him as his own people would." Ürbon said. "And we cannot honor him by the customs of our own. We can't even do a standard burial at sea as we do not have his body or something of his to give."

"But we can pray for him," Tlupic interjected, but he was quickly corrected by his stone companion.

"Ha, no. We go to a tavern, get completely drunk, tell stories about him, and if by the end of the night, we're sober enough, then we pray for him."

"I cannot get drunk. My people need only to be in the presence of gold to sustain themselves, the last *gift* of the God of Greed." Said Maka.

"Aye, I understand the feeling. After the Mountain Birth, normal alcohol no longer had an effect on us, but we found a way. If we find a brewery and a smith then I will make you some Jödmun Fire Mead. That will surely knock you down like an avalanche, if it doesn't kill you. But by Yanvild, I could use a drink myself."

Tlupic was pleased to see his friend more lively, but now they had to deal with the situation at hand. "So what do we do now?" the Geck'tek asked Ürbon.

"Now? We go to Venova, fetch the artifact for the golden boy, and then we find a different path. Hopefully one very far from him and very close to my ship and crew. But first, dawn is almost upon us and with our current wind, we should arrive at the island by sundown. Vampires can make good ships when they want to, so for now, you rest. Lioness, you can help me with tying up some ropes and following my instructions."

"I am a princess. You do not get to command me!" Maka said, stamping her foot and looking at Ürbon with her eyes ablaze before gesturing to Tlupic and adding "Why doesn't the lizard contribute?"

"Do you know how to use a ship? I think not. That makes me the captain and as long as I am the captain, you obey my orders. Tlupic, go and rest underneath. You've had a couple of long days and nights, especially for somebody who needs to sleep and eat. Speaking of which, help yourselves to some of the slave gruels. I know it's...well...slave food. But we don't have anything else."

Tlupic went under the deck, feeling better knowing that his partner no longer had the Snake Madness. Once down in the cargo hold, he had little trouble with the darkness, and quickly made himself at home. Deliberately ignoring the empty chains and cages, as well as the bottles obviously filled with blood, he focused on finding this gruel thing that Ürbon mentioned.

Finally, he found some sort of stew made with water seeds and other plants that transformed into a strange grey paste. Surprisingly, it did not taste as terrible as he would have thought. It was definitely better than the meals his tribe gave to their sacrifices, but he would have still preferred fresh meat. Once he was full, he drank from a water skin found next to the slave food and laid down on the wooden floor, closing his eyes for some much-needed rest.

***

Ürbon decided to simply let his mind go blank and be consumed by the water churning beneath the ship. It helped to keep his mind from spiraling into a foul mood. He started to chant a Jödmun sailing shanty.

"What will we do with a drunk maldoran?

What will we do with a drunk maldoran?

What will we do with a drunk maldoran?

Early in the morning!

Run run to collect the buckets,

Run run to collect the buckets,

Run run to collect the buckets,

Early in the morning!

What will we do with a drunk maldoran?

What will we do with a drunk maldoran?

What will we do with a drunk maldoran?

Early in the morning!

Steal his gold and toss it in the ocean,

Steal his gold and toss it in the ocean,

Steal his gold and toss it in the ocean,

Early in the morning!

..."

As his mind wandered and the hours passed, he realized he could see the majestic buildings of Venova ahead. The sparkling white stone buildings highlighted its presence against the blue sky. The navy could also be seen at the harbor, battle-ready ships prepared to repel any pirates or unwelcome visitors. Ürbon called out for the others to be ready, and steeled his nerves for the undoubtedly long conversation that would ensue.

As soon as the Venovan ships spotted them, they formed into a defensive half-circle and slowly approached the lone vessel. Ürbon felt as if something was wrong with this situation, as did his companions, who looked warily at the incoming fleet. Before he could even say anything, the incoming ships each shot out a jet of liquid flames, ejected out of a strange metal contraption at the helm of their ships.

With mere seconds to act, Ürbon threw his companions into the water before being hit with the full force of the blast. As he sank into the depths, the alchemical flames still hugged his form and Ürbon sank into a world of darkness.

***

Ürbon rose from the cold water with a cry. He looked at the warm sun while he focused on breathing, glaring at his assailant upon the shore as he began walking out of the water. The one that was responsible for his current situation laughed uncontrollably as he rested on the shore of the lake next to a campfire.

Sigard, his brother in all but blood, was his best friend ever since they were children. They had both grown up in Pongül, a small settlement hidden by the Lost Crag mountains and the Moon Forest, and the dumb bastard had pushed him into the freezing lake.

When he finally got out, he was greeted by a warm stew and a laughing friend. He laughed with him, took the stew, and pushed him into the lake.

The world faded to black once more.

***

Ürbon cried out in fury. He lunged for the Beast of the Moon Forest, ignoring his own wounds as he raised his shield and struck down with his sword at the foul beast. Behind him, Sigard clutched his wounded leg with one arm and a hunting spear with the other.

The Beast had only appeared a month ago. Still it had already killed two of their people, and its third victim died only a few days after being rescued, the badly wounded survivor describing a monster they had never heard of before.

The horrid creature was bigger than both Jödmun, covered in white scales white white tufts of fur in between. It had eight clawed paws and seemed capable of using the first four as arms while the others were used as legs. Its thick tail had four sharp spikes that had mangled Sigard's leg, its long jaw and flat face reminding him of that animal the humans called a crocodile, only with the snout of a pig.

But none of that was too troubling, even if they had never heard of anything remotely similar to it on their island — or even outside of it. The truly worrying thing about the monster in front of them was not only its endless bloodlust, but its ability to heal itself rapidly. Steel, rocks, wood, and fire had failed to harm it permanently. They had even used the poison of a Snow Snake, but no matter how large or grievous the wound, it would always be back up on its feet in a heartbeat. Even when they sliced off its tail, it had just regrown — that was how Sigard's leg had been mangled.

Both of them knew that unless something unexpected happened, this would be the end for them. Ürbon wouldn't leave without Sigard, and even if he carried him, they would still be too slow to outrun the beast.

He looked at the dark forest around them in a panic, and for a second, he thought he saw two golden eyes looking at him from the darkness.

***

When Ürbon woke from his memories, he was still underwater and noticed that his hands were in a death grip around Bjarl, despite him not remembering grabbing the axe. Although the flames that enveloped him had died out, he could still see the burning carcass of their stolen ship above the water. Only then did he see Tlupic tugging his arm. He gestured for him to follow and then swam in the direction the others had probably gone. While the Jödmun could not swim with them, he could easily walk on the seafloor, though it was a slow progress.

The long walk gave him time to sort out his thoughts, and he reasoned why the Venovans would have attacked so ruthlessly. Sure, he had never actually talked to them, but still, attacking without warning was a bit excessive, even in his opinion. What troubled him more were the memories that flooded his mind after the flames had struck him. Sigard was his friend. The two had been raised together, ever since Sigard's parents had died fighting in the War of the Wall against the demons.

The two young Jödmun had a dream of building a ship and sailing off to acquire fame and fortune. But they would never travel the world together, as Sigard sacrificed his life defending Ürbon from an attack from the Beast of the Moon Forest. Ürbon used that same moment to attack and kill the Demon that had created the Beast. When the Demon died, so did his Beast, but it was too late for Sigard. When Ürbon finally returned to his village, they were hailed as heroes. Sigard was given a proper burial, the last Jödmun burial Ürbon would ever see. In time people forgot about Sigard, since only a few months later the Mountain Birth happened, turning them all into what they were now. That's when Ürbon decided he had to fulfill his promise. So Ürbon and his father built *the North Wind*, then he formed a crew out of his most talented and trusted friends and set sail, never setting foot on the Isle of Fusterig again.

All thoughts of the past left him as soon as his feet touched dry land. He joined an exhausted Tlupic on the sands, as well as a wet Maka, a very amused Hydrulian, and a creepy horse. Maka was less than pleased, and she glared at Ürbon while tending to Stixerio.

"What was that?" she said. "I thought you would be able to talk to them!"

"I thought so as well. Obviously we were both mistaken," the Jödmun replied.

Hydulian stood in between them and addressed the lioness. "My lady princess, allow me to fix your current situation."

With a flick of his finger and a small spark, Maka and Stixerio were now completely dry, leaving Ürbon and Tlupic still completely soaked. "Tadaaaa!"

Tlupic decided to interrupt and change the subject.

"Where are we now?" He asked.

Ürbon, unable to answer the question, took a moment to get a better look at their surroundings. From the position of the setting sun, he could spot grey mountains faraway to their east, and a deep lush forest of pines and other trees.

"Hmm, let me think. There are mountains to the east and to the west, and the Inner Sea is to the south. We could be either in the kingdoms of Artaria or Ravenburg. Both are good places to be." The Jödmun said. "We only need to walk along the shore to find a friendly town, and from there we can find some answers."

Having successfully shifted Ürbon's attention, Tlupic continued with the next question. "So where to? East or west?"

"If we are in Artaria and we go too far west, then we will end up in the desert, again. If we are in Ravenburg and we go too far east, we will end up in the Wasted Coast, which is full of orcs and brigands. Neither are particularly good places to be, but I've had more than enough of deserts. So we'll go east."

The Jödmun then looked at the Sentriel. "I don't suppose you could just scout ahead and tell us."

Hydulian smiled at the Jödmun and turned invisible, even though they could clearly see his footsteps next to theirs.

After only a short while, they spotted the mouth of a wide river and a small fishing pier that doubled as a makeshift bridge. Ürbon chose not to use it as it would crumble under his weight. Next to the pier, a small rowing boat was tied. Taking a closer look, they saw a bucket of fish thrown down to the ground. Farther ahead, they could see a man on a rowboat furiously rowing up the river and away from them, in spite of the strong currents.

With no other clues of civilized life, they followed the river bordering a dark forest, and were quite surprised to eventually see a village up ahead. It was a humble settlement, though it had sturdy-looking wooden palisades. It was obvious that it was abandoned and dilapidated, as if nobody had touched it for some time. The buildings themselves were made predominantly of wood and only a few had stone foundations, and all the roofs were made of thatch, some blown off by heavy winds.

The village had proper cobblestone roads, and after walking a bit more, they were surprised when they spotted another wall, this one larger and sturdier. They found a wooden gate and with ease Ürbon forced it open, breaking the wooden planks used to protect it with a single sweep of Bjarl.

It seemed the village had sprung up around the road and the bridge, people drawn by trade and the promise of wealth. Around a large well, a center square of sorts had formed, complete with a surprisingly large market, a church, and something that looked like a town hall. From there they could clearly see a castle on a hill overlooking the village.

But the most curious thing was that it was completely empty, even though the goods in the market, as well as the fish, looked fresh. Yet there was no one outside. Tlupic's keen senses were able to detect the smell of sweat and fear all around them, inside the houses. Thankfully for them and the residents of this place, he could not sense any immediate magic.

Only after Ürbon called for their hidden viewers to come out did a large mob of human peasants appear, wielding farming tools and makeshift weapons. They quickly surrounded the unimpressed group of travelers. After the wave of infantry, a group of archers came out from their hiding spots on top of the roofs, and nocking their bows. The peasants were shouting in a thick tongue that Ürbon barely understood at all. It was either Ravenspeak or southern Artarian.

He could hear Hydrulian giggle unseen beside him. While Maka, seated in a queenly manner upon Stixerio, looked entirely uninterested in the assorted rabble around them, and had already unsheathed her swords. Tlupic seemed to have the same idea and was already mentally marking the locations of all the archers.

Ürbon, who was as close to tired as a Jödmun could get, decided to intervene before the little village turned into a little pile of ash.

"We are not here to harm you." He said.

As if on cue, a small group of mounted knights made their way to the front of the nervous mob, weapons drawn. Thankfully, their leader spoke the Common Tongue.

"As Knight-Captain of the city of Clavenstil, I hereby hold you under arrest by order of the Markgraf Reinhold Westermann. Surrender yourselves to the law of King Odwin van Ravestern of the kingdom of Ravenburg, horrid beasts!"

Ürbon took one quick glance at the scared peasants and the nervous looks of the knights and made a choice. "We surrender," he said.

The entire town and even his companions gave him a bewildered look.

Tlupic groaned, Stixerio neighed to show his dissatisfaction, Hydrulian audibly smacked his forehead, while all Maka could do was say.

"By Dedpheker, not again."

The villagers and knights were suitably surprised at the turn of events.

"G-good, good choice, creature. The punishment of the law shall be swift. You must relinquish your weapons and any other items." The captain stammered.

But Ürbon surprised everyone yet again. "No, I don't think I will."

"But..."

"No buts. I'm going with you as a show of good faith. Now take us to the castle."

The knights looked at each other nervously. Regardless of their doubt, they accepted, and led the strange group to the castle, firmly seated on a large hilltop.

Once inside, they were directed to the dungeons. None of the jail cells were large enough to comfortably hold the Jödmun, and none of his companions were at all willing to enter them. So the weary knights decided to leave them just outside the gates and increase the number of guards, leaving ten in total to watch them.

Ürbon sat down on the cold stone floor, leaned Bjarl against the wall, and reached for his journal. He was pleased to see the water protection enchantment had worked perfectly. The pages turned magically, as they had before, bringing a smile to his face. The page it landed on had a list of all the enchantments that he had placed on it.

-*Infinite pages.*

-*Water protection.*

-*Fire protection.*

-*Time degradation protection.*

-*Increased durability.*

-*The ability to allow the reader to find the page he desired the most.*

-*The ability to make certain pages "locked" so that only the owner may access them.*

The enchantment had cost him much time and coin but they had been worth it. He'd had this journal ever since he was a child. It had been a gift from his mother, though back then, the journal was a normal black book made for a young boy with vague dreams of adventure and heroism. In those days he still had the need for sleep and his mother was still alive. He closed the journal before it changed pages and his mood soured even more.

He looked around the dungeon and found nothing of note. It looked exactly like one would expect — cold stone, moss, the odd torture tool. Ürbon saw Maka resting against Stixerio. Tlupic was taking in his surrounding area and Hydrulian was...talking to someone?

Indeed, he had cast off his invisibility and had begun talking to a human. Though the guards did not seem to notice the large humanoid dressed in exorbitant golden clothing, with large metallic wings emanating a faint golden glow.

The human had blue eyes, long dirty brown hair, and the beginnings of a beard, as well as dirty clothing and boots made from seal leather, which was surprising as there were no seals even remotely close to here.

There were four jail cells in the dungeon. The dirty man shared a cell with a younger-looking human in peasant clothes. This human had black hair, green eyes and looked very tired, as well as anxious.

Rumbling snores could be heard in the other cell, as it housed a sleeping black-bearded dwarf.

The third cell housed a blue humanoid, with several aquatic features such as gills, webbed fingers and joints, as well as a few fins. It was the size of an average human and was only wearing rags, though it didn't seem to mind. Sitting in a corner of the same cell was a significantly smaller creature, which somehow simultaneously looked like a child and an elder. It had floppy ears like a dog, a large nose and eyes, its crooked yellow teeth peeking out of its mouth. It also had seven fingers on each hand and black greasy hairs growing sporadically over its entire body.

In the final cell, there was a Gataran. It was malnourished, but it's crocodilian head and large, strong body gave it away. Why it was here was a mystery, as there was a whole continent and ocean separating this area from the jungles of the Gatarans. Next to it was an ugly looking creature. Seven-feet tall and with pale skin, it was built like a warrior. Grey and white hair grew over its entire body, except for patches where there were many crisscrossing scars. It had a hugely squashed-looking face; it didn't have any nose, though it did have large bat-like ears.

Ürbon didn't recognize some of these other races, but he knew at least some of them should be the Artarian slave races that he had heard about. After a devastating famine, the population of these races had drastically declined in Artaria, leaving humans as the vast majority. The humans did what they often do, and took advantage of the situation. With relative ease they took over the realm and enslaved whatever was left of the remaining races.

He tried to focus on the conversation Hydulian was having, but was distracted when the pale-skinned brute started making a weird noise. It sounded halfway between a growl and a whistle. While he made that strange noise, his face contorted into an ugly frown, and he bared his sharp teeth at him. To anybody else, the display would have been intimidating. But to Ürbon, it just looked like a particularly ugly and hairy Jödmun child about to throw a temper tantrum.

The ugly thing was silenced once the Gataran placed a clawed hand upon his shoulder.

"Calm down, Tlog. You are half his size. You don't have to intimidate every single person you meet." He then turned to Ürbon and added apologetically. "Beggin' your pardon, please excuse him. Ever since his tongue was cut out, he's felt the need to prove himself."

The scarred creature made a grunt-like noise and relaxed, but he kept looking at the newcomers who didn't have a cell. The Gataran then looked up to address the strangers in the Common Tongue, though not without a heavy accent.

"Who are you all? I don't know your races. What did you do to end up here?"

Tlupic chose this moment to launch into a string of insults at a speed that the giant had trouble understanding. But he did catch the words, *heretic, slave, sacrifice*, and something about a *cow*. Weird, he didn't know that Tlupic knew what cows are. Ürbon once again glanced at the guards. They seemed to not have noticed the shouting despite being able to easily see Tlupic, which confirmed his belief that Hydrulian had placed some sort of charm on them.

The Gataran just looked on, confused at Tlupic's furious response.

"What is the small one saying?" he turned to Ürbon.

Now that did make Ürbon smile. "What is it, Gataran? You do not even know the language of your people?"

"Gataran?" it replied, now even more confused. "I am a Lazar. My name is Odyx. My people speak Artarian. That is our native tongue."

Ürbon almost didn't believe him, but then he remembered that long ago before Artaria existed, this territory belonged to the Empire of Artimus. Many records remain of that civilization, and they point out that it also had access to the sea, a real sea, and was renowned for having races shipped from all over the world to serve as pets and slaves.

"Then the gods must be amused, having two people so far apart that look identical." Ürbon scoffed. "To answer your question, we are travelers, evidently not very good ones since we always end up lost. That was our only crime. I don't believe you would recognize any of our races even if I told them to you, but I will provide you with an answer. I am a Jödmun and come from Fusterig, an island to the far north, so far in fact that it is perpetual winter there.

"My small friend is a Geck'tek. He comes from the marshes and jungles of the continent Aleasaric where everything is wet and green. The woman. Maka, is a Nebu-Gi, a warrior-princess of the golden desert. It is not too far from here, but her people prefer isolation. The annoying golden one is a Sentriel named Hydrulian. His homeland is far to the north and is now destroyed. Now tell me, Odyx, how did your friend lose his tongue?"

"We used to be slaves in an Artarian mine. He spoke up too much, complained too much and resisted too much. So they cut it out." Odyx replied.

"That sounds rather harsh..." Said Ürbon, thinking of ways to change the subject. "Who are the others? What grave sins have you committed to be here?"

"My friend here is called Tlog; he is a Northerner." Odyx said, introducing the other prisoners one by one. "My small friend is called Srikk, he is a Gar. Their kind is used in mines and crafting. My aquatic friend here is a Mys called Blueli. His species are enlisted in the defense of Lake Rhonis, a large lake in the middle of Artaria that goes both to the north and south, but they are just as much a slave to the Artarians as the rest of us. Aligar Bruven, that green-eyed human, was once a prisoner to our masters. Eventually, we ran away. We made a group and tried to cross the border."

The Gataran then gestured at the two prisoners left who were yet to be introduced. "The dwarf and the other human were different. They joined us because they could not enter these lands by themselves." He then pointed a scaled finger to the young man with the vivid green eyes. "He helped us, said that he had contacts that would protect us. Noble intentions, but bad result. There are many more of us, fellow escaped slaves and human prisoners of Artaria. We planned on becoming sellswords to pay for our freedom."

The young man moved closer to the bars. "It was not supposed to be this way. I have...I had an uncle in Whitehill, a town northeast of here. He was an influential merchant, but I was unaware that he had passed away. My plan was for him to harbor us until we were able to form a militia or mercenary company of sorts. Then we would earn some coin and be able to live off that. It was never a good or safe plan, but it was better than staying in the mines."

Ürbon now had a better chance to look at the young man who the gataran had introduced as Aligar. He looked tired, but his clothes didn't hide the broad shoulders and strong arms. He didn't have any noteworthy scars visible, but he did not know if he could truly make it as a mercenary. Most young sellswords only managed to make it through thanks to the advice of older members."

"Mercenary life is hard, Aligar. Do you know anything of actual battles? What makes you think you could survive?"

Aligar straightened up and looked directly at the Jödmun with steel in his eyes. "My father was the Knight-Captain in the Capital, Ravenburg. He and his men taught me all about combat, from pikewalls to shield walls, from swords to hammers. I've never been on a battlefield, but I've had more than one tavern fight and more than one bad run-in with the local authorities. Plus, I once escaped from a convict mine, so I feel like I'm not half bad. The others also know how to fight. Many of the Lazar and the Northerners have fought in pit fights and the Mys are trained to be guards.

"I can teach them how to fight in unison. My mother taught me quite a bit of alchemy. I know how to create a few simple potions, like the ones that grant strength and speed. I can also make healing poultices, to help fight off sickness and other such things, nothing too akin to witchcraft."

Ürbon was still unsure about the survival odds of the group, but that was better than what he expected. "What about the other human and the dwarf?"

Suddenly the sleeping dwarf awoke with a jump. "Who are you to challenge me, mate? I am Grodsug, The Black Pick, killer of Zuggzag the Ugly, and burner of the summer horde! I represent two hundred years of anger, drunkenness, and killing. I've been fighting orcs, goblins, dargoons, and vampires since you were a child. So don't you try and cross me, you ugly stone freak. My people have been mining rock since the beginning of time, so come and fight you if you dare, damned pebble!"

The dwarf continued to ramble on, but Ürbon could only laugh. He hadn't heard such banter since he had been split from his crew. Oh, how he had missed the familiar sound of angry drunken shouting. Dwarves and Jödmuns always called each other brother and few times did the sentiment feel so true as now. So he responded the only way honor could allow — by rising to the occasion.

"Only two hundred years? The youngest Jödmun alive has lived for more than a thousand years by now, and you think fighting vampires is hard? How about fighting an entire army of Hassimsi orc hussars, or a Warband of Norsmen Manhunters? And what is that damnable greasy thing on your face? I thought Dwarves were supposed to have beards, not pieces of driftwood!"

It looked like their verbal duel fueled only by their own egos would continue forever. But it was interrupted by the sound of the door opening and boots thundering against the stone floor.

Ürbon glanced at the Sentriel, only to notice that he had turned invisible again. As the door opened, the guards were released from the pacifying spell. Through the door, five people entered — two new guards, the Knight-Captain they had talked to outside, some sort of noble in decorated yet battle-worn plate armor, and an old and experienced-looking knight.

The old knight had an eye patch over his left eye with a large scar peeking under it, a bald head, and a well-groomed white beard. He wore pitch black plate armor with a dark blue tabard with the symbol of a Raven perched next to a raised spear. The noble stepped forward, flanked by the old knight and the Knight-Captain.

"I am Reinhold Westermann, Markgraf of the city of Clavenstil. It is my duty to protect every man, woman, and child within these walls. You represent a threat to the peace here, so tell me who you are and why you have come before I call for the executioner."

Before Ürbon could speak up, he was interrupted by Maka. "I am Maka Rabymat, the Golden Lioness of the Desert, the Warden of the Nebu-Gi, and Princess of Osharis, the Last Golden City. This is my entourage. The Jödmun is Ürbon the Wanderer, son of Ongul the Wise, and Slayer of the Beast of the Moon Forest. The lizard is Tlupic the Sky Seeker. Finally, there is the winged one, Hydrulian, the Last Sentriel. We were traveling with the intention of entering Venova when their fleet suddenly and brutally attacked us unprovoked and without warning. That is the reason why we are in your land. After the unjust attack, we ended up stranded and lost, with you being the first sign of civilization we have seen. I request safe passage to the Island of Venova so the wrongs done to me might be corrected, and those responsible be brought to justice."

The whole room was quiet after the imperial and commanding voice of the Lioness.

The Markgraf made a deep bow before addressing the warrior-princess with a much more courtly voice. "Excuse us, Princess. Our most sincere apologies. Here in Clavenstil we respect royalty, we did not mean to trouble you. I shall prepare an escort to accompany you to the Town of Ethan tomorrow morning and from there, an escorted ship heading straight to Venova. But tonight, you are our guests. We will find suitable chambers for you and prepare dinner."

As the group moved to exit the cell, Ürbon paused to stare at the prisoners. "What will happen to them?"

The Markgraf stared quizzically at the giant and the cells. "The prisoners? Well, The slaves will be returned to Artaria. Any human with bounties on their head will be exchanged for coin. The rest will be executed." He then pointed at the young human. "That one will be executed one way or the other. He had past grievances in the Kingdom. We're not sure about the dwarf yet."

Ürbon looked at the young man. He was probably around Askia's age, and like Askia, he saw too much of the world too quickly. An idea was starting to form. He would execute his plan at dinner.

**

Time passed like a breeze. Maka was quite pleased with herself for having the correct courtly behavior. They were all offered baths, but he refused, seeing that none of the tubs were big enough to fit him. Neither was the room he was given, but after the first few hundred years of traveling, he had gotten used to cramped spaces.

At dinner, he actually ate food, though he did not need to. During their stay in the desert, he did not eat or drink to preserve provisions, but now he could. He never got hungry, but the food tasted nice. He liked the chicken and the wine was spicy. Though even a barrel full of this pitiful beverage couldn't hope to make him even slightly tipsy. He was seated on a beautiful carpet with ample pillows, seeing that any chair offered to him would break. Beside him Maka made an attempt to be courtly, but did not eat the food.

Tlupic was gorging himself after days of meager provisions and water. Hydrulian was still invisible, but he could see that the love-struck fool was observing the Princess from the way the air rippled. They had been told that Stixerio was being treated like royalty back in the stables. The damned beast was probably royalty among horses anyway.

"I hope you're enjoying the wine." The Markgraf said as he set down his goblet. "It's Artarian, the finest around these lands. There was a time we would have served our famous mead to our guests, but due to the plague, we don't want to risk it."

The Markgraf used dinner to explain to them the current situation of Ravenburg. The population was recovering from a recent plague that had ravaged the land. The start of this "Dark Decade", as the people of Ravenburg called it, began with the "Thirstful Plague." After a dry summer came a disease that infected hops, and leeched off the energy and food of other creatures. As mead was being served in countless taverns, the Plague spread like a wildfire. Ürbon could swear he heard Hydrulian make some sort of sound before he giggled and muttered something about vampires. So as the disease ravaged the country, in an attempt to avoid an outbreak, the Artarian army closed the border and the Venovans stopped trading with them. This greatly affected the economy, and even as the plague subsided, this issue spiralled out of control and crime started to rise. The two years between the plague's end and the present was known as the "Quiet Two" because of the uncertainty that the plague was indeed over.

Still, the Artarians and Venovans had just reopened trade with Ravenburg. No pirate dared attack them, giving them time to gather their strength as slowly traders started returning to Ravenburg. However, people often burned the plague-ridden bodies, and a few summers ago, the uncontrolled flames set the woods near Whitehill ablaze, destroying a majority of the White Wood. The forest areas were very slowly recovering but in the meantime, they did not have access to the precious trade goods. Their troubles did not end there, for when the plague struck, almost all the mines were abandoned. And surely now many of these mines were overrun with beasts, bandits, and other fiends, cutting the trade of iron and other metals, and to a lesser extent, gemstones.

The mood at the table had turned grim, but once there was a lull in the conversation, Ürbon made his move.

"Markgraf Westermann, I believe I have a solution to your prisoner problem. Returning them to Artaria is not going to make you any coin, seeing as they will consider them their lawful property. Bounties are always rather poor, especially when it's just a rabble and not a real threat. Killing all of them is just a big waste of time and you can't just keep them as prisoners forever. Perhaps they could buy their own freedom.

"Those men are ready for battle." Ürbon said in response to the Markgraf's silence. "Some of them even have formal training. Just focus them against a target. Repeat this until they all die or they have compensated for their wrongs to the people of Ravenburg."

Though the silence continued, Ürbon only took it as a sign to continue presenting his argument.

"Think of it. You said yourself that your prisons are full, that bandits and beasts threaten your kingdom. These men will kill the enemies of Ravenburg or die trying, and you will be able to profit from both situations. If this ends up being a waste of time, then the prisoners will die having at least killed some of your enemies. Though if it ends up successful, you will be remembered as the man who brought new, although unusual, hope to the kingdom."

The Markgraf pondered on the proposition for a bit before nodding to the old knight in the eye patch. "Commander Ulrich, what do you think?"

The old knight stood up and addressed both Ürbon and the Markgraf. "The idea has merit. Turning our prisoners into disposable fighters may prove a worthwhile idea, especially if they can be given proper equipment and better training. They would be a considerable and expendable force, but the Artarians won't like that their slaves are gone permanently. They are so fractured and busy with factions infighting that they might not even notice, but the young man, Aligar Bruven, must die. His mother was sentenced for witchcraft and we cannot allow the son of a witch to go free."

Ürbon cursed inwardly but on the outside, his face revealed nothing. He gathered his thoughts to try and find a way to save the young man.

"His father, however, was a Knight-Captain of the city of Ravenburg." He said, "From the faces that both of you are making, he must have been a rather good one. The boy knows how to fight, he knows how to lead men, and he knows the lay of the land. From my brief exchange with him, he did not have any kind of anger or resentment towards the kingdom, and he has expressed a desire to fight the orcs that trouble you so much. Let him fight for you and prove himself. Besides, the boy has already shown his distaste towards witchcraft and his own heritage."

The last part was a lie, but a little trickery couldn't hurt.

"Hmm, very well." The Markgraf said. "Tomorrow they shall depart. I will write a letter with instructions to determine their fate as convicted sellswords."

Ürbon felt as if a great weight had lifted from his shoulders, but he knew his job was not done yet. After the dinner ended, he gathered the others and discussed the events that had transpired. None were annoyed at his decision, Hydrulian even congratulated him on his chaotic choice.

They quickly descended to the dungeons, where there were now only two guards guarding the cells. With a flick of his wrist the Sentriel quickly put them to sleep while the rest awoke the prisoners.

In hushed whispers, Ürbon gathered the prisoners and explained to them the situation. They were more than pleased to have been given a chance to fight for their freedom. The outcome would no doubt be better than execution.

But they had to prepare, as it was unlikely that the knights would allow them to properly organize and train for an extended period of time before they saw battle. So they had only this night to help them prepare.

Ürbon pulled Hydrulian to the side, "Do you know how to enchant weapons?"

The Sentriel froze.

***

Ürbon gathered Aligar and the other human whose name he still did not know. As well as Grodsug the Dwarf, Odyx the Lazar, Tlog the Northerner, Blueli the Mys, and Srikk the Gar. Each had retrieved their weapons from the storage.

The dwarf told them that they could go lick a vampire's ass if they thought he would allow them to enchant his superior dwarven pickaxe made out of secret dwarven metal and covered in ancestral family runes.

The dirty human held in his hands something that Ürbon immediately recognized — a musket, a Yanvild damned *Glavieri musket* at that. The man didn't appear like he was from Glavier, but everyone knew the Glavieri would never ever allow anyone to get their hands on their secret weapon. The Glavieri would hunt him down to the end of the world to retrieve the stolen weapon.

Hydrulian got closer to the weapon. "So that's a...musket...thing that you spoke about. I can't enchant that. It has too many parts."

"I've seen enchanted crossbows." Ürbon said. "A musket can't be that different. Sure, the Glavieri don't enchant theirs, but they aren't really known for being masters of enchanting weapons."

His three companions looked equally confused at him.

"Who are the Glavieri?" Tlupic asked.

That was the disadvantage of traveling with members of lost and isolated races.

"The Kingdom of Glavier is a very powerful and influential human kingdom." Ürbon explained. "They are allied with Maldora and have many colonies around the world. They also know the secret of grey powder, the fuel for their muskets and cannons. Very few races know the secret to it, not even their Maldorans allies. Maka, it might interest you to know that they are the most powerful descendant of the now sunken Alleanari Empire."

Maka looked at Ürbon puzzledly "Truly? The Sea People were good allies to us before civil war doomed their island empire. Maybe old pacts can be reforged once I return to my people."

"Yes. After the fall of the island, the survivors of the empire formed many nations. Maybe some of them still remember the old ties to the Nebu-Gi." Ürbon then gestured to the crossbow. "Now, this here is called a crossbow, the contraption that some of the southern dwarves that ambushed us had. It's a lot like a bow, but much more dangerous at short range and easier to use."

"Oh, the tiny shooty things." Hydrulian nodded excitedly, "Anyway, I don't know how to properly enchant that thing!"

After this conversation, the group began to focus on training the prisoners in the basic skills they would need to survive in their new services. They only had a few hours but, in that time, they managed to roughly organize the prisoners into areas of specification and establish a few fighting strategies. The Lazar and Northerners would be good at swarming the enemy with their brute force and ruthless attacks. The dwarf decided to stick with that group and the Mys were able to organize themselves into a proper phalanx formation.

The Gar would be useful in quickly digging trenches or building barricades, or simply gathering resources in general, but were weak in melee combat. Then there were the humans. While most of them had varying experience with fighting, it was eventually decided that the best idea was to just give everyone a weapon and shield and teach them how to fight in a shield wall.

Fortunately, Aligar had spoken the truth when he said he knew how to fight, so he was capable of teaching these men the basics of organized combat. A few of the humans had experience with archery and exchanged their swords for bows to become proper rangers, commanded by the other man whose name Ürbon still did not know.

As the sun was rising, it was time for the team to say goodbye. The prisoners were being put back in their places and the leaders brought back to their cells.

"Thank you for everything," stated Aligar before being escorted back to the dungeon. "If not for your intervention, we would all have died or worse. And thanks to your help, we will survive the coming battles. We are forever in your debt. If you ever have need of us, don't hesitate to ask for our aid."

***

In a candlelit room inside the castle, Markgraf Westermann and Commander Ulrich of the Raven Spear were looking over a map of Ravenburg, slowly nursing their wine as they focused on the parchment.

The map depicted the country as a triangle, with the tip facing northeast and the base making the shoreline of the Inner Sea going from west to east. The triangle was solidified by two mountain chains that formed a natural defense and protected the kingdom. To the west, bordering Artaria, was the city of Clavenstil, far from the mountains, but still divided by the river Thurbrook. To their south on the coast was the town of Eathan, their largest port second only to the capital. North of them near the top where the two mountain chains met was the city of Whitehill, directly west of the Whitewood forest.

Farther past the eastern mountain range was the northern continuation of the Titan Divide and the coastline that was called the Wasted Coast. The coast got its name from the Steppe Orcs, who had, for untold years, crossed the Divide and ransacked both Artaria and Ravenburg. The Wasted Coast was full of war-hungry orcs and goblins, whose only desire was to push even further inland, with the mountains and the Raven Spear being the only defense between civilization and their brutality.

"The Graf of Whitehill will not be pleased with the order." Commander Ulrich sighed. "Even if he agrees with the idea, he doesn't like to be reminded of your uneven position."

"I don't care. I'm the *Markgraf*. It is my honor and duty to protect the border, and that outranks him by far."

"He won't be the only one." Said Ulrich. "I know the Grandmaster, he is a pragmatic man. He will approve this project, but not the king. The king will be rather displeased that we pushed him aside and made such a decision without his approval."

"We have to. The orcs are gathering in large numbers for yet another raid, you know something has them in a frenzy. Our army won't be sufficient to fight back the orcs, but these prisoners are not ready yet. They need training and experience. We need to throw them against small threats to toughen them up before the orcs reach here." The Markgraf said, as if trying to convince not only the Commander, but also himself. "Gods protect the king, but by the time we tell him and he makes a decision on what to do, the orcs will have already arrived. We will have to sacrifice a lot of our own soldiers if we don't have the prisoners fighting for us."

"Even so, these prisoners will not be enough on their own."

"No, but they will be the shield to our spear."

***

When the sun was high in the sky, the party was escorted to the courtyard of the castle, where a carriage was waiting for them. Hydrulian had already disappeared into the sky and a sleepy Tlupic climbed into the carriage. It was clear that it would be a rather slow journey. Maka was riding Stixerio next to the horses despite the stallion continually scaring the other horses. As they were preparing to leave, they saw the Markgraf along with Ulrich and the Knight-Captain talk to the leaders of the newly formed mercenary warband.

"Commander Ulrich Von Steiner will take this letter and give it to the Graf and the Knight-Captain of Whitehill." The Markgraf said to the assembled sellswords. "You will accompany him, and once you reach Whitehill you will pick up battle-ready prisoners to join your group as well as supplies to make it to your next destination. You will then travel to the Fortress Monastery of the Raven Spear and speak to the Grandmaster of the order, Sigvald Zandler, where you will do the same thing again. You will also be accompanied into combat by one hundred knights of the Raven Spear as well as Commander Ulrich Von Steiner himself. They will be your wardens and commanders. If you survive, they will judge if you are worth keeping. The Grandmaster shall then determine your next target. Before you see any action against orcs, you will likely be sent against brigands and monsters that have taken the mines or stalk the roads. Don't fail, and may the gods be with you." He said, ending with a salute.

***

The journey towards Venova was both boring and relaxing. Tlupic was sleeping peacefully. Progress was swift and they arrived sooner than expected. Deep forests gave way to the city called Ethan with buildings closely resembling Clanvestil. As they went through the center of the town, people gawked at them and the group of knights escorting them. No doubt this was an event likely to be retold and exaggerated for years to come.

Finally they arrived at the ship, and once onboard, the captain saluted them proudly, bragging how the entire Ravenburgian, Artarian, and Venovan fleets were built almost exclusively out of wood sourced from their Whitewood forest.

The only notable conversation was Tlupic asking him how there were also orcs here, resulting in Ürbon explaining the difference between the mostly civilized Jungle Orcs and the savage Steppe Orcs. Despite some similarities, they were most definitely different races, unlike the Gatarans and the Lazar, but he kept that to himself.

From there, it was smooth sailing. Once the ship and its two escorts approached the Venovan fleet, one of the escort ships advanced to meet a lone Venovan ship that had left its formation to meet the oncoming ships. Then, after a minute or so, a loud whistle was heard and the whole convoy advanced. Within half an hour, the white city was getting closer, as was their target, one of the many mysterious artifacts they sought.

***

To the far north of Faladon, beyond the obsidian peaks, a disturbance shimmered in the air. The lands to the north were seldom visited, and if so only ever once. The magical activity was volatile within that empty wasteland, and not even the most practiced of mages could harness its power. And yet, along the stretch of ash and dust, a cloaked figure stood, proud and tall.

He strode amongst the blisters of the earth towards a red-hot flicker in the air. Like an ember catching wind it disappeared for a second before catching alight once more. The flicker seemed to twist outwards then in, keeping a hold on reality with fiery fingers. Until finally, as the cloaked figure stood before it, it took hold of the air and tore itself forth. It flexed and twisted, a large circular form of raw power, shimmering in the dim light. With a surge of power, it stabilized on the plane, growing wider to show dark spires deep within its depths. It was a sight unimaginable to a being of Faladon, yet the cloaked figure stood its ground, as if awaiting something more.

Suddenly the dark spires within it disappeared, as a dark form appeared to hide it from view. It stepped forth from the rift like a shadow and the very air seemed to warp from its presence. Another figure also stepped through the rift close behind the first. They stood there before the proud cloaked figure, and their metallic wings screeched as they moved, like hundreds of obsidian throwing knives unfolding behind their backs.

For several moments the three stood; the cloaked figure unmoving while the two newcomers surveyed the landscape. They inhaled the air as if able to breathe for the first time in years, gazing wide-eyed at their surroundings. Finally the first shadowy form looked behind it and gave a curt nod. Without pause or answer, the second stepped back into the reopened rift, disappearing into the fiery embers.

Upon its departure the cloaked figure took a step forward, as if reminding the other of its presence.

"Your efforts to bring us back to this realm are commendable." The winged being said to the cloaked figure, its voice was thin and raspy, as if the air was too thin for it to speak clearly. "I imagine it is no simple matter for which you've gone to all this trouble, and risked the consequences of our return," it chuckled.

"Enough. We have much to discuss, and my patience already wears thin."

Chapter 12:
Old Friends

It had been ten days since Askia had seen the sun, the only way he could note the passage of time was whenever a guard came down to feed him and the other prisoners some sort of gruel.

Escape seemed impossible, whenever he had the time to think of a plan the ghostly pains of his hand would haunt him.

When was Ürbon coming? Was he coming? Maybe he was dead. Or had they given up on him?

He did not know how much longer he could last.

***

Ürbon stepped down from the ship and saluted the Ravenburgian crew as they departed. In front of him stretched the Golden Port, the civilian port. It was abuzz with activity — fishers, sailors, merchants, and common workers all fluctuated in and out. Directly south, large fortified walls indicated the limit where the Golden Arsenal began, the center of the Venovan navy and the first line of defense of the Islands.

He paid it no mind. He was not keen on meeting their accursed alchemical fire again. To the east, rising over the other buildings was the royal palace, its white columns glistening in the sun. Further east towering over the palace was Mount Olympia, the lone sacred mountain of Venova, where the inhabitants believed the gods, such as the Ocean Man and the Green Queen, lived. At the peak of the mountain overlooking the islands was the Colossus, a gigantic bronze statue representing a Titan, a mythical race that, according to Venovan beliefs, was created by the gods. The Titans in turn created Venova and its races. The Venovans said the Titans mysteriously became extinct after some unknown cataclysm.

As Ürbon walked down the cobbled streets of Venova with Tlupic resting on his stone shoulder, he marveled at how they had managed to get there in one piece. In looking just at his own trials, he wondered whether to praise the fates, or curse them.

Glancing down at his side, he found Maka atop her horse checking the aged map once again. It was supposed to lead to the artifact of great magical power apparently located in the city. But from what the group could sense, there was nothing even slightly magical for Tlupic to pinpoint its location. For this reason Maka had been rather unapproachable since their arrival in the city.

Hydrulian was somewhere ahead of them, having cloaked himself in invisibility at the first sight of civilized people. Ürbon could only hope that the Sentriel wasn't making a fool of himself, or causing any further mischief.

The city around them was quite diverse, one of the most tolerant places in the world for separate races, though nearly all the races in the city were native. There were humanoid creatures with arms layered in multicolored feathers, as well as large lumbering shapes towering over the populace. There were over half a dozen different and unique species in view at all times — a true testament to the island's racial tolerance.

Ürbon was at least somewhat versed in the history and lore of Venova, but there was nothing, to his knowledge, that stood out as an obvious place to search. There was the Maceford University on the far side of the island. It was a place where scholars from all corners of the world studied science and mathematics. But he doubted they would have information about any hidden magical artifacts that just so happened to be on their island.

Ürbon turned back towards the Nebu-Gi beside him as she beckoned for him to listen. Tlupic leaned in from his shoulder and even Stixerio flicked an ear upwards to better listen in to the conversation. Ürbon had a good feeling he knew what it was about.

"I know what you're about to say, but first we need to find a proper map of the city." Ürbon said as he looked at the old, poorly detailed map in her hands. "This old piece of crumbling parchment doesn't detail the island beyond a large stain of ink."

"The artifact is here..." Maka said, exasperated from constantly getting sidetracked, but Ürbon shook his head, interrupting her. This was not the place to speak of such things, especially in a city where any talk of magic would be a great excuse to get them thrown in jail. The Jödmun motioned towards a nearby building, an inn of some type with a worn sign reading 'The Blind Cyclops,' its gold text faded from time and the elements.

Maka nodded her head in agreement, and the group walked through the doors of the inn. Ürbon was barely able to fit through the entrance.

The interior of the building was much more pristine than the exterior. Circular tables were scattered across the hardwood floor, supporting the food and drink of the creatures who occupied them. Among them were many of the native races of Venova. A nearby table housed a trio of harpies. Another closer to the wall seated two cyclops and three satyrs, appearing to be playing cards. Others were distributed among the rest of the tables, minding their own business. A woman with snakes for hair was currently sweeping, a pair of sunglasses on her face despite being indoors, while talking to a woman with the lower body of a snake. At the other end of the room and standing behind the bar was the innkeep. He was quite surprisingly a human, who had his gaze fixed on the group, sizing them up and trying to determine if they meant business or trouble.

As the group approached the man, they drew several stares from the field of people. While many of them had lived in the shadows of cyclopes and the rare minotaurs, none had seen someone tower over them as Ürbon did. Maka's returning glare tried to fend off the opposing gazes, but she was mostly unsuccessful due to how many people were present in the inn.

Crossing the room and ignoring the glances of the other customers, Ürbon approached the innkeep. The human remained relatively calm, no doubt due to his prior experience with giant creatures.

"How much for three rooms?" Ürbon rumbled.

"Five silver Ducma, each," the man replied.

"Food?"

"Two."

"How much is that in Raven Shields?"

"Two Gold Raven Shields makes a Silver Ducma."

As the Jödmun continued to bargain with the innkeep, Tlupic and Maka both noticed the two harpies returning. With them were two new people wearing matching uniforms of blue and white and several pieces of bronze and steel armor. One of these newcomers was another harpy with a bronze leaf-shaped shortsword, while the other was a cyclops with a large bronze hammer. Both approached the group with a determined look set on their faces. Maka turned to meet them, glaring distrustfully at the duo.

The cyclops with his longer strides reached Maka first, looking down at the woman with the same impassive look. It was met with annoyance from the Nebu-Gi.

"I'm sorry, madam, but you're going to have to leave Venova as soon as your business here is finished," the cyclops stated this plainly.

Maka raised an eyebrow questioningly. "Excuse me? We've only just arrived!"

"Sorry lady, but the law states that magical beings are forbidden on the island. Your horse tied outside and the talking golem will have to go."

Ürbon stopped haggling with the innkeep to look at the guards. His impassive face showed that this was not the first time that he had been confused with some sort of stone elemental or even a soul-fueled necromantic construct.

"I think there has been a misunderstanding. I am no more magical than the rest of the inhabitants on this island. After all, I was born the same way most are. As for the horse, he is my lady's trusted steed, bred from an exceptional lineage and trained since youth by the best horsemasters riches can buy. We would not want my lady to have to cut her visit short because of some minor mix up. That would certainly impair her opinion of this fine island, especially when she returns to her palace to talk about her trip with her father, the High-King of Osharis."

The confusion in the guards' faces showed that they didn't recognize the title, not that Ürbon expected these guards to know the non-existing political situation of an ancient and supposedly destroyed kingdom. But he didn't need them to. Well-paid guards in merchant cities were trained to never disturb wealthy-looking foreigners without good reason.

But Ürbon had forgotten something. Venova did not have guards; it had Magisters. They served as the guards, soldiers, and secret agents of the kingdom. The two Magisters looked at each other and their doubt was replaced with determination.

"I am sorry sir, but the law is clear. You need to leave." The Magister's hands moved slightly towards their weapons. The worried look in their eyes and the fact that they were wearing armor confused the Jödmun. He had heard that Venovan Magisters almost never wore armor. Something strange was going on.

The Jödmun crossed his arms, moving them away from Bjarl strapped to his back and gave a side glance to the Lioness. He hoped she understood his silent message. It seemed Yanvild had blessed him at that moment, since Maka did not reach for her weapons.

"Very well." she said in her most regal and commanding voice, reserved for courtly and political matters. "Tomorrow morning we shall depart. After all, we have just arrived and acquired lodging. Finding transport for tomorrow shall take time."

That seemed to pacify the Magisters, at least for now. They left the inn but the Cyclops remained not far from the exit while the Harpy flew away, presumably to inform their superiors. Ürbon quickly turned back and paid the innkeep, who now looked at them with judging eyes. Without further ado they group retreated to the privacy of their room, and away from the prying eyes of the inn's other residents.

They walked into the small and fortunately comfortable room. Though not as well kept as the luxurious accommodations back at Ravenburg, it still had a bed for each of them.

"I'm surprised you didn't just let them arrest us. You seem overly fond of that trick." Maka said

Her words carried with them an edge built up over several days of harsh travel, and while not incorrect, Ürbon still had his honor to defend.

"You'd be surprised just how well that trick works with a group of Jödmun. Me and my crew pulled it off more than once. It confuses the enemy and lets them drop their guards. After that, escaping and causing havoc is child's play."

Maka's pointed glance shut him up. She was not in the mood to console a hurt pride of a Jödmun.

***

Hydrulian lazily flew in circles over the city, looking for a source of magic that might belong to the artifact. He had found plenty of magical spots all over the city, however they were all shrouded and despite his prodding he couldn't locate a single source. So he resolved to observe all the people swarming over the various roads and paths like little insects, while routinely checking his invisibility ward. He was utterly bored. He had been trying to find anything interesting in this city for an entire fifteen minutes and nothing but a robbery, which was immediately halted by surrounding authorities, was remotely interesting.

In discontent, the Sentriel folded in his wings and began plummeting towards the street. As the ground came closer and closer to his face, he found his thoughts idly wandering toward Maka, the golden figure who had his mind's eye captivated. The beauty of her face, the fullness of her lips, and her eyes...

He was snapped out of his thoughts by the ground, rushing up to give him a stone and dirt hug. With a curse, he levelled out as fast as he could, though even so his metallic wing scraped through the cobbled road, leaving a gash in its wake. Unfortunately, as the Sentriel's gaze cleared, he realized that the road was not exactly *clear*.

As he rushed down the street, he was forced to dodge and weave through countless civilians, folding and extending his wings to avoid the strollers with the wind whistling in his ear. Eventually, he emerged from the crowds and wasted no time extending his wings and flying skyward to get away from the sorry masses.

He glanced down at the path he had taken to avoid crashing into the cobbled street. While he himself had not collided with anything except the road with the tip of his wing, the displacement of air he had created a considerable disturbance among the civilians. He checked his spells of soundproofing and invisibility, and sighed in relief in finding them intact. No matter what the civilians heard or saw, they would never in their wildest dreams be able to figure out that it was him. For all they knew it was just an incredible gust of wind brutal enough to split rock.

Even though it all ended up fine in the end, Hydrulian was still annoyed. Whatever magic the princess had wrought on him was growing stronger and stronger and he couldn't figure out how to stop it. Frustrated, he frantically looked around for any kind of distraction to ease his mind. His head swiveled constantly, his eyes piercing through the crowds of the city until they settled on one that stood out from the rest. A grin spread across his face as he remembered the efficiency of the Venovan law enforcement and he immediately set to work.

***

Arthurian observed all the different races around him, all walking the same road and working together. He never would have believed that the world could house so many different sentient species, even less so that they could all live together in harmony. Certainly not with the humans, who were so dominant over others in the west. Even in Maldora, with its ideals of equality and freedom, humans still dominated every facet of life.

It had taken quite a long time for the elven mage to get to this place, especially after he had teleported himself back to his home island and found himself in the care of his family again. A little island inside the archipelago that formed the Forgotten Isles, a place relatively unknown to the wider world. With few alive who knew the Isles' location, it had become the last refuge of the last truly independent elves. He scowled at the thought. He had purposefully used his magic to escape from them to gain his freedom aboard *The Pinnacle*, even if Caultere had been a bit useless to begin with.

With elvish populations being so low, his family had sought to keep him on their islands and use his growing magical talents to bring prosperity to his homeland. But Arthurian had not been content with his life being entirely planned out for him from start to finish by others. Despite his frequent attempts to change his fate through negotiations and occasionally feigned magical ineptitude, his parents still wouldn't let him go. On one fateful day, however, a human named Caultere raided his uncle's lowly ship while at high sea. He spared their lives and asked for volunteers to aid him on his quest to conquer the seas. Needless to say, the young elven mage had jumped at the opportunity.

But all that was in the past now, and Arthurian had a score to settle. He wouldn't rest until he found the stone monstrosity and overgrown lizard who had left his side a crimson mess the last time they had met. Despite magical treatment from his family during his brief visit, he still occasionally felt a dull pulse of pain when he turned too fast or exerted too much energy.

After having been healed at his family's estate, he had teleported away to one of the neighboring islands of the archipelago, despite the strain it took on his body and soul. There, he heard of a group of stone pirates that had been captured, though one had escaped. Immediately he realized that the stone creature that had wounded him and left him in such a state had also dared to raid his home.

He would not allow that slight to go unpunished. He asked two of the mages that captured the group to scry and find the location of the escaped giant. It cost him more in the way of coin than he had hoped, but he learned that his quarry was heading towards the city of Venova and made all due haste to catch up.

Over the course of several days, he had teleported to the nations neighboring Venova. There he listened in on bewildered villagers talking of a massive stone giant with a lizard on his shoulder. He knew he was incredibly close, and wouldn't let anything get in the way of his vengeance.

That being said, there was one major problem blocking the way. There was no easy way of finding where they were in the city. Even if the stone man was larger than almost all the other locals, he would still have a hard time finding them. The lizard would be even harder to spot. If he asked around, he could possibly find out more, as no doubt they would have left a lasting impression on anyone who saw them.

Unfortunately, while magical travel was extremely fast, it was also taxing on the soul. He found himself relying far more than he would have liked on his staff, the piece of gnarled wood serving as his only companion in his travels. It wasn't required to use magic despite many folktales throughout the lands, though it and other similar items were useful for focusing magic into more intricate and complex forms.

With a sigh of determination, he looked around his surroundings for somewhere to start his search. As he scanned his immediate area, he saw a glint of gold in the air above him. He barely had time to react before a beam of golden light smashed into the cobbled street in front of him with the thunderous sound of tearing stone.

***

"Oi! Get off the damn road!" A furious rider shouted at the elf amidst the traffic. Hydrulian watched the dazed elf stumble onto the pavement, barely dodging the passing rider. Hydrulian giggled at the effect of his neat little trick. The silly elf was quite disoriented. But that was not all, as the elf's innocent disregard for street etiquette had caught the attention of some nearby Magisters.

"What's the matter with you then?" one of them said.

Poor, poor Magisters, Hydrulian thought, spending their days running after ruffians and keeping the drunkards in line. In a second, their day was going to get a whole lot more interesting.

"Nothing! I-uh..." Arthurian stumbled on his words, squinting and bringing a hand to his temple. But his hand didn't reach his head.

With just a glance, Hydrulian sent a rock straight into the elf's grasp.

"Magic?! You're coming with us, elf!" said the other Magister.

Before Arthurian could say a word, his arms were firmly held behind his back and he was being dragged along the pavement.

Not ready for the comedy act to end, Hydrulian followed close behind the excited Magisters and arrested the elf.

***

Ürbon layed down the map of Venova they had finally found on the table of their room, studying it and explaining its details to his companions.

Venova was an island chain with a large central island and two smaller islands to the east and west. The main island was divided into north and south by a large handmade canal, and connected by three great bridges. The northern half was dominated by the Golden Port and guarded by the Venovan navy stationed in the Golden Arsenal that protected the entrance to the canal. To the northwest was Mount Olympia, a volcano separated from the rest of the city. At the foot of the volcano was the entrance to the Forbidden City which housed the legendary Oracle. The center of the island was overshadowed by the royal palace — the seat of the Titan King's power. The southern half had its own landmarks, such as the temples for their different gods, Maceford University, and other places less likely to house a hidden magical item. The western island, however, was named the City of Magisters, and Ürbon didn't want to go there unless absolutely necessary.

"So, what now?" Tlupic said from atop Ürbon's shoulders. Maka could still feel the stares at their backs as they walked out of the tavern.

"We split up. We'll cover more ground that way," replied Ürbon.

"Agreed," said Maka, "we'll meet you both back here at sundown."

"Before we go, remember not to call too much attention to yourself. The guards gave us a day, but something is off about this. The Golden Fleet is not normally so needlessly aggressive and the Magisters even less, so keep an eye out."

With that warning the three split off, each heading off into different directions.

Maka wandered the markets of the Golden Port atop Stixerio, with the intent of crossing over to the southern island. Out of the corner of her eyes she spotted a group of armored Magisters pushing their way through the crowd. Maka guided Stixerio into a side street in hopes of avoiding the guards.

The side street turned out to be narrower than Maka would've liked. Stixerio carefully plodded through, mindful of the brick walls closing in as they moved forward. The narrower the street got, the darker it became.

"We told you to get out of town, Madame," came a familiar voice from behind them.

Were these two waiting for me? How did they know I would enter here? She thought.

Not having enough room to turn Stixerio around to meet the Magisters face to face, Maka turned her head to reply, "We'll be gone by the morning."

"I think you better come with us," said the other.

Oh how I'd love to shut those stupid mouths, she thought. But to do so would cause more harm than good. And so, gritting her teeth, she agreed to go with the Magisters.

***

Having Sent Tlupic in the opposite direction of Maka, Ürbon observed the street, pondering where in such a place the artifact could be. Engrossed in his thoughts, he didn't even notice the three satyrs walking out of the tavern behind him.

"Jödmun."

"We've been expecting you."

"Cards get boring after a while," the satyrs said, barely a second after one another.

"Expecting me? How could you even know I was coming?" Ürbon replied, steeling his patience as the three satyrs jumped to and fro in front of him.

"Our king knows many things!"

"Many things no other knows!"

"To him you must ask and to him we will take you!" The three satyrs giggled and jumped.

"Oh? And if I don't want to go?" growled Ürbon, his hand edging towards Bjarl upon his back.

"Oooh! The Titan King also knows of this question!"

"What answer did he give?" and the three satyrs finally ceased their jumping, standing still as if in deep contemplation. But a moment after, they all said in unison, "Artifact! Artifact!" and continued their erratic acrobatics.

Ürbon growled. Of course the Titan King would know of an ancient artifact within his city. Muttering a silent curse, Ürbon agreed to follow the satyrs and meet their master.

***

"Get back here!" they yelled after him as Tlupic ran along the cobblestone streets. It was not long after splitting up from the others that he was cornered by the Magisters and — as a result of panic — had wacked one across the head.

Luckily, the magisters weren't used to running around the city. Not long after the chase began, the pursuing footfalls of the Magisters turned into ragged huffs and puffs shortly lost to the deafening bustle of Venova.

Just to make sure of his escape, Tlupic crawled through a gap in the wall beside him. Not a chance they'd follow him now.

On the other side of the gap, he found himself in a dark and dilapidated building, surrounded by dusty crates filled with empty bottles. His eyes quickly adjusted to the sudden darkness, and he saw an unstable wooden staircase leading upwards and another built of stone descending.

With a jump, he scampered down the stone stairs as a beam of timber fell from above.

The lower level was even darker and dustier. But within seconds, it didn't matter. His eyesight was used to the lack of light from a lifetime spent underground.

"At last you have come, Sky Chaser." A voice spoke from the darkness. It sounded feminine, yet also hoarse with age. Grabbing his spear, Tlupic squinted to see the source, edging closer to meet it.

"What are you?" Tlupic called out, close enough to see the being before him. It leaned upon a crooked wooden staff with long and pale fingers, and its back was bent beneath a dark and tattered robe. However, the Geck'tek could see beyond the normal eye and the same aged figure was enveloped by magic, but in a way Tlupic had never seen before. The figure looked as if it were haunted, as something similar to a ghostly bull cloaked and circled around it.

"I am the Oracle," it wheezed in an ancient whisper. "But who I am does not matter. What matters is what I have seen."

Tlupic had heard of oracles before, ancient beings with prophetic sight, a skill revered by his tribe, and he remembered Ürbon mentioning that there was one here in Venova as well.

"Tell me what you have seen," the Geck'tek edged closer.

"I see a world at the edge of death. Many will stand against the abyss and many more will fall. To be ready for the coming war, you must relive that which has passed. Once more, you must venture through the depths, and once more you must chase for the sky. Each of your allies have paths they must take. Yours, young Geck'tek, you must take alone."

Tlupic stood before the Oracle, considering its laden words.

"Take this lantern," the Oracle broke the silence, handing Tlupic a lantern made of black iron. A glowing turquoise stone could be seen inside it. It glowed brighter as Tlupic grasped it in his hand, illuminating his surroundings. "Take it and venture forth through the Undercity," the Oracle added.

At that moment Tlupic heard a high pitched melodic whistle that resonated in every wall and every pebble. The ground between the Oracle and the Geck'tek opened to reveal a dark tunnel.

Tlupic gazed down into the unending darkness, as if the abyss the Oracle spoke of had appeared right before him. He tried to make sense of where the darkness would lead, but the darkness was absolute.

"Let the lantern guide you," said the Oracle as if sensing Tlupic's hesitation.

Without any further words, the Geck'tek stepped forth, holding the lantern aloft. Usually he wouldn't have trusted a magic user, but he decided to make an exception for the Oracle.

At first, he took small steps and then, gathering his confidence, his strides lengthened. The Oracle's chamber disappeared in the dark. The lantern guided him through the series of tunnels with a beam of light. It seemed to bend with the corners, illuminating some paths and ignoring others as if choosing Tlupic's direction of its own accord.

***

Ürbon followed the satyrs along the narrow streets, their erratic jumping clearing a path as those passing by kept their distance, avoiding the odd entourage.

At last they made their way to a building of architecture unmatched in the city, held up by multiple marble pillars so spotless they seemed to exude a light of their own. It was a welcome change to the dark tunnels and dusty caverns Ürbon had become accustomed to traversing of late.

The Jödmun and escorting satyrs made their way in. They entered a vast hall within which stood a man of ordinary appearance, though he stood with an air of majesty. His head was covered with long white hair and a beard of matching length. Ürbon met his gaze as the man turned to regard the approaching group, his eyes shining with a bright intelligence.

"So pleased to finally meet you, Ürbon the Wanderer. Welcome to Venova. I'm sorry for the way my Magisters have treated you. They're still working on...old orders, which is why I had to send for you directly." His voice was strong and echoed through the long hall while the satyrs scampered off and out of the way.

"How do you know my name? How did you even know I had come here?" Ürbon asked, more wary of the man's omniscience than the man himself.

"I am Mace, the Titan King," he replied with a hearty chuckle, "I know a lot of things — where you've been, and where you're going."

"Where I'm going?" Ürbon said, his annoyance threatening to get the better of him. Nobody spoke even a modicum of sense in this Yanvild damn city.

"The Oracle often speaks of the world's end," The Titan King said, turning away from Ürbon. "The rebirth of an abyss long thought vanquished threatens to return, bringing with it the death of countless lives. She's the one to blame for our unfortunate mix up; she can be quite infuriating at times. She has a terrible habit of keeping her prophecies to herself until the last second."

"Can someone please speak in clear terms, for once?" Ürbon shouted, his voice echoing through the hall, bouncing back and bringing with it shameful evidence of the Jödmun's temper.

"Souls. Only the collection of souls will save my city, my people." There was a certain tightness in the king's voice as he turned to meet the Jödmun's exasperated gaze. The king's eyes were grim. "With enough souls, I can transport Venova somewhere safe. Somewhere far away from the calamity fast approaching."

Before Ürbon could protest, the King added heartily "Come. I must show you something," as if suddenly snapping out of distant and grim thoughts.

***

At last, Tlupic reached the end of the winding tunnel, the lantern's bright light branching out to reveal a damp cavern held up by pillars cracked with age. If the city above was white and glistening, then the one below him was a labyrinth of brown buildings on dark rock. He could hear the drips of water falling down from above. The maze-like cavern must've been built long ago as he could barely make out platforms of stone and hallways branching down before him. Peering from above and planning his next steps, Tlupic could see he was not alone as he spotted shapes slowly moving along the narrow corridors with tired and shambling steps.

Tlupic dropped down from the platform into the cavern itself, finding himself within the series of pathways. Once again, the lantern's light united into a beam, leading him onwards and showing him the way through the maze-like cavern.

Occasionally, he would walk past one of the creatures and they would stop their awkward gait to peer at the Geck'tek. They had bovine-like faces covered in wiry hair. Each had a pair of horns protruding from their foreheads, some large, some small, and some cracked or misshapen. Tlupic had seen their kind before at the inn; Ürbon had called them minotaurs.

They walked along upon cloven hoofs except when Tlupic passed them by. They stopped to gaze at the unexpected visitor, occasionally snorting upon recognizing the lantern within Tlupic's grip.

After much walking and having made no progress, Tlupic stopped by one of the shambling beasts, who peered back at the Geck'tek with dark beady eyes.

"What is this place?" Tlupic asked the minotaur.

"Those who live upon the surface call this place the Undercity. But we who live here call it the Eternity Puzzle." The minotaur looked at Tlupic's lantern with keen interest. "What brings you here, traveler?"

"The Oracle sent me."

"She sends many to find the Warden. Many who do not return."

"Where is this Warden?"

The minotaur merely looked at the lantern once more and replied, "You already carry the answer with you."

The lantern's beam of light swerved around the corner and, having fewer answers than what he started out with, Tlupic followed the beam through the cavern.

After more walking, Tlupic found himself in front of yet another minotaur. This one was much larger and, unlike the rest, was completely white. Even stranger was the minotaur's magical aura. Eerily similar to the Oracle's, the only difference was that it lacked the ghostly bull. The minotaur watched Tlupic approach with blazing red eyes.

It seemed to Tlupic he had reached where he had to go, for the lantern's light dimmed, as if gathering itself back into the black iron cage.

"You're the warden," Tlupic said to the outstanding minotaur.

"Usually travelers ask me that question rather than just stating it so outright." The minotaur's red eyes flared with enthusiasm. "So, who has the Oracle sent me this time?"

"I am Tlupic, champion of the Geck'teks, and I come bearing the Oracle's lantern."

"That's not much to be proud of." The minotaur chuckled and motioned to the lantern in Tlupic's hand. "She gives one to everyone who must pass the trials of the Eternity Puzzle." The minotaur paused, his gaze still on the lantern. His chuckle faded away. "But it seems you do have reason to be proud. That is truly the Lantern of the Lost."

"The Lantern of the Lost?"

"Yes, the Lantern of the Lost," The minotaur stated wryly. "Given to the one who has passed the trials and to whomever the Oracle deems worthy." The minotaur lifted its heavy white head, as if listening to something far off in the distance. "But you must go now, little Geck'tek. Your friends need you."

The bull let out a whistle almost identical to the one Tlupic heard near the Oracle, and opened a passage behind him, this one without the presence of any minotaur and shrouded in darkness.

"None may pass through here, for to do so would mean to never find your way back to the surface. Fortunately for you, the holder of the Lantern of the Lost won't meet the same fate."

As the white minotaur watched the small lizard disappear in the darkness he allowed himself a weary sigh.

"Oh sister, I hope you chose correctly."

***

The Titan King led Ürbon down the staircase, followed by a small retinue of Magisters. The chamber was lined with iron bar cages, mostly empty apart from an elf he had seen somewhere before. He scowled as he saw the Jödmun, and —

"Maka?" Ürbon exclaimed as the Nebu-Gi met the Jödmun's gaze. She seemed unharmed and clearly unamused about being locked up in a dungeon.

"You know this one?" Mace asked. It seemed the Titan King wasn't entirely all-knowing after all.

"Yes, and I demand an explanation for why you've locked her up!" the Jödmun shouted, his patience altogether gone. "In *clear* terms."

"The souls of those who die in these cells are what will allow me to teleport my city away from the world's end."

"No magic can perform such a thing!" cried the elf from the cell next to Maka's.

"The Sentriel, an ancient race long thought to be extinct, are able to harness such power. Though twisted and corrupted by the magical dimension they escaped through during the War of the Wall, they have returned. I made a deal with them to save my city. I had no other choice!" the Titan King said defiantly.

A maniacal cackle echoed through the dungeon, as outside the elf's cage an illuminating light appeared and morphed to form a giggling Hydrulian. "Not even *I* would be able to come up with that one!" he laughed. "The Sentriel are all gone, except for me, you silly king! You must've dreamt them up in your sleep!"

His laughter came to an abrupt halt as two dark globes appeared. The globes enlarged and transformed into humanoid creatures fitted with tattered black robes and pitch-black plate armor. Metal feathers of dark iron protruded from their backs, screeching as they moved. Their skin was a pale purple, covered in sinister markings and grisly scars. They seemed uncannily like Hydrulian, but twisted and menacing as if conjured by the darkness of night itself.

With only a glimpse, Ürbon could feel that these corrupted Sentriel were not of this world. One of them, with greasy long black hair, looked back at Ürbon for only a moment. Her pure black eyes seemed to sear into his brain. The other, a male with a bald head, kept his eyes intently on Hydrulian.

"Look who we have here. Hydrulian and some pet mortals!"

"Calivex," Hydrulian said, his eyes regarding the male. And then moving to the female. "Alivex. Must be terribly annoying having to share one wig between the two of you. But then again, you know what they say about twins!" Hydrulian spoke with mirth, as if the beings in front of him were products of his own broken mind.

"Do you know what they say about you?" cackled Alivex. "Too cowardly to go through a portal, preferring to exist in this pitiful world filled to the brim with pathetic creatures."

"No, no sister, it isn't his fault. Look at him; he was probably too busy talking to the voices in his head to even know there was a war going on. Pathetic," Calivex joined in his sister's cackling.

Ürbon watched as Hydrulian seemed to glow, his arms and legs tense, looking as if he was about to burst. With a tremendous flash the room erupted as Hydrulian sent a beam of light straight at the twin Sentriels. With a wave of her hand, Alivex deflected it back, forcing Hydrulian into a corner.

Seeing that the Sentriels were busy fighting Hydrulian, Ürbon seized the opportunity to free Maka and the semi-familiar elf. Grabbing a firm hold of the iron cage's door he pulled and heaved. With a screech the cage-door hinges snapped and he set the door aside. No longer stuck inside the cage, Maka sprung into action, jumping atop Stixerio she was about to aid Hydrulian but at the same moment her path was blocked by demons appearing out of nowhere.

It was then that Ürbon saw the portal Calivex had conjured and the hellish looking demons stepping forth in large numbers. He gripped Bjarl and charged the Sentriel as a purple blast shot into the spot he had just been.

Ürbon roared a mighty war cry and charged at the cursed fiend, toppling and crushing any demons on his way. The elf was hot on his heels. His hands crackling with purple energy as he prepared a spell, Calivex held a whirling black vortex in his hands. The giant was about to reach him when a hellish green fireball from across the room hit him in his flank, making him stumble backwards and cry out in surprise and pain.

The magical attack left no mark but the pain it caused made the Jödmun fall to a knee. Bjarl nearly fell out of his hand, but he found his footing as the axe shot a lightning bolt straight at the Calivex. The effect was masked by Calivex unleashing the strange dark vortex upon Ürbon and Arthurian, who managed to raise a magical shield to protect both of them. The shield did not hold, and once it faltered the vortex swallowed both the Jödmun and elf, leaving no trace of either.

On the other side of the room, Maka, atop Stixerio, was slashing away at the horde of demons, making a beeline towards Hydrulian. As she reached him and grabbed his arm, an explosion threw them both to the floor. They looked up just in time to see Ürbon and the elf be entirely consumed by a spell that took them in a flash of dark magic. Alivex turned and smiled at both of them. The wretched being's jaw was dangling off in a grotesque manner, reminiscent of a broken marionette and disrupting the otherwise beautiful face.

"Princess. Hydrulian. We'll have to take you home now. We're sure the others will be ecstatic to meet you!"

He was interrupted by the sound of thundering hooves. Maka and Hydrulian watched as Stixerio gloriously collided against the corrupted Sentriel's broken face.

Hydrulian used the temporary respite to charge a spell. It seemed frantic and unfocused, as if Hydrulian himself didn't know what he was about to do.

In the meantime, Stixerio was bravely holding the attention of both Sentriels, but it wasn't enough. The twins each conjured fantasmal swords coated in wicked green flames and made them hover in the air. With perfect synchronization, they unleashed their swords, skewering the poor horse and cloaking him in unnatural flames. Maka watched in despair as Stixerio gave one last painful cry and turned to ash and dust.

The Lioness abandoned all reason and elegance and just ran with both her golden khopeshes drawn and poised to strike. The twins had fun parrying and avoiding her attacks. Alivex conjured a barbed magical whip and struck the princess. The whip snaked around her right leg and burned her, leaving a wound circling her calf and thigh. As the two disfigured and sadistic figures approached the defeated and outmatched survivors, Hydrulian unleashed his spell, with all madness gone from his eyes for just a moment.

And at that, Hydrulian created a golden portal that engulfed both him and Maka, transporting them elsewhere.

***

Ürbon awoke alone with no trace of the battle, with no remnant of the smells of magically created sulfur or the extreme decay he had just experienced. Slowly regaining his awareness, he stumbled to his feet and noticed that Bjarl was not near him. He felt a slight pull towards the south and somehow knew that was where Bjarl lay. He failed to notice the shadow lurking behind him in the tree line.

***

The first thing Maka saw was sand, black sand. As she tried to stand up, her right leg buckled under her and she fell, landing on an unconscious Hydrulian. Turning onto her back, she saw the black pyramid. They were in Necrophantis.

***

Tlupic continued into the endless labyrinth, his eyes superbly adapted for the dim light. He survived on rats, lizards, insects, and any critters that crossed his path.

The oracle had told him the voyage would be long and that his companions would scatter to the winds, but it had been many days since he had seen the sun. He started to doubt the usefulness of the lantern given to him. Suddenly, the blue flame turned turquoise and the glowing stone shone brighter. The earth around him gave a slight tremble and a perfect staircase formed out of the wall. He climbed, not hesitating for a second.

At last he reached the top of the ceiling, which opened effortlessly and allowed him passage to the world above. Once again, the Sky Chaser was free.

***

Calivex and Alivex cursed their luck and were discussing what to do. "Damn Hydrulian. That pathetic wretch. Track his portal. We need to find him and the girl."

"I'm afraid that will have to wait."

The twins had been interrupted by the Titan King, whose face revealed nothing of his true intentions. "Before you do anything, you should pay attention to the axe."

Just as he spoke, the two Sentriels noticed the axe left by the giant. It had a faint static field glowing around it, growing in intensity and frequency as if it was unstable. Calivex got closer to investigate, but took a step back as the axe rose up from the ground and started to levitate. It reached a breaking point when the axe shot out towards the Sentriel, completely ignoring the hastily summoned barrier. The axe slashed his throat and threw him back, pinning him to the wall.

The electric field started again, charring the flesh and burning the hair on the head of the Sentriel. He would have cried out in pain and despair had his lungs and throat not been ripped out. Alivex ran towards her brother and tried to remove the axe. But as her spindly fingers touched the handle she was blasted back. She could only watch helplessly from across the room as the axe froze her brother into a perfect ice statue. Fear and pain were clearly painted on his blue face before a surge of electricity turned him into a pile of snow and chipped ice. But the horror wasn't over.

Although invisible to normal people, she could *see* her brother's soul as it was ripped from the melting snow on the floor. It swirled towards the soul gem that the Titan King was holding, and disappeared into it.

With all of her rage, she tried to summon a spell only to realize that her arms were limp and useless, an electrical pulse surging through them. Looking down she could see how they shrivelled and crumbled into white ash.

What sort of weapon could do such a thing? She thought as she looked to the axe before turning her gaze back to the Titan King looking at her with disdain. She opened her mouth to speak, but was silenced by a wave of his arm, and she melted down to a stain on the marble floor.

She, or what she used to be, looked like a drop of paint that had been dropped in a glass of water. Her soul mixing into the life essence of so many others trapped inside his tiny jewel.

The Titan King was admittedly pleased by the resultant deaths of the Sentriels. They might have been necessary allies, but he was still revolted by their corrupted existence. Indeed, he almost felt nauseous having their souls inside his jewel. But he couldn't allow anyone or anything to know what had happened here, and he knew well how dangerous a stray soul could be to his plans.

He turned around towards the axe. Though it still crackled with energy, it had unlodged itself from the wall and floated serenely in the center of the room. The death of the two Sentriels had somewhat appeased it.

"You're a willful one. It is not often that one comes across such a powerful weapon," he said

The axe gave no response, it did not need to.

"Go on, don't keep him waiting. He will need you."

The axe made a low noise, like the growl of a tired beast.

"Ah. I see. I'll help you just this once. But soon enough both of you will need to learn to do this on your own."

With a blinding flash, the axe let out a thunderous burst of lightning and the world flashed white for a second. When the light dissipated and the colors returned, the axe was gone.

If he had been a mortal or even an over-glorified immortal like the people that had previously fought in this room, the Titan King would have been blinded.

But he wasn't.

"That went well." A familiar figure materialized behind him, hidden under a black and tattered garment. It was hard to tell where its robes ended and the darkness began.

"Did the lizard receive the Artifact?" asked the Titan King. The figure's silence was the only response he needed, "Good. You were right about the battle, I thought they would at least have a fighting chance. I hope you were right about the rest. If not, you've cost us a powerful ally."

"When have I ever been wrong?"

Contents

Chapter 1: Into The Deep 7

Chapter 2: Through Uncertain Waters 31

Chapter 3: The Sands of Death 61

Chapter 4: Deserted Plans 91

Chapter 5: Deal With Death 99

Chapter 6: Bury The Dead 125

Chapter 7: A Long Way to Go 153

Chapter 8: The Titan Divide 167

Chapter 9: Schemes and Soldiers 185

Chapter 10: Now or Never 205

Chapter 11: The Depths of Sorrow 233

Chapter 12: Old Friends 271

Printed in Great Britain
by Amazon